ANGLED FOR REVENGE

Sarah Ickes

August, 2022
ISBN-13: 979-8-9860137-2-5
Ebook ISBN-13: 979-8-9860137-3-2

Cover art and all illustrations have been created from the author's own hand.
www.sarahickesart.com

"The full moon illuminated the landscape before her,
    Hazed, lines were undefined,
        All that remained was light, and shadows,
            With three tiny stars to comfort thy night.

        The deep sea of sky, and gray of grass
            Were split only by a forest darkened to hide all foes,
                Small light of guidance pure and strong,
                    Will steer me true to one's internal peace."

MURIAL ROBERTSON SERIES

The Serpent's Star
Angled for Revenge

Murial's mother, Nora Robertson, stepped out of the topless carriage just as she and Jack came up to the front door of the family farmhouse. Seeing Nora's radiating smile, Murial couldn't remember a time when her father was alive and that same sense of happiness spread across her mature face. Her dirty blonde hair's vibrancy had faded, but her eyes were still as authoritative as when she was a young woman many moons ago. A pastel pink dress with a high fitted neck collar adorned her slim figure and a cream colored shawl wrapped around her shoulders. Upon her head sat a matching cream hat with a pastel pink flower that laid delicately over its brim. Various pleats and ruffles extended over the dress's bodice in a deliberate attempt to reveal the white fabric hiding underneath the overskirt.

The gentleman helping her down from the carriage, stood to the right of the hired transportation and bent down to kiss Mrs. Robertson's hand, bidding his farewells for the evening. His gray washed facial hair bore wisdom whilst his clothes had the aroma of refinement brought on by his tailored dark blue suit and newly crafted black shoes. Acknowledging Murial and Jack with the tip of his English riding hat, the man gave them both a dramatic sweeping of his hand in a grand gesture of a bow.

"Dramatic as always, Mr. Shetron." Murial spoke with a smile on her lips while Jack stood to her right, both of them now out on the front porch. If it had not been for the eastern backdrop to the farm, one could have sworn that Jack had never left Conestone, Arizona by his daily attire. Brown boots sat squarely on his feet with worn marks etched into the leather. Tan pants accompanied his blue buttoned down shirt and dark brown vest while a pipe rested in his pants pocket, unseen except for a slight bulge on his left thigh.

"And you are as lovely as always, Miss Robertson. I bid you all good night." Mr. Shetron instructed his driver to begin the journey back toward Philadelphia, settling down into the passenger seat of the carriage as the horses' hooves patted the dirt. Nora Robertson watched with longing in her hazel eyes as Mr. Shetron's carriage traveled down the road and eventually out of sight. Murial walked down the stairs in order to stand next to her mother, her outfit quite dull in comparison to Nora's exquisite looks. Leaning closer toward her mother's ear, Murial lowered her voice to a mere whisper.

"Don't look now, but your face is that of a dreamy-eyed school girl." Mrs. Robertson abruptly turned about to look into her sassy daughter's playful expression. Her eyes scanned Murial up and down, displeased with the way her daughter constantly kept her outward appearance. Instead of the fanciful dresses of the higher society, Murial was more partial to dresses suited for the working class. An apron would often be present over her simple dress, displaying bits of oil paint scattered like stars against its striped fabric.

"I don't know what you are talking about, Murial. And do stop dressing like the hired help. It is so unbecoming of a Robertson. Why, your grandmother is probably rolling in her grave this very minute." Her mother glided gracefully up the stairs and through the front door with poise as Jack joined Murial on the ground and placed his arm around her shoulders. No matter how hard she tried to joke with her mother, or to even have any decent conversation for that matter, her efforts were always smacked away with coldness and critique. It had been a taxing mental battle, to say the least, when both mother and daughter moved into the farmhouse last August.

Murial's uncle had bequeathed the deed for the farm to her upon his death in what had become the start to both a liberating and difficult past year for the Robertson family. With the Senator laid to rest in the Territory of Arizona, Mrs. Robertson had been forced to sell their home, as well as most of their possessions, in order to pay off the plethora of debts he had left behind. Months had gone by since the vultures had laid claim to their bittersweet memories. However, that devastating moment remained silently frozen in Nora's mind; as if it had just happened yesterday. With a simple hand scribbled signature, Mrs. Robertson's life had been changed in more ways than she could not have dreamt possible.

After moving into the family farm with Murial, her strained relationship with her daughter eased to a certain extent while being magnified in others. Nora had lost no love upon her husband's passing, but she adhered to the code she was taught and dawned mourning black since the announcement of Senator Robertson's death; until she met Mr. Shetron. The adjustment took weeks for Nora to acclimate to the new "normal" she would endure, clumsily trying to conceal her struggles from her youngest child.

Rumors had spread like wildfire around the social circles in regards to Mrs. Robertson's sudden displacement. It was rare that she was ever invited to a social event anymore, except by extended family members for holidays or birthdays. When it came time to celebrate Walter Crancin's birthday, Murial's cousin, just four months prior, the whole family was in attendance, along with a few outside friends and some hopeful marriage prospects vetted by his mother. His parents had been not so secretly trying to persuade him back into his family's business of butchery and enlisting the help of others to encourage him against staying on as Murial's foreman on the farm.

That was the same day Murial's mother had been introduced to Mr. Shetron; a successful man from New York whose money came as a result of investments in shipping companies before ultimately deciding to start a cattle ranch out West. He was a friend of Walter's father, Harold Crancin, from when they were kids and returned to the East to tie up some loose ends before heading out West for good. Roped into attending the party, Mr. Shetron was not familiar with the outcast stigma that clung to the Robertson family and was a refreshing change to their usual company of a twice removed cousin. Since then, her mother and Mr. Shetron had been spending many hours together and Murial feared for the day when he would break her mother's heart and head back to his ranch without her. In her eyes, her mother was not made for the West.

"You should know better by now." Jack pulled Murial closer into him while her thoughts remained as far away as the Pacific Ocean.

"I know, Jack. It's just that," Murial pulled at one of her rolled up sleeves, staring after her mother's empty trail into the house. "Well, it's just that…she was actually more friendly with me this past evening, in an enlightened demeanor at that, and then," she pointed her left index at the vacant doorway, "you saw how she stared me down and walked away as if I were some unruly maid in need of a scolding." Jack grabbed a hold of her left hand, trying to downplay her frustration by removing her accusing finger. "Every time I finally think that we are getting along a little better, more like how I have always envisioned we would be, she straightens her back and sticks her nose up in the air." Her eyes looked up at him in sudden thought. "Do you think she is afraid of something?"

"It's possible." Jack smiled down at her, taller by a mere two inches. "But you also know that a man is hardly an expert when it comes to what a woman thinks." Murial playfully smacked him in the shoulder right as Jack was raising his hands up in surrender. "Hey, I'm only speaking the truth here."

"The truth according to whom?" She smiled and arched an eyebrow.

"Every man who has ever lived, and every woman who has ever talked to a man." Jack's tone turned more serious. "Murial, you can't change her. She is who she is, and you are who you are."

"Now that is the truth of it." Her eyes squinted. "But suppose she is afraid of something?"

"Like what?"

"I am not sure. She doesn't normally shut me out that briskly unless she has something to hide."

"Murial, forget about it. You are probably just imagining things."

"That's what you say now, but mark my words, there is something she is not telling us."

Turning to walk back up the porch stairs, Jack and Murial could not see Walter bolting across the fields toward them. He had lost a little weight since returning from Arizona, and a little hair off the top of his head as well. His rounded face was wrought with panic and his blue eyes conveyed urgency as the chain from his new pocket watch flapped against his stomach while he ran through the knee high vegetation. Stopping a few yards away from where Murial and Jack were, Walter began shouting and waving his arms as if he were a king's jester, trying to grab their attention.

"MURIAL! MURIAL!" He paused while his cousin swung around to see him slightly panting, his hands now on his knees. Walter took a moment to catch his breath before continuing. "IT'S FIRESTORM AGAIN!" Murial turned out of Jack's arm around her shoulders and raced over to join Walter in the fields. Jack ran to catch up, all three of them heading towards the brown barn where an eruption of squeals and stomping hooves rang out from behind its wooden walls. Ever since she had purchased the young colt from a neighbor six months back, she had suspected that he had been the victim of abuse by a previous owner. Her suspicions had been confirmed within a week of his arrival when his past haunts began causing him to behave erratically from time to time. There didn't appear to be any pattern to what triggered his sporadic behavior, but according to Walter's hurried ramblings, one of the new farm hands had gotten a pitchfork too close to the horse, causing him to panic.

Cautiously, the threesome swung the large barn doors open to get a better look at the current situation brewing from inside. Murial stepped into the barn first, being the only one that Firestorm ever calmed down for. She surveyed the stalls and found him staring down Thomas in the second box to her left. Straw had been tossed everywhere, coating all visible surfaces with a thin layer of the dried, yellow grain stocks. Watching the streaming sunlight pouring into the darkened space, the American Quarter horse's bay coloring took on a fiery presence. Compared to the mares they housed, he was a striking beauty. Kicking at the stable walls located behind him, Firestorm's back legs ended up launching a bucket straight at Murial's head.

Ducking in the nick of time, Murial heard it slicing through the air as it sailed past her ear. "Be careful." Jack whispered. She rolled her eyes with irritation at such a childish remark. *Like I am a baby or something? I've handled this horse before. He is mine, after all, and you are not my husband.* The young farmhand's breathing was extremely labored in the corner he huddled in, trying to keep his body away from the stomping hooves of the terrified horse. Thomas's pitchfork rested haphazardly amidst the straw on the ground to his right, with the stall's closed gate being guarded on his left. Firestorm pawed at the dirt each time Thomas tried to move an inch in either direction.

Murial quietly approached the stall, keeping her steps methodically placed so as to not knock anything over as she creeped up to the open gateway. Sweat was beading down the back of her neck from the sunlight's warmth. Closer and closer, she inched her way across the dirt floor and started speaking softly into the air once she was approximately three feet from the stall's wall. "Firestorm, it's okay. Shhh. It's alright." She paused to see if he was listening to her. "Thomas doesn't want to hurt you. He has no idea what you have been through." *Actually, none of us have.* His head bounced up and down, not giving a sign either way of whether her words were working. "Just…calm down. It's alright now." Gently raising her hand, Murial eased over to Firestorm's right shoulder. "It's okay. Shhh. Everything is going to be alright."

Her hand graced along his neck in a rhythmic motion while she simultaneously moved herself closer to the opening of the stall. Suddenly, the maroon fabric of her dress caught on the fragmented corner of the stall's door, causing the hinges to creak sharply into the air. Firestorm reared up on his hind legs and squealed into the air once more as Murial backed up from her horse. "Whoa, Firestorm." In her peripheral vision, she could see Jack and Walter take a couple of huge steps toward her from their station near the barn doors. "Back up. Back up." She motioned with her free hand for them to not come any closer. *I do not need them spooking him more than he already is.*

"Murial…" Jack cut his message short when she whipped her head around to give him a fierce stare. Returning her focus back to Firestorm, she continued sweet talking him until her hand was able to reach his head again, stroking his forelock as Thomas crept along the back stable wall. He forced himself not to rush through the open gate and calmly exited without the pitchfork. Murial slowly shut the door and Walter came over to pat Thomas on the shoulder, asking the shaken man if he was hurt at all. Sticks of straw were protruding from various angles throughout the farmhand's chestnut hair and the fear of death echoed in his blue eyes. After a moment, he brushed some of the dirt from his clothing in an attempt to shake himself out of it.

"Only my ego." He cleared his throat, trying to be nonchalant about his recent scare, but Walter knew better when he saw the young man's hands trembling at his sides.

"Why don't you call it a day and head back over to the bunk house?" Walter suggested. He wasn't sure if it was the right thing to do, but all of the other chores had been finished for the day by the others. "That horse is liable to put a good scare in everyone working here. I think Daren is the only one left who hasn't spooked him."

"Yeah…thanks. I think I will, Sir." Thomas wiped the sweat from his face with his shirt sleeve and headed out of the barn without so much as a backwards glance. Jack also gave him a pat on the back in passing before making his own way over to Firestorm's stall. Standing just beside the second stall to his right, Jack studied the resemblances shared between the two Robertson women. Their stances were identical, both with the same authoritative presence and stubborn attitudes he had not fully grown accustomed to dealing with as of yet. Even though their hair and eye color were different, there was no mistaking their familial traits. Some nights, he could see a bit of her Uncle Seb in the way she watched the breeze rolling through the fields. It had been a favorite pastime of his; saying that if one listened hard enough, one could hear the voices of the past being carried on the winds.

"Wait a few more minutes before giving him an apple, Walter." Murial placed her head against Firestorm's forehead, listening to his heartbeat pulsing through his veins. Her lips formed a smile. The stallion was a gentle beast when properly handled and she was glad he was at a better home than where he had been before. She switched positions with Walter, continuing to speak gently to Firestorm as she backed away. "It's okay now. Walter is going to give you a treat, my little blaze of fire." It was her favorite way to spoil him and he didn't seem to mind his long nickname.

Jack waited to speak until Murial joined him on the other side of the barn. "That horse should be destroyed. He will never be fit for riding, much less anything else for that matter." She shook her head in disagreement. "You always give me that same reaction when I mention it."

"And I always will. That is not an option and you know that." Her arms crossed her chest. "The mere fact that you would even suggest such a thing is beyond my comprehension."

"Murial, you know I love animals, especially horses, but he is just too unpredictable and dangerous to keep around." A sigh slipped from his lips when he saw his words were not making a difference. "Then sell him."

"I can't do that either. This is my farm and MY decision." Murial could sense a new irritation festering under her skin. She reached behind her head to remove the apron strap from around her neck.

"You cannot or you will not?" Murial tightened her mouth at his question. "Because you know as much as I do that anyone else would have already been done with him."

"He just needs to be given a chance."

"A chance? You have had him for six months and he hasn't even successfully plowed one field or allowed anyone to ride him."

"Except me." Murial's focus remained steadfast on Firestorm as she spoke. "I rode him."

"For a whole two seconds before you were flat on your back." Jack walked out of the barn with Murial in tow, the argument being far from over.

"And how is that any different from breaking in any other horse?" She challenged, swinging her painting apron into a ball around her arm; the ties sailing through the air haphazardly.

"Because he is not like other horses, Murial. There is something in the way he acts…I can't put my finger on it, but it's like he…"

"Now who is imagining things?" Both eyebrows

11

raised on Murial's face.

"I am being serious here. I just don't think that horse is going to ever work on a farm. And I do not want you to get hurt trying, or anyone else." Murial's gaze fell to the ground. She knew Jack was just trying to look out for her, but sometimes it felt more annoying than helpful. Grabbing his hands in her's, she looked up at him once more.

"And I appreciate that. But I am not a little girl who needs constant protection. I would have thought you would have known that by now."

"There is a reason that Thomas was the last farmhand who would even attempt getting close to that horse." He countered.

"Walter isn't scared of him." Murial bit her bottom lip when he arched his eyebrows at her. "Okay, he is not fully scared of him." She drew herself closer toward Jack. "Tell you what, give me a few more weeks with him and then we can decide on what to do with Firestorm. A solution that does not involve destroying him."

"I thought this was your farm and your decision?"

"I do have the final say, however, suggestions are always welcomed." Her arms rose upward and wrapped around his neck. "Besides, I put up with you don't I? What is one more invalid?" Murial waited for Jack to come back with a playful retort, but instead, his attention was being pulled by something in the far off distance. "What is it?" She looked over her shoulder as Jack removed her arms and began walking into the fields. "Jack?"

"There is someone along that tree line over there," He mumbled under his breath, inaudible to her ears. Without another word, Jack dashed through the wheat and after a shadow that was dodging behind some pine tree branches on the opposite side of the field. Murial skedaddled after him in the hopes of finding out what was going on.

Rocks along the edge of the property made the final leg of the chase a bit slower for Murial, who tried to keep herself from twisting an ankle in her boots. Suddenly, she froze when silence met her ears. She could no longer hear the rustling of humans through the underbrush nor the sound of feet pounding against the rocks in pursuit. "Jack?" Murial whispered into the trees. The strong shadows created a cave like atmosphere under their thick branches and crowded needles. "Are you there?" Sunlight was barely reaching past the rocky fence line she had scrambled over just a moment before. Her ears listened for a sound, struggling to hear anything more than the buzzing of a few bees hovering around some wild flowers to her right. "Jack?"

As fast as lightning, a hand clamped over her mouth from behind. She wanted to scream, to shout, to call for help against the stranger who was restraining her. Fear was electrifying her senses while she flailed her arms to keep the stranger from being able to control her movements. "Hey, relax. It is just me." Jack's voice brought a rush of relief to her panic-stricken face. Turning around, she saw him intensely studying the shadows. "I lost whoever it was that disappeared."

"All I can say is, do not ever do that to me again!" Murial's breathing was labored from the sudden stop of adrenaline. "Don't you remember anything from a year ago?"

"You were the one calling out my name. What else was I supposed to do?"

"I whispered it around to see where you were. It is not my fault you rushed off like you did without a word as to what you were doing." Murial patted a few stray hairs back into the bun on the back of her head. "Who do you think it was?"

"Not sure. By the few footprints I was able to analyze, I would say that it was a man with a slight limp in his stride. Larger foot in size, so perhaps a taller man at that."

"The only man I know with such a limp is Silas from the hillside. But he lives in the opposite direction and does not care to venture around people unless it is imperative for him to do as such." Murial looked down at the rocky ground they were standing atop of. "That was fortunate for your 'Shadow Man' to have come this way. Not only obscuring his footprints as he fled, but adding some extra obstacles to slow down any pursuers."

"Meaning he was either lucky or knew the area."

"He could have just been a homeless gentleman or a wanderer." Murial moved her head six inches to the left, almost poking her eye out with a branch from the nearest tree. "We best be heading back now." A strange feeling was beginning to sprout within her. *Just when it seemed that all was forgotten.*

"Wait a second." Jack reached down and batted away at Murial's boot for her to move her foot. "There is something under your shoe." Stepping to the right, Murial looked quizzically at the small tubular object Jack picked up amidst the fallen needles and underbrush.

"Is that the end of a cigarette?" She carefully prodded a couple of rock crevices with her boot, just in case there were more clues to be had. "I don't see anything else. But the end is still smoking, so it had to have been dropped by your 'Shadow Man' before he fled." Her mind started grinding away. Up until this point, she had hoped that Jack was imagining things.

"The tobacco mix has a unique smell to it." Jack brought the cigarette up to his nose, breathing in the strange aroma. "Not from around here, that I am certain of. The tobacco must have been imported." He rolled the curled paper between his finger and thumb. "Hand-rolled too."

"That's not much to go on. Manufactured would have narrowed it down, but lots of stores import goods from all over the place around this area." Murial looked back over the partial cigarette again.

"Yes, but it costs more to import. This person could not have been on the poorer side and afford such a mix to smoke."

"Perhaps. But maybe such a mix was a gift from someone who could afford it. Either way, there is not much to go on here." Murial shook away a nagging feeling in the pit of her stomach that was causing her grumbling pains for some much needed food. She wanted to forget all about the 'Shadow Man' before her memories started flooding her mind. "I'm hungry and it is almost time for dinner. Race you back?" Jack playfully pulled her into him, sneaking the cigarette butt into his pants pocket, before Murial pushed him off with a laugh. Racing him all the way to the house, she maintained her distance to stay out of his reach.

They ended up on the steps of the farmhouse where he caught up to her and gave her a kiss on the lips. With a soft thud, the front door opened and closed as Nora stepped onto the porch. "Dinner is ready. You two might want to get washed up." Murial rolled her lips under themselves and straightened her dress before walking past her mother and into the house with Jack following sheepishly behind her. Mrs. Robertson rang the metal triangle attached to the overhang of the porch for the dinner call. Shouts of joy from Walter and the farmhands filled the air and she watched as they emerged like ghosts from a battlefield.

The table had been set and dinner cooked by Katy, the only maid Mrs. Robertson kept on since selling their house in the city. Nora's blue and white ceramic ware, once having belonged to her Grandmother, made the room fit for the President and brought a smile to her face when she saw it glistening in the candlelight. Being one of the only possessions she had been able to salvage from the debt collectors, it was important to her to have the place looking special for when she broke her news to her daughter. Their ornate design accented the beautiful landscape paintings that Murial had skillfully painted and hung on the walls of the eating room. Sitting upon an oak table hosting four chairs around its rectangular shape, the plates and bowls stood in sharp contrast to the wood's darker stain. Centered above the table, a cast iron chandelier held up eight candles that illuminated the room while the foursome took their seats.

Katy's heels clicked on the wooden floorboards as she made her way over from the kitchen and spooned piping hot soup into their bowls. Mrs. Robertson slowly swallowed the broth, peering up from time to time in order to glance at either Walter, Jack, or Murial. Her nerves caused her breathing to shake a little when she noticed Murial's constant sideway peeks in her direction. Placing her spoon back atop the napkin nestled beside her plate, Nora decided it was best to get it over and done with so that there were no more elephants in the room. "Bernard, Mr. Shetron, has invited me to visit his ranch out in California. He is leaving at the end of the week and would like for me to join him on his trip."

Walter and Jack stopped with their spoons in midair and gave Mrs. Robertson their full attention, mouths gaped as far as their jaws would allow. Murial glared over at Jack. *I knew she was hiding something.* Turning back to her mother, Murial was the first of the trio to speak up. "And have you accepted his offer?" She rested her spoon in the bowl of her remaining broth, grabbing the glass of water at her table setting. It's refreshing taste cleansed her palette and was helping to keep her temper at bay. *Now what is she up to?*

"I was thinking about it." Mrs. Robertson responded with a very stoic facial expression. Murial almost choked on the water when she heard her mother's reply. She was shocked beyond belief, having thought of her mother as being too cultured into the high society of the East to even consider the notion. *It would be just like her though. I had ventured out West and now she wants to as well. Always trying to do everything I do.*

"Go out West? Mother, have you lost all reason? Have you gone insane?"

"I believe I can make my own decisions in life without consulting you, Murial." Mrs. Robertson resumed eating her soup while Walter and Jack silently sat like statues, passing glances between the two ladies and waiting for the verbal showdown to commence.

"But you have never even set foot out of this area, let alone Pennsylvania. What makes you think that you will like it out there? Not to mention, survive?" Murial countered her mother's statement. "The West is far different from the East. Almost as different as two sides to a coin, if you will." She stared over at Jack, still frozen. "Tell her, Jack."

"If you could make it out there, my dear, then it cannot be all that difficult. Now, I would like to finish my soup in peace please, Daughter. Katy has a wonderful roast for us to enjoy after this scrumptious first course."

Murial could feel her anger mounting from within; frustration that had been silently increasing since the day her mother had arrived at the farmhouse. Closing her eyes, she slowly breathed in a deep breath for a moment. *Give me strength*, she spoke in her mind as she reopened them, staring up at the ceiling. Walter finished his soup, excused himself with some roast-to-go, and called it a day by heading out to his accommodations on the farm. It was a small cabin style building and had an amazing view of the valley that sprawled out before them. Jack went out back to check in with the other farmhands, and to have a smoke from his pipe, while Katy cleaned up their dishes. Nora continued to sip the broth until it was no more and promptly walked into the parlor room when she was finished.

"I suppose that it makes you feel better by belittling me in front of others?" Murial started round two of their conversation while following her mother into the other room.

"You are the one that spoiled dinner. Why come after me?" Nora sat down on the sofa.

"Me? You are the one talking about leaving with a man you know little about. I would say that that the topic was far more off putting than my questions."

"Jack's tales of the West intrigue me and I think that some traveling would do me good."

"There you go again." Murial's hands flew into the air. "You have always tried to do everything that I do."

"I have not."

"Remember the time you used my paints and created a 'landscape' to show your lady friends that afternoon you were hosting the weekly tea meeting?"

"I had already explained to you that the other ladies all had hobbies they were showing off and I wanted to let them see mine." Nora didn't look up at Murial.

"That would have been fine by me. Except for the small detail, you have so purposefully left out, about passing off my artwork as your own." Murial crossed her arms, refusing to allow her mother to get off so easily.

"I could not show them my landscape after all. You saw it. It was…"

"A wreck." Murial interjected. "Face it, Mother. Why did you not choose to live with Shannon and her new husband? You do not ever seem to give her as many issues as you do with me." Nora grasped her hands together and clenched them with all her might. It was not going to be easy for her to tell Murial what she had to say. A woman of any substance was supposed to withhold her feelings from all but oneself, according to her upbringing. A bead of sweat formed on her brow. With a deep breath, and closing her eyes, Nora began to explain.

"Take a good look around you, Murial. I am not a young woman anymore and your father's misguided compass in life has left me totally dependent upon you. No one wants me around their social gatherings and I have been completely left out of society altogether; left to rot away like discarded vegetables." Her mother tried to hold back the tears from welling up in her eyes. Murial was stunned, having never seen her mother cry except at Uncle Seb's funeral. "Everything I have ever known has changed, Murial. Maybe heading out West will be a new beginning for me. I understand that it will be challenging for someone who has been brought up in a certain way for a certain lifestyle, but…" Her mother's voice trailed off when a tear dropped down her cheek and she quickly dried it up with a handkerchief. Looking down at the initials "BS" embroidered on the square of fabric, she continued. "I really like Bernard and I haven't felt this way in a long time. Only one other person…" Nora's voice faded into nothing. That was a secret she would never reveal.

Murial wasn't sure what to say. Part of her was scared for her mother, knowing that she would really be out of her element, while the other part was happy for her, for having found Bernard after dealing with misery for so many years alongside her father. She wished there was something she could say with wisdom and comfort in a time like this. *How come the words rarely present themselves to me at the moment I need them?* "You need to do what's right for you,

Mother. Not based on the opinions of other's, but because you want to do it. If you want to go out West with Mr. Shetron, then we will support you in your decision." She embraced her mother in a hug, something unfamiliar in their family, and her surprised mother placed her arms around her daughter in a grateful and loving reception.

"Thank you." She whispered in Murial's ear. "Now we will have to tell your sister." Katy called for Mrs. Robertson from the kitchen in regards to some of the silverware, so Murial quickly found herself alone in the parlor room with only her thoughts and the ticking of an old clock for company. Through the window on the far side of where Murial sat, she glimpsed a portion of a gorgeous sunset and decided to get some fresh air on the front porch. Murial walked toward the door, talking to herself along the way in a self-discussion over what she was thinking of doing. The door creaked open as she exited the house and allowed it to bang against the threshold. *I think I must be certifiably nuts.*

She gazed out over the land that had been in her family's name since the Revolutionary War and inhaled the sweet aroma of the wild grass. The summer evening was cool and refreshing as the gentle breeze carried the clouds at a slow pace. Pink and purple undertones accented the golden rays reaching out for one last glorious display before succumbing to the darkness of night. In the distance, the mountains were hazy with humidity, casting everything in a hue of gray and shrouding the terrain with a mystic presence. This slice of heaven was her's to call home, something she had dreamed about for as long as she could remember, and she didn't want to leave it for anything in the world. But her mother was going to need all the support she could get for taking on such a big risk. *It will not be forever. Just for a few weeks.*

"I am not so lost in thought that my hearing is impaired." Murial smiled when she heard Jack's sigh of disappointment. The one thing he was not successful at was sneaking up on her. He wrapped his arm around her shoulders and kissed her forehead. Although she normally treasured being alone, Murial could not imagine having the farm without Walter and Jack to help run it. Those two men worked well together and the farmhands respected them, giving her more time to work on her paintings.

"Something is bothering you." Murial stared down at her hands, fiddling with her fingers. She missed her uncle's sheriff star whenever life was troubling her. Three years of having the small metal object at her side had created a habit that was hard to break. Her thumb began twitching while her mouth remained silent. That was all the response Jack needed to know that he was right. "You might be surprised, Murial. Maybe your mother will like it in Bracken. That is where I believe Mr. Shetron's ranch is located."

"Maybe. But she is so…proper. I am not sure if she will even last a day once we step off the train."

"Want to bet?" Murial rolled her eyes up and tilted her head back to look up at Jack.

"Are you serious?"

"Sure. Walter is already in on it. You might as well be too." He smiled.

"And what is the bet?"

"Walter thinks she will last a week. You want to bet a day?" Murial's lips pursed in thought as Jack brushed some hairs away from her forehead.

"A day and a half." Her eyes glistened with amusement. *I wonder what Mother would say to us betting on her?*

"What if she does stay?" Jack watched Murial's head lower and moved away from him. The wooden steps creaked under the pressure of her feet. Her arms swung along her sides in a careless manner.

"I think that's what I am afraid of." Murial's right hand rubbed her left arm.

"Why?"

"My mother has lived all her life on the East coast, used to a certain style of life, and has no idea of what's out there. Sure, she has listened to your stories about Conestone and my father's stories about his campaign trips, but that's all they are to her. Stories. To see it for yourself is something completely different."

"That's why she wants to go with Bernard. She wants to see what it's really like."

"Then what if she ultimately decides to live out there? Then what? One day she might realize what she has gotten herself into and then it will be too late."

"Whoa, slow down. If you ask me, the way you are talking sounds more like you are more scared than she is." Jack joined her on the dirt lane at the bottom of the stairs. He grabbed a hold of Murial's hands. "Come here." She wrapped her arms around his torso, laying her head upon his shoulder.

"As much as she annoys me to death, she is still my mother, Jack. Apart from my sister, who has CLEARLY chosen her side in all of this, she is all I have left. You know how the Drouthers are."

"You will always have Walter." He smiled at her, causing Murial to chuckle.

"Ah, yes. I cannot forget about Walter."

"Listen, there was a first time for you and me at one point, as there is for everyone at anything. It is her decision, Murial. You cannot make her choices for her. Besides, her annoying you is an understatement. You two argue like a pair of stray cats. Do not believe for a second that I could not see you were about to blow your top at dinner this evening."

"Was it that obvious?" She bit her lower lip. "But I was right about her hiding something. Wasn't I?"

"Yes, you were right." His eyes rolled. "You are not going to let that go for a little while, are you?" Murial shook her head in satisfaction.

"Nope. Not a chance." Jack's face lit up with an idea.

"Hey, what if we accompanied your mother on the trip?"

Murial's eyes widened with excitement. "I was just about to suggest that."

"I know. I overheard you discussing it with yourself a few minutes ago." She jokingly slapped his arm.

"I see your manners haven't improved."

As the stars began to twinkle in the night sky, Murial and Jack re-entered the house to go over the travel plans with her mother. The end of the week was not far away and there was a lot to do if they were going to head out to California.

3

His perfectly groomed mustache tickled the back of her neck as the smell of his cigarette smoke filled her nostrils. Murial could feel his calloused fingers over her mouth and the growing fear rising in the pit of her stomach. The Arizona sun beat unmercifully upon her skin, baking her uncles' blood onto her face after it almost sprayed into her eyes. Suddenly, her mouth was free and although she could feel it still hanging wide open, no sound came forth no matter how hard she tried. Uncle Seb was lying dead on the remaining porch of the bank that blew up. Lifeless eyes stared out of his skull at her, shattering her soul into unhealable fragments with the broken pocket watch that lay in the middle of the street.

Murial's body sprung out of bed like a rocket, a cold sweat running down her neck and face. Gulping, she managed to somehow catch her breath and ripped the bed covers off in an attempt to cool herself down. Her right hand wiped away the beads of moisture from her forehead before they ran into her eyes. *I thought I was over this by now.* Slamming the bed with her free hand out of annoyance at herself, Murial felt as if she was slipping into a darkened abyss. Finally, after so many months of nightmares plaguing her sleep, it seemed as if she had gotten them under control and was able to close her eyes without visualizing what happened in Conestone.

Killing a human being was an action she had not thought herself capable of committing a few years ago, but she reasoned that any person could kill if the motive was strong enough or a particular situation drove them to doing it. Now that she had experienced it first hand, she almost wished she had never agreed to be on her father's last political campaign. *There were two good things that came out of it.*

Self-defense had been the cause, pure and simple, but the aftermath effects were far more damaging than superficial wounds. The man had been a thief, a crooked gambler dealing with an even slimier snake for a boss. It was clear to everyone concerned that the world was better off without him in it. However, if that was truly the case, then why did Murial feel so guilty about what she had done? Pulling herself up to a standing position, her nightgown falling down to her calves, Murial picked up her housecoat that was draped over a wooden chair in her bedroom. As quietly as she could muster, Murial tip-toed her way down the stairs and walked out onto the front porch, making sure that the door closed behind her.

Fog had filled the surrounding land around the farm, reflecting the recent deluge of rain and increasing humidity brought in by the earlier storm clouds around midnight. Oddly enough, the moon shone in all its glory amidst a clear backdrop as the clouds dipped under and above its rusty hue. An eclipse was causing its unnatural coloring; a celestial event that would have piqued her interest if it had not been for the darkened trees looming slightly to her left. Thickly consuming everything in sight, darkness swallowed even the smallest glimpses of light and she could not ignore the feeling of being watched. Murial pulled the blue housecoat closer to her neck and sat on a wooden rocking chair next to a parlor room window.

Her clothing clung to her skin, latching on as if it had a life force of its own. Murial's dark brown frizzy hair laid limply over her shoulder. *It must have been the way that Jack grabbed me under the trees today. That must have been what triggered my nightmares again. And they are always slightly different each time.* She knew that the scene her unconsciousness produced was not what really had occurred, but enough of the elements were right.

When Murial had arrived on that hot Monday afternoon in July, she had been but a trapped soul, muted by her father's tight grip on her life. At the time, Walter Crancin was the manager of Conestone's only bank and she had sought out his help when her father's life was threatened by someone claiming to be "The Serpent." She was closer to him than to her own sister, which was the reason her heart became severed when her cousin was thought to have been killed by an explosion; only to find him alive outside of town days later.

As for Jack Fulton, Murial had not seen him for years before that week in Arizona; a fact that suited her quite fine in the past. She had first assumed that all of Jack's buttering-up to her father, the Senator, was just in the hopes to establish the beginnings of his own political career; back when they were both barely twenty. However, it was in the first few days of her arrival to Conestone, three years after her Uncle's funeral, that she had learned the real motive. Sometimes, she still felt a little guilty over the way she had treated him before. *Oh well, no use dwelling over unchangeable events.*

Fidgeting with a loose thread of hemming on her sleeve, the air was beginning to feel more oppressive. Some nights, she wondered if the visions would ever truly disappear with time or if they would continue to lurk in the crevices of her lost thoughts for as long as she lived. Goosebumps began to rise on her arms as her eyes caught a quick glimpse of a faint light by the line of trees. It was only visible for a brief moment before being snuffed out by something in the shadows. *Did I really just see a light? There, over there*…

Murial's back became more rigid with worry. She stared as hard as she could into the thick of the night without any success at seeing anything else. Only the tree outline was barely noticeable against the landscape, but that didn't settle her nerves any. Gently, she rocked the chair back and forth in a steady motion. The unsettling creaking from the wooden joints only added to her paranoia, so Murial hastily stopped rocking and toyed with her hair instead. Usually being outside was a way for her mind to ease by reminding her of where she wasn't: Conestone.

That dreadful place had been both a blessing and a curse to Murial. It had brought Jack back into her life and each time she looked into his eyes, she couldn't help but notice a wild, untamed look that one would imagine was born from the West. But alas, growing up on the same street as his family meant that she was not so easily fooled. All the dime novels about the Wild West were based in truth, no matter how small, and inspired young boys to travel away from home for all the action and adventure they believed to be awaiting them in a small town located in the middle of nowhere. His feisty spirit had always been there, and just like those other overeager lads, had led him into a life of being a Sheriff just like her Uncle Sebastian. *Uncle Seb.* Thinking about her uncle saddened her heart.

Jack had been there through it all at a time when she needed help the most and he stayed with her over the past year. *Funny how life sometimes parallels.* Her father had not approved of Jack's affections toward Murial when they were younger, regardless of how self-serving her father's interests had been, and now it was Jack who found himself in a quandary with his parents over their courtship.

At first, Jack had been hesitant about seeing his family in person after returning home with Murial and Walter. Even though he had written letters to them while he was away, he wasn't sure how they would react to seeing him face to face. He had been his grandfather's favorite out of his grandsons and his abrupt departure caused the aging gentleman to enter into a faster decline of health. At least, that is what his father told him. During the same week of Walter's birthday party, Jack took a chance and arrived home that Tuesday evening.

Unexpectedly, his parents accepted him home with

loving arms and his brothers, Edgar and Daniel, were each happy to see their brother. But when his mother brought up the issue over Jack and Murial courting, the merriment ended there. Murial gave an absent half smile at that memory. *Amazing how all of notable society has declared us garbage and yet we are still whispered about at their gatherings.* It did not escape her keen observations though that the gossip floating around the circles was for nothing more than their hollow amusement. Senator Robertson had owed a lot of people money and that sort of stench didn't remove easily.

At various times, Murial had tried asking Jack about what happened between him and his parents that resulted in him staying with Walter for the unseeable future. But each time he would just shrug it off and change the subject. She had even resorted to bribery in an attempt to get Walter to talk, knowing that he was closest with Jack. However, his mouth was sealed against all of the temptations she had dangled in front of him. Jack had not been the same since his family's reunion and it tore her up inside to think that she was the reason their family was being divided apart. *Is life supposed to feel like a string of issues with no end in sight?*

An owl sounded off from about five hundred feet away, bringing her back to the present and her feeling of being watched returned to the forefront of her mind. Sitting on the porch was a dumb move if she was being targeted by a stranger. She was a sitting duck; handing the person a prime moment to do whatever it was they wanted to do to her. Murial tried focusing in on the tree line once more.

Nah, I'm being silly. My imagination is running wild. Who would want to harm me?

"I would not use it all up if I were you." A tall man crept along the jutting rocks to join a thin squatter resting behind a pine tree near the rocky fence of the Robertson property. It had been a day since they had spoken last and he was eager to see how his new "friend" was getting along in his task. Most of the land was shrouded in darkness thicker than a sandstorm, but he was able to see enough through the use of a dark lantern attached to his belt and found his way between the undergrowth and the clump of pines.

Being careful to keep the light aimed at the ground, the tall man kept his face obscured. He had found the squatter a somewhat surprising gent back in town and did not want to kill him if at all possible. The less his face was seen by the squatter was better for the poor man's life to be spared. Despite the fact that the tall man had killed sixteen men before, he considered himself a fair man for giving his partners a chance to live.

"You ain't me and that's a fact 'cause I am me." The thin man replied. He lovingly pulled the cigarette out of his mouth, moving his fingers up and down as if it were a flute. "And I say that this tobacco is too ripe for wasting. As me father used to say, back home in Donegal…"

"If you are really from Ireland, then I am really the Queen of England." The tall man snuffed the light out from his lantern, pulling his hat off his head and stroking the wide brim. It was a tan hat with a singular brown feather stuck through a woven band and had been through more gunfights with him than most of the people he knew. A single bullet hole pierced through the right side of the brim just last year, becoming the only scar it now carried. His thumb poked through the hole, remembering what had occurred to give his treasured hat such a noticeable mark.

All of a sudden, a faint glow cast a fuzziness on the edge of his hat's brim and the tall man shot a murderous glare at the small flame of a freshly struck match. "Put that thing out!" Lunging for the match, the tall man almost stumbled over one of the rocks and the squatter dropped it out of fear. His bottom lip quivered.

"Needed to see who I was talking with. Just in case…"

"In case I was one of your past targets from one of your cheap cons back in the day? Given how thin you are, I'd say you weren't very successful at it."

"Maybe I was, and maybe I was not." The squatter pouted before placing the cigarette back in-between his lips. "How'd ya know I'm not from Donegal?"

"Worked with a man from Ireland once. Good worker, but he had the strangest way of talking. His words only made sense to the other Irish boys and it took quite a while to get used to."

"What happened to him? That Irish feller."

"My brother couldn't understand him and thought he was spilling his guts to a copper. Shot him between the eyes." The squatter took a hard gulp. "Wasn't until after he killed O'Sullivan that a'other Irish boy informed my brother that the badger was really protecting us by pinning what we did on a local thief." Laughter disrupted the chirping of the crickets as the tall man stuck his hat over top of his sweaty head. "That was a few years back now. Sully, that's what we called him, was a right ol' sort." Staring into the darkness, the tall man locked eyes with the squatter, returning to all seriousness. He couldn't quite make out the man's outline, but he had a good sense as to where the man's face was located. "Did they spot you at all?"

"That feller she has with her, stays in the foreman's cabin, he saw me in the shadows this afternoon." The tall man stepped forward, losing his temper and grabbing the throat of the squatter in one decisive move. Through the calloused hand constricting his airway, the squatter managed to get a few words out while the pressure mounted in his veins under his skin.

"He…chased…I…lost…him…didin't…see…me." Letting go of his accomplice, the tall man waited for the squatter to catch his breath. For a split-second, he thought about striking a match so he could talk to the disheveled wanderer face to face, killer to man. It was getting quite frustrating to be arguing with an endless sea of black. It was not the same as hashing out a conversation in the light of day; especially when he was fuming with anger. The squatter had been on the job for four days and he had already been made.

"They cannot find you. That was our bargain. Now they are aware that someone is keeping an eye on them."

"There is no need to worry. I am handling it. She is on the front porch right now. That red moon makes it hard to see, but she is there alright. Heard that door open and shut, a rocking chair creaking before long, and the door has not been opened as of yet." The squatter massaged his neck and chuckled. He could feel that his employer was hardly satisfied with that response. "She thinks I am a 'Shadow Man.' Me? Guess I am in a way. Been livin' in the shadows all me life." Shaking his head and reaching down for the cigarette that landed on the rocks, the squatter pulled at his ripped cardigan. "Besides, I thought you wanted to taunt that woman, Murial Robertson. Thought you wanted her to know y're after her." His hand continued to forge for the lost roll of tobacco. "Now, where is that smoke?"

"I don't care if she thought you were a creature from the stars, I need you to remain hidden. You hear me?" The tall man's teeth grinded together. "Or the rest of the deal is off and so is the money."

"I hear you…I hear you; loud and clear as it w're. I may not have been by this way for a spell, but the land has not changed. There is no way they will escape my watchful eye." He tapped his index finger near his left eye socket as if the tall man could see what he was doing. "Damn it!" The squatter muttered while continuing to comb the terrain with his hands. "Now you've gone and done it. I have to roll me 'nother one. Do you know how tough that is in the dark?"

"Why should I care?"

"That's right. Why should you care? It's not y'r

problem." The disheveled man pulled a small bag of the tobacco mix from the worn left pocket of his cardigan and pulled some paper from his sack. "Best I use it all up soon anyhow. Seeing as how you will most likely shoot me dead after our bargain is done. Just like that Sully guy, huh?"

"Who knows. You're not all that bad. You have at least until I get what I came here to get."

"And just what are you after? Might I ask?"

"Blood." The tall man gritted his teeth. "Just like that moon up th'r. Blood."

Shannon and Samuel Drouther had just returned
home from their honeymoon in London after a beautiful
wedding hosted by Samuel's father. Whilst overseas, he had
treated her to all the finest things her heart had desired,
sparing no expense. All paid for by his very generous father,
as according to Murial's sister. She showed off the necklace
Samuel had given her on the second day of their trip and
twirled around in one of the twelve new dresses they had
brought back with them, designed in one of the finest dress
shops in all of England. Mrs. Robertson was pleased that her
eldest daughter had married such a desirable man, in all the
right aspects, but still kept her reservations about the family;
especially after Murial had informed her about the dirty
deals between Senator Drouther, Murial's own father, and
Clive, Senator Robertson's manager. Not wanting to shatter
her daughter's happiness, Mrs. Robertson had decided to
keep the story to herself and instructed Murial to do
likewise.

Sitting on the handcrafted couch, Mrs. Robertson
gawked at the spacious parlor room that held beautifully
gilded frames displaying numerous members of the

Drouther family and sat in awe at the over-designed wallpaper coating the sides of the room. A mahogany piano rested in a corner to her right, and large windows on her left allowed for plenty of natural light to bath the area in a soft warm glow. The floor to ceiling curtains were made of silk and the suit of armor watching over the passageway, branching between the parlor and the kitchen, had been imported from Scotland. Shannon tried making her mother feel welcomed in her new home, but the snobbiness of the decor was a little overdone, even for a woman who had lived her entire life within the higher social class.

"My goodness, my dear. That necklace is quite beautiful. It is stunning on your neck." Mrs. Robertson sipped the coffee in a teacup that had been imported from Italy, watching the necklace glitter in the sunlight against her daughter's fair skin. "I will say that you do have some good taste in jewelry and tea cups."

"Those were a gift from his mother." Shannon smiled with pride. Her eyes lit up when she remembered something she had been dying to tell Nora. "Oh, Mother, I almost forgot to tell you. Remember that Marmalade Water Ice I wrote to you about? The light refreshment we were served while visiting with Lord and Lady Asherby of Canterberry?"

"I believe so." Nora pondered in thought. "Yes. Had you not described it as an orange tower of marmalade flavored ice with some candied peels around the base and top as decorations?" Shannon smiled.

"Your memory is as sharp as ever, Mother. That is the one exactly and I managed to hornswaggle it out of the head cook at the Hall. I instructed Margaret to make some the minute I received your message about coming over for a visit. I promise that you will not be disappointed. It is just like…" A sound from behind caused her to stop in mid-sentence, turning to see Murial entering the room from the kitchen doorway. Shannon rose to hug her sister. "Murial, it is so good to see you."

"It seems like forever since we saw you last. Sorry I'm late. I was stuck at the servant's entrance due to a delivery of vegetables from the local market." Murial smiled as best she could, but couldn't help the feeling of being shafted by her own sister. It used to be that the pair of them were closer when they were young girls, not deemed even old enough to ride a horse by themselves. But as the years passed, Shannon grew more distant with each one.

"Sam thought that it would be best if you didn't come through the front door because of, you know…" Shannon broke off before finishing the statement and stared down at her hands for a brief moment.

"What? Father's death leaving our family destitute, or are you referring to when I told Senator Drouther that his family were gutless swine at their California party a year ago when…"

"Murial, behave yourself!" Mrs. Robertson eyed her daughter. "They are part of our family now." Nora watched Murial's cheeks flush slightly when she realized she almost revealed too much. As it was her mother's decision to keep the truth hidden from Shannon, Murial would obey it. But there were times that she thought it was best for her sister to know what type of people she married into. Now was not that time, however, and even if she were to clear her chest of all she had learned, it would do nothing but add unnecessary pain to her sister.

"I have no hard feelings toward them, Mother. I said my peace in California, and do not wish to repeat the past." Murial smiled at Shannon, letting her know that she was genuinely happy for her sister. With Shannon's hair braided and pinned up as a bun at the back of her head, more attention was brought to her blue eyes that dominated her facial features. She gave her sister a smile in return as they silently agreed to let the past be the past.

"I'm glad for that." Senator Drouther stepped into the room with a voice that fire could not warm. "I would hate to have my daughter-in-law's sister go spreading her rubbish imaginations with complete strangers that would involve irreparable harm to our distinguished family name." Samuel stepped in behind his father, taller by nearly a foot and with red hair that came from his mother's side of the family. His thinner build was in stark contrast to his father's stocker frame, but there was no mistaking their eyes were mirrored twins.

"I must respectfully disagree with your opinions of my imagination, Senator Drouther. But to each their own opinion, as clearly stated in our Bill of Rights." Murial matched his gaze, an uneasy feat to do. His stench was the kind that inflected all he touched.

"Oh, do have some coffee, Murial." Shannon handed her sister a small plate with an ornate design and a cup that equally matched in its pattern. She knew her sister's tendency of stirring the pot and wished that this one time,

Murial would not intentionally begin to do just that.

"Thank you." Murial tried a sip before offering a compliment to her sister. "This tea set is very beautiful, Shannon. Where did you acquire it?"

"My wife picked it out. She has impeccable taste, unlike some people." The Senator's eyes fell upon his son's new wife, and Shannon cast her eyes at the floor. Murial glanced between the two, and ended with a look at her mother who was staring into her coffee, drinking softly and slowly.

"I'm afraid I must disagree again with you, Senator. I believe that your son picked a stunning necklace for my sister." Murial turned and saw Shannon smiling at her with gratitude. "He must have received such fine taste from his mother's side." She was surprised to find that even Samuel was attempting to hide a smirk from his father after her last statement and felt some inner pride for having accomplished that much.

"I must apologize for my daughter's behavior, Senator Drouther. Unfortunately she has yet to learn some refinements when it comes to holding her tongue. Something that my daughter, Shannon, has observed beautifully." Nora stated flatly.

"Your apology is accepted, Mrs. Robertson. I still miss your husband when we convene in Washington, looking back at the many years we served this great country together." He dipped his head respectfully at Nora before resting his eyes upon Murial, whose composure was as strong as ever. "Perhaps, if your daughter would like some help in acquiring such skills, I could provide the services of the Headmaster at the local finishing school. In order to teach her where her place truly lies. After all, our children are the reflections of their parents." His mouth bore an evil grin that curled at the ends. "I wouldn't want Shannon to have to bear the shame of having such an uneducated sister." He refocused his attention back onto their mother. "Nor, to have all your work go to waste in such an ungrateful daughter."

Murial glanced over at Shannon to find that her eyes were reflecting an invisible cage quietly strangling her. It was a feeling that Murial had felt herself; allowing the demons in her mind to chain her limbs within the bars everyone had in their own lives. Her sister may have married the man she dreamed about, but it came at such a high cost in many other ways. *I wonder if I could put up with such awful family members just so I could marry someone?* Calmly, Murial stepped forward and addressed the Senator in a very pleasant manner.

"Thank you for the offer, Senator Drouther, but I am disinclined to acquiesce to your request." Murial dipped her head in respect, ending with a sinister grin of her own and asked her sister to accompany her into a private discussion away from prying ears. As the two ladies left, Samuel turned to his father.

"What did she say?"

"She said 'No'." Mrs. Robertson responded and smirked into her cup of coffee as Senator Drouther stared up at his son in disappointment.

A thud sounded out against the farm's wooden wagon just as Jack and Walter dropped the last of Nora's things into the back. Not a single white cloud hung in the gorgeous blue sky that spread above their heads while birds flew across the fields and bugs zoomed about the plants growing around the base of the house. "Nice day. Humidity seems to have finally cleared out after those storms from last night." Walter looked over at Jack in puzzlement at his stoic friend. Neither one enjoyed the humidity, which is why Arizona had been such a draw to both of them, and Jack never hesitated to speak up when the air was not as thick. "You have been quiet this morning. Thought you would be delighted to be heading out West again." Jack suddenly realized that Walter was talking to him and faked a smile in order to please his friend.

"Oh, yeah, I am." Walter eyed him skeptically, given his less than enthusiastic response.

"Wow. Hold on there, Sheriff. I know you are excited and all, but simmer down." The sarcasm was oozing from Walter's words as he spoke.

"No, really…I am excited." Jack's feigned interest

was not fooling his best friend.

"Your mood would not have anything to do with the telegram you received this morning, would it?" Jack shook his head.

"A lot has been churning away in my mind as of late. That's all."

"In regards to your parents, Murial, or your inheritance?"

"All of it really." Jack rubbed the back of his neck with his left hand, pulling a red handkerchief from his pants pocket with his right and wrapped it around his neck to soak up the perspiration. It would have been better if it was soaked with water first, but his canteen was already in the wagon ready to go and the closest water pump was stationed at the back of the house.

"Is your grandfather still set on his mandate?"

"You are full of questions, are you not? Of course he is. He is the most stubborn man I have ever known. Once his decision is made up, that is the end of the discussion." Jack's eyes appeared distant in thought. "Is it weird, that as the Sheriff of Conestone, I knew what I was doing, and yet here...between my parents, my grandfather, Murial, this farm...I feel so lost?" Walter patted him on the shoulder.

"That does not sound the least bit weird to me. In fact, that sounds only human. Better watch yourself though. You would not want those fans of yours to hear that their hero is fallible." He chuckled. "Why just the other day, a boy came running up the lane asking if he could see the famous Jack Fulton." Jack's face showed his amusement.

"How those kids find out all their information is

beyond me."

"Not hard to fathom really. You are spotted in town, purchasing something at Bryan's Store or visiting McGrew's blacksmith shop, and a young boy overhears your name being spoken. And ta-da! Your secret life has been discovered, Detective."

"Thanks for being my number one prowler Walter."

"Hey, that grapevine is as strong as when we were kids. Once one boy knows where you live, the others are destined to find out. Or have you gotten rusty since you left your post as Sheriff?"

"And what about the infamous Walter Crancin who all the eligible ladies come in search of?" A teasing melody painted Jack's words. "To find the one who will follow in the family's footsteps by keeping the butchery business thriving and whisking them off to riches built from selling cut meat."

"Never thought I would ever say this." Walter's one eyebrow went down, along with a corner of his mouth slanting upward.

"What?"

"Thank the Lord above for animal manure. One deep smell of that stench and they run faster than a wild horse in the valley." Both men broke out laughing at one another. It was the first time, in a long time, that Jack's laughter was actually real and not some facade. *How such a simple act of pure happiness can lift dead weight from a soul is remarkable,* he noted to himself. All joking aside, the visit with his parents had stirred up mixed emotions from his past that he had not quite anticipated. Seeing the family home initiated a tidal wave of memories, both bitter and kind, smashing into him with the force of a wall. He hadn't mentioned to Murial about the time he spent with his grandfather since they returned, having told her only half the truth by saying he was visiting an old school friend for two weeks. Not even Walter knew the whole story since some secrets were too dangerous to reveal.

Just then, Nora's voice rang out through the air, catching the two gentlemen off guard. "Murial? Murial? Are you ready yet?" She stood just outside the front door, her hand still clutching the knob in case she had to re-enter the house in order to retrieve her daughter.

"Coming, Mother." A moment later, Murial popped out from behind her mother with an overstretched bag in her hands. "Last item." She handed the medium piece of luggage to Jack with a look of relief when the weight had been transferred to someone else.

"We are taking a train, not booking passage on a stern wheeler."

"Ha-ha. Very funny. This happens to be only my second piece of luggage."

"Yeah, the first one was the wagon." Walter quickly dodged behind Jack as Murial cast him a death glare.

"If she starts throwing punches, you are on your own my friend." Jack tossed the bag on top of his near the rear wheel.

"Some friend." Walter made his way around the other side of the wagon to check in with Thomas as Nora pulled her daughter into her side. Gazing up at the farmhouse, the two women took one last long look. The two story building consisted of a beautiful porch that wound halfway around the ground level and its pale yellow colored sides stood out against the tree line of the woods that rose beyond about half a mile back. Windows marked where the different rooms were held inside its wooden walls and cream colored drapes framed the rectangular shaped glass. Flanking the worn stairs leading up to the porch, purple and orange flowers were wilting in the midst of the summer heat.

Walter and Katy gave each of them a hug, wishing them the best and safest of travels for the long journey ahead. Mrs. Robertson wiped away a tear cascading down her maid's face before it reached her neck. "Oh, my dear Katy, you will be fine. Watch the house while we are gone." Nora gave Katy a motherly embrace, to which Murial was not sure what to think of when she saw her mother's unorthodox gesture. She knew that Katy and her mother were close, having nurtured Katy into the job as a maid since the girl was all but fifteen, but even so, the first time her mother hugged Murial in over seven years was that night earlier in the week. Such a show of compassion was not normally displayed by her mother, let alone to the hired help.

"Yes Ma'am. I will still miss you, just the same." Katy's voice held a shadow of her former British accent. Her parents had immigrated to America when she was a young child and most of her homeland's mark had faded in her tone and speech patterns. All that remained was the food she loved to cook and Murial could not foresee that aspect changing much.

"You better not damage my house." Murial warned Walter, giving him a teacherly warning.

"I promise to not break more than a plate or a dish." He teased back.

"No wonder you will never marry. Always joking and playing around just like a school boy."

"Yes, Mother." He pulled his watch out from the small pocket of his brown vest. "Time is ticking and you better get going to make sure you arrive in time for the train."

"Do you think you will be able to handle Firestorm while we are gone?" Murial grew more serious in her tone of voice. She had been worrying over how the young horse would behave in her absence, knowing full well that he only responded to her whenever he was spooked. "I don't know how long we will be staying out there."

"Everything will be fine. I have it under control." Walter assured his cousin before helping her to climb onto the wagon's front seat. Turning to Jack, Walter shook his friend's hand and pulled him in towards himself so no one else would hear what he was about to say. "And maybe it will be a good time to ask her?" His eyebrows rose up, waiting for his response.

"Jack, we are going to be late." Murial called down to them. Obligingly, he piled into the back of the wagon without giving his friend an answer and silently watched Walter and Katy's waving silhouettes grow smaller against the morning sun as the horses pulled them down the lane.

Thomas was not as experienced at driving a wagon as the other farmhands on Murial's payroll, but he had been getting better with practice and maintained the two mares at a moderate pace along the dirt road. The farmlands sprawled around them were so peaceful that none of the passengers disrupted it with any sounds. A small breeze helped to keep the warming air not so stifling whilst dandelion puffs used the currents to spread their quiet wishes whispered by the children on McBanister's farm. After thirty minutes had passed, Nora's fingers fiddled with one another nervously beside Murial, who sensed the uneasiness coming from her mother. *Maybe some conversation would help her relax?* "I've never been to Graver's Station. Have you Jack? When you visited your school friend for those two weeks?" She raised her voice so that he could hear her in the back of the wagon.

"Nope. Used the main one in the city. Graver's Station is much newer, but I heard good things about it." He tipped his hat down over his eyebrows, slouched his back against the left wall of the wagon and kicked his feet up. It was going to be a warm day and a long ride.

Murial turned around to see him settling in between the luggage. "Were you there with me when Evelyn Thatcher told me about how her cousin got the job as the ticket agent at the station?"

"I don't believe I was."

"She said that he was in talks with the original architect when it was being built, just casually talking while walking their family dog, and the gentleman asked him for his name. Only when her cousin said 'Thatcher,' the architect misheard due to all of the construction noise and thought he had said 'Hatter.' Apparently Mr.Hatter is a man on the city council and the architect, I forget his name, offered him the position as the ticket agent." Jack used his right thumb to pop the cattleman hat upward, looking up at her from under its brim.

"Murial, you know Mr. Hatter." Nora interjected into her daughter's story.

"I do?" It took her a minute to remember, but when Murial did, her face took on a disgusted look. "Yeah, I do."

"Would not the man have noticed that his last name was different when Mr. Thatcher showed up for work?" Murial was delighted that Jack was bringing the topic back to the present story.

"The architect informed the railroad company who figured that it was just a simple mistake in last names and hired him anyway. It wasn't until the architect talked to Mr. Hatter a month later that he realized Evelyn's cousin was not the man's son and by that time, it was too late." A sudden thought occurred to Murial and she glanced over at Thomas on the seat to her left. "You do know where you are going, right?"

"I believe so. Walter gave me the directions." Thomas pulled a wrinkled piece of paper from his pants pocket and handed it over for Murial to unfold. Her eyes widened at the smudged writing that was illegible.

"That is just great."

"What?" Thomas heard the sarcasm in her voice and scanned over the ruined directions to see what was wrong. "Oh no! That must have been when I spilled the water from my canteen earlier this morning. It drenched that side of my pants." They both looked at his right pant leg that had not completely dried yet.

"Well, when we get closer to the edge of the city we can ask someone there. If you don't already know where we are going Jack." Nora turned around to look at the man almost asleep in the back. His nose wrinkled as if it was bothered by a foul smell.

"Pull over, Thomas." Jack's voice came out from under his hat. "I'll take over the reins." He remained frozen while Thomas did as he requested and slowed the horses down until they stopped near the side of the road. Murial's nose sniffed the air. Since the breeze had calmed down, an unusual scent wafted up to her instead of being pushed downwind in Jack's direction. It seemed to be coming from underneath the seat.

"Jack, do you…" Jack raised his hand up for silence, breaking off Murial's question in mid-sentence. He quietly nodded his head in agreement and hauled himself up from where he had been lounging. Instinctively, Jack reached for his gun that was no longer at his side. With life being far more subdued in the East, there was little need to carry his Colt. Rolling his eyes, Jack remembered that he had packed his gun belt away in his bag and bent over to pick up the closest piece of luggage he could find to use as a weapon. Carefully, he inched his way across the wagon and over to a large bump draped in a red blanket underneath the front seat.
1…2…3…

Whipping the blanket back, Jack brought the piece of luggage into the air and primed it to strike if need be. He stared down at the man huddling in the tight corner of the wagon. Dressed in a faded blue cardigan, the disheveled man was sweating worse than a pig and tried to look up at Jack through the blinding sun. "Who are you?"

"Nicholas Smith is the name." Using his hand as a shield against the overpowering light, Mr. Smith pulled a torn handkerchief from his pocket to wipe his dirty face off with. Much to his chagrin, the combination of dirt and sweat only smeared the grime around his sunken cheeks and made him resemble a pig even further.

"Really?" The man clasped his hand over his heart in offense over Jack's disbelief.

"On me honor, Sir. Me father was John Smith."

"And what is a hornswoggler, like you, doing in our wagon?" Murial peered down from the seat. All eyes were transfixed on the stranger curled up in their midst.

"Just using it for a ride into the city, Ma'am."

"You have an unusual smell about you, Mr. Smith." Jack studied the man up and down as the wanderer uncramped himself in an attempt to sit upright.

"This time of year makes every man sweat. So I may have not had a good washing in a month. That doesn't make it right for you to point out my stench." Nicholas shook his head and clicked his teeth together. "Shameful manners, you have, Sir."

"May I remind you that you are the one stowed away on our wagon without permission." Murial's hand wanted to give the man a light hit on the back of the head, but she stopped herself before making contact.

"Alright, alright. You do have a point there me lady." Nicholas held up his hands in defeat. "Let me just grab me bag and I shall not inflict myself upon you any further." Reaching for the brown sack to his right, a small pouch of tobacco popped out of his worn cardigan pockets.

"Pipe or cigarette?" Jack put the luggage bag down; his focus now changed more onto the tobacco than the possible violent nature of the thin man.

"Huh?" Jack pointed to the pouch with a peculiar design imprinted on the cotton bag it was in.

"Oh," Nicholas's eyes fell to the half-used tobacco. "Cigarettes."

"I still prefer to smoke a pipe my grandfather gave me when I was seventeen. I've tried cigarettes but sometimes I find it difficult to roll them correctly."

"Yeah. Sometimes they are a bit hard to get right." Nicholas awkwardly stuffed the pouch into his sack. His eyes shifted side to side, almost like a trapped animal.

"What blend do you use?"

"Huh? Come again?" Jack could tell that Nicholas was becoming more rattled by all his questions into the tobacco. Mr. Smith's hands fumbled around with his sweater nervously until a failed roll came spilling out of the same worn pocket.

"Just something a friend gave me. Nothing real-fancy like." Nicholas wasted no time to climb out of the wagon. "I'll be on me way now. Thanks for the ride." Without looking back, the thin wanderer made his way along the lane and disappeared around a thick batch of bushes as everyone watched on with curiosity.

"Hey, we have a few more questions for you!" Murial called out. "Jack! Go after him!"

"I think he was the man who has been following us."

Jack muttered. He switched places with Thomas, taking the driver's spot on the front bench, and sat next to Murial on the seat. "Get in the back, Thomas."

"Then why did you not ask him why he was watching us from the pine trees if you suspected that?" Murial was not happy with the way Jack had handled the situation. She would have gone after the stranger herself if it had not been for her being sandwiched between two people. By the time she would have climbed down from the wagon, the man would have had a good head start.

"What are you talking about?" Nora was lost in the dark as to what her daughter was referring too. The rapid movement of the horses starting up on their journey once again made her grip onto the back of the seat to keep herself from falling off the crowded bench.

"Jack thought he saw someone hiding in the line of pine trees opposite our house and we found a cigarette butt of the same mixture of tobacoo that Mr. Smith had on him." Murial looked over at Jack. "At least that is what I presume caused you to ask all those questions about his tobacco mixture."

"But his story could have been true. Did you find any evidence to suggest otherwise?" Her mother pulled an ornate hair pin out of her hat.

"No." Murial looked confused. *It is not like Jack to let something so mysterious go.*

"Then there is no reason to suggest that he is nothing more than a wanderer who was spending the night under those trees and tried to obtain a way into the city for free." Nora repositioned her hair under the hat and reinserted the pin. "Besides, we must make it to the train station in time."

"We could have at least asked him about it." Murial shifted her focus over to Jack. "I really did not think you were going to let him go so easily."

"Because a man like that is not going to give us a straight answer. He was nervous alright, when I inquired about the tobacco, but if I were to ask him who gave it to him and why, he would just end up with more and more excuses every time."

"We could have offered him a reward for telling us the truth. That would put your mind to rest whether he was following us or not."

"The train is due to arrive within the hour and we have to meet up with Mr. Shetron before that." Jack encouraged the mares to quicken their pace with the reins. "The company's mark on the cotton pouch is from South Carolina. It is a premium grade and was most likely given to Mr. Smith as payment for some sort of services rendered, whatever they might have been. So I doubt that he would talk to us when someone else has already paid him quite handsomely."

"Perhaps. But since he now knows exactly where we are going, we should know either way soon enough. That is, if he manages to get another ride in time." Murial dabbed away some sweat from her forehead. "Say, if the wind was carrying the scent of his tobacco straight at you, how come it took you so long to pick up on it?"

"That patch of honeysuckle back there." Jack tipped his head in the direction they came. "The flowers must have just bloomed because their sweet smell would have washed out freshly spread manure."

Turning the wagon onto East Graver's Lane, Jack managed to get the group to the train station with fifteen minutes to spare. To their right, people walked up and down the sidewalks with parasols dangling from their arms or dogs strapped to their wrists. Stores and businesses hummed to the dance of a busy lifestyle in the small town and the air was filled with the noise of horse hooves clopping against the road while transporting people to and from work. Murial and Nora were both delighted to finally have some shade from the intense heat that was fixated on them as young Thomas jolted awake from his nap due to a rough pothole.

The station's building was rather unusual in appearance and confused Mrs. Robertson as to what the architect had been trying to achieve with its design. From the front of the building, one could see the semicircular tower that protruded upward from the back and the different styles of dormers that were haphazardly used. Painted wood and brick were just some of the materials that gave the man-built structure a whimsical feel. An extended canopy arched over the entrance so that people could disembark from their carriages and wagons under protection from the weather.

"When was this place built?" Nora asked.

"About four years ago, Mother." Murial pointed to the metal plaque placed in the wall of the building. "1883." Jack pulled the horses to a stop under the wooden canopy and Thomas jumped out of the back to start unloading the luggage while a black carriage parked to their left.

"There you are." Mrs. Robertson smiled when she saw Bernard walking over to join them. He helped the ladies get down from the tall seat before giving Nora's hand a kiss. "I am so glad that you have decided to come along. I've already sent a telegram to my daughter, explaining as much, so she will be expecting us." Bernard waved for a porter to come over and collect their belongings. "I've already paid for our tickets. Nothing but the best for my closest friends." Mr. Shetron gave each of them a boarding pass for first class travel. "We still have a few minutes before the train is due to arrive. Come. Let me introduce you to someone." He motioned for the others to follow him into the waiting room. Jack handed the reins back to Thomas before bidding farewell and caught up to the ladies inside the unique station.

"Frank!" Bernard called to a gentleman in a blue suit who was about to walk onto the platform. "Over here!" He waited until the man maneuvered his way through the crowded area to reach them. "May I introduce you to the architect who designed the very building we are standing in."

"My, it is a pleasure to meet the man who envisioned such a staple design." Murial looked over at Jack with widened eyes. Walter had informed her that Bernard knew lots of people from all different aspects of life and he was not exaggerating. It seemed that no matter where they went, Mr. Shetron knew someone.

"Thank you, Miss. I wanted to establish a look unlike others as a way to easily identify the structure. A bit of expression through the design, if you will."

"You must be thrilled that your station is so busy." Nora commented while standing in the middle of the overpacked space. Women and men struggled to get anywhere through the massive line to purchase a ticket against the flow of people trying to head out onto the platform. Voices chattered in their own separate circles, adding to the chaos encompassing the small room. Murial felt hotter amidst all of the warm human bodies than being outside under the direct sun and it was beginning to get to her. She could see the architect's lips moving, but had to strain her ears to hear what he was saying against the commotion.

"It's the rioting Ma'am. Some of the train workers have shut down the other stations on the line and everyone is trying to get on here as a result."

"Do you think we will have any issues getting through?" Nora almost stumbled into Frank from a young child forcing her way through the people's legs. "Oh, I'm terribly sorry Sir."

"Don't mention it. People are like vultures when they need to be somewhere in a hurry. And I'm not sure. Where are you all heading?"

"To Chicago before continuing out to California." Bernard stepped closer to Mrs. Robertson as a shield from another youngster wanting to push their way between the group.

"I think you should be alright. But be careful around Lebanon. There are two cousins who own competing rail lines that run parallel in some of the areas. I even heard about a time when they raced their locomotives because they are so competitive. If you have any issues, it might be around there. Sometimes things happen between those two lines."

"It has been very nice meeting you Sir, but this crowd is a little much. Please excuse me." Murial bid her farewell and followed the flow of the traffic moving out to the platform. She did not even notice who was behind her until a man shoved her out of his way and she fell backwards into Jack.

"Watch it, Lady." The man's sour tones cut through the heat.

"You are the one who shoved me…Sir." Murial was in a right foul mood already without a pompous suit and tie trying to tell her what to do. The chestnut haired man, about Jack's height, stopped to look back at Murial. His hazel eyes went straight through her to glare at Jack.

"If she is with you, Mister, then might I suggest you tell her where her place is." Murial's nostrils were fuming. She was about to give the man a piece of her mind when Jack pulled her back a step.

"I don't think that would be wise."

"Then she is not with you?"

"Oh, she is with me alright. But, you see, she is my boss." Jack gave the shocked man a canted smile.

"What is this world coming to?" The man flung his attaché to the left and continued on his way. Jack peered down at the small show of amusement that Murial was trying to hide from him.

"Was that better than telling him a piece of your mind and having a platform of people staring at you in bewilderment?"

"Maybe." Murial looked up at the large overhanging they were standing under. It reached over the tracks where the train was due to come in so that all passengers could safely board in all sorts of weather. "I haven't seen a train station like this one before."

"No. Can't say that I have either." Jack pulled his hat off to wipe his brow. "Sure is warm today. Walter may have been right that the humidity is gone, but that does not mean that the high temperature vanished." Murial couldn't wait for the train to come in so that she could get out from the crowd. People didn't bother her but the heat did. Adding a large quantity of both into the mixture was not a good combination for her.

"How much longer until the train arrives?"

"About five minutes by my reckoning." He noticed that she was becoming more unsettled. "Do you want me to get you some water?"

"No. I'll be fine. But thank you."

"There you two are." Nora weaved through three families and a group of college students to reach the edge of the platform where Murial and Jack were standing. "Bernard says that the first class boarding will be taking place near that second pillar this way." She led the other two past a small boy whose shirt was unevenly tucked into his pants and his socks sat unevenly on his legs.

"Gingerhead is guilty. Mill is mo'ving. Lady has a date with death. Read it here! Read it here! Get your copy! Seven cents." The boy raised his arms in the air in an effort to capture more attention his way. His short stature almost left him lost in the sea of adults if it weren't for his loud voice projecting over the talkative passengers.

"Murial, stay close to me." Nora grabbed hold of her daughter's hand for the final length of their journey through the masses to catch up with Bernard. A train whistle blared from somewhere down the tracks, around a bend in the nearby hillside. Smoke puffed into the air over the tops of the trees in a warning to all that the train was coming into the station. Patiently, all the onboarding passengers waited for the train to empty first. Then, in a somewhat calm manner, the new passengers began to make their way onto the steaming locomotive. Time seemed to move at a snail's pace for Murial, who clutched onto her ticket with an iron grip. There was no telling what thieves would be sneaking around in the hopes of pocketing some valuables or tickets from oblivious men and women.

Suddenly, an outcry from a nearby child caught Murial's attention, and she turned to see a little girl desperately trying to pull her mother back after losing a homemade doll that slipped from her grasp. The mother, aged and worn past her earthly years, did not heed her daughter's pleas but continued to run toward the train in a hurried fashion. The line for the third class passenger car was an interwoven mess, resembling that of a snake coiled within itself. Murial rushed over without another thought and collected the doll just before a man's boot was about to crush its small form.

She took note that its eyes were made of old buttons seemingly rescued from a trash bin, filled with straw that could have come from a nearby stable and sewn by hand out of fabric probably cut from a discarded dress. Murial scanned the crowd with her eyes, searching for the little girl whom the doll had belonged to when she heard a chilling voice in her ears that transformed her bones to ice. "I will get my revenge." The man whispered the frightful message as he passed through the horde of people. Swinging her head around to look at the man's face, Murial wasn't sure if she was relieved or disappointed to find that he had vanished as quickly as he had appeared. For a brief moment, she considered the thought of trying to search for the mysterious person, but the train's whistle blew its five minute warning, forcing Murial to resume her previous goal of locating the little girl instead.

Closing her eyes, Murial tried to visualize the girl's blonde hair and faded dress with worn boots, then reopened them to find the child and her mother about to board the train. "I'm sorry, Ma'am, but you have to purchase a ticket before boarding." The train's employee was attempting to explain their company's rules to the distraught mother.

"But I don't have any money until we reach California. Our family is out there and I do not have another way of getting there." The woman begged the man denying them entry into the car. Murial instantly fished out her purse from the pocket in her dress and counted out enough money to get them to California.

"I'm very sorry to hear that, Ma'am, but I must follow our company's rules."

"Here, this should cover it." Murial gave the gentleman the money from her purse. "That should cover both their fees." His eyes widened and the distraught woman started tearing with joy.

"Thank you, Miss. I cannot thank you enough for this." The woman reached over and gave Murial a hug out of gratitude for her unexpected generosity. "If you would tell me your name and where you are going, I can repay you once I reach my family."

"No need for that. Just glad I could help. Oh, and I believe this is yours." She handed the doll to the little girl who snatched it up immediately from her hands and thanked Murial for having saved "Patty." Another blast sounded from the train's whistle, indicating its final warning to all boarding passengers as Murial wished the mother and her daughter the best of luck.

Maneuvering her way back up to the first class car, Murial listened to the sound of the train's wheels beginning to inch their way forward. The engine roared to life and steam billowed throughout the station while the smell of coal filled up the platform. Jack called out Murial's name, standing at the entrance to the first class car and extending his hand out to her when he caught sight of her running along the platform's edge. Thrusting her hand into his, Murial managed to swing her body into the car just before it had left the platform altogether; the heel of her boot almost sliding off the last inch of the wooden floor.

"Thanks!" Murial smiled, her breathing labored from the jump.

"I was wondering where you had wandered off to in such a hurry." Jack followed her inside the car and over to where her mother and Bernard were seated by a medium sized window. The forward motion of the train felt weird under Murial's feet. *Been a while since I had to walk in a different direction than I was traveling.*

"Murial! Thank heavens you made it. Where did you disappear to? The train almost left without you aboard. And what did you think you were going to do then? " Her mother's eyes were as hard as bricks. Jack sat down in the chair closest to him, leaving Murial standing alone to face her mother's judgment.

"I saw a little girl lose her doll in the crowd and returned it to her." Murial sat down beside him, settling into the padded chairs as soon as she could.

"Don't be so hard on her, My Dear. She made it onto the train in the nick of time." Bernard gestured with his hand at all of the beauty that first class had to offer them. "What do you think?" Murial's mother had never seen the inside of a first class passenger car before and her mouth gaped slightly in awe at the luxuries that were at their disposal as Bernard rattled them off to her. "We can have the porters send telegrams for us, we can order a drink if we are thirsty, they have snacks to offer us, and they even provide footrests if we so desire." He beamed when he saw how enamored she was with their surroundings. "And if you think this is impressive, then just wait till we get to Chicago and switch trains. The Pullman cars will fulfill your every whim."

8

Chugging along down the metal tracks, all of the passengers were given a wonderful view of the countryside that passed by their windows; alternating between farms, woods and towns in patchwork while they rode across the fabric of the country. Murial speculated that the birds must see an enormous quilt designed by something far bigger than just any one person. Studying the terrain, she watched it with wonder and admiration as if it were for the first time she was witnessing it. "As many times as I have traveled over this vast country, it still amazes me with all its raw beauty." Speaking softly to herself, Murial was debating on whether or not to unearth her drawing supplies for a little bit of sketching. "Do you miss Conestone?" She raised her voice slightly louder and tilted her head away from the window while awaiting Jack's reply, who had been flipping through a newspaper he had purchased from the young lad at the station.

He briefly looked up from an article about the mill being moved out of the county. "A little." Murial glanced over at the paper and read the headline "Lady Has A Date with Death." She skimmed over the first few lines about a woman who killed a family with poison because they did not approve of her courting their son.

Murial's eyes suddenly widened the instant she remembered an appointment with Jack's mother and bolted upright in her seat. "I forgot about your mother's lunch date next week. I was supposed to be meeting Elizabeth for the first time." Jack snickered, folding the paper up in his hands.

"Edgar's fiance is Edith, and don't worry. I figured you would forget and took care of it by sending her a note with a message explaining as to why you could not attend."

"Thank you. I cannot believe I forgot." She laid her head against the back of the chair. "Oh, how did Daniel's birthday celebration go…while I am on the subject?"

"It went well. My brother was picking on Edgar for asking Edith to tie the knot with him. My mother apologized again for the engagement party invitation that just happened to have 'disappeared' in the mail." Jack's voice was edged with sarcasm.

"You know she has never really cared for me. I am not very gentrified in her eyes." Murial looked down at her hands to rid herself of a pestering fly swirling around her fingers. When she looked up at Jack again, his eyes were unsettled. "Jack, is something wrong?"

"Nothing I can't handle." He returned to the newspaper in his lap, unfolding it and returning to the story about the mill.

"That was not the question." She watched him clear his throat and continue to ignore her by burying his face into another article.

"Excuse me, Ma'am, I was told to give you this." A

porter bent over to give a rolled up piece of paper to Murial. She thanked him, studying his face for any sign that she had seen him before. But, she had not. No one should have been trying to contact her on the train. The piece of paper was crinkled and dirty like it had traveled across the desert and floated down the Mississippi River before getting to her. Murial gave the surrounding passengers a quizzical look just as Jack lowered his paper once more. *Unless it is from Walter…but why is the paper so dirty looking?*

"What is it?"

"I obviously have not opened it yet. Give me a chance to read it first." Unrolling the note, a frightful chill went down her spine. Awkwardly, she shrugged it off in an attempt to downplay the harsh words written on the paper. "Nothing. Just Walter joking that he has already broken a plate." Her lips quivered within the fake smile she bore. Murial could tell that Jack was not convinced and she hastily got out of her seat in order to question the porter as to who the sender was.

"Murial, where are you going?" Nora's question may have been spoken aloud, but it never reached her daughter's ears. Murial walked down through the aisle of seats, toward the back of the car, and found the porter taking a sip of water from a cup.

"Excuse me, Sir."

"Yes, Miss. Is there anything I can do for you?"

"Who gave you this note to give to me?" Murial held the paper up for him to see the message he handed her only seconds ago.

"Don't know his name, Miss. A thin man in a

cardigan sweater."

"Is he on this train now?"

"I do not believe so. He gave it to me at the train station. Said that there would be a young lady with a Mr. Bernard Shetron and that I should hand the note to her once we were five miles down the track." Murial's heartbeat was beginning to race. Jack had been right that the man was indeed following them. And for some unapparent reasoning, he wanted her to know that.

"This man…could he be in the second or third class cars? I know that you had your job to attend to and all, but if you can remember, it would be much appreciated." She smiled pleadingly at the man.

"Last I saw of the gentleman was just after we arrived at the station. He handed me the note, told me who to give it to, and then walked back along the platform. I'm sorry Miss." The porter's brows furrowed. "Is something wrong? Should I contact the conductor?"

"No, no. That's quite alright. Thanks for your help." Murial made her way back to her seat in silence.

"Murial, what are you doing? You keep disappearing without saying a word?" Nora placed a hand on the back of her daughter's seat. "That is rather rude and un-lady like."

"I am sorry Mother. I just wanted to check on a few things." Her voice was distant and her words hollow. "Jack, do you think that Nicholas Smith could have made it to Graver's Station before this train left?"

"It's possible…if he managed to get another ride into the city. He would not have made it if he had to walk the whole way." Jack observed her face. "Does it have

71

something to do with the note you are not telling me about?"

"No. I just thought I saw his face in one of the seats towards the back of this car." She lied, hoping he wouldn't read through the façade.

"You did?" Jack whipped his head around to see the other passengers' faces.

"I'm probably wrong. It is not like he could afford first class anyway." She tried joking the matter off.

"His employer could have paid for it." Murial placed her hand on his arm.

"Do not worry about it. I'm most likely a little shaken up from almost falling off the platform earlier today." She crumpled the message up in her free hand and asked a porter passing by to dispose of it immediately. Jack was about to counter her request, still on the hunch that it was not a message from Walter, but grumbled to himself to keep quiet. He knew that it would be a losing battle to get Murial to tell him. They were both stubborn in that regard. Returning her gaze to the tranquil countryside, Murial leaned her body against the window with the intention to place some separation between herself and Jack.

The words on the message had been emblazoned in her mind and they echoed between her ears. *My brother's blood is on your hands, and soon, yours shall be on mine.*

As the train came to a complete stop at the station in Chicago, Murial reluctantly pulled herself up from the chair, careful not to make eye contact with Jack. Lying was not her strong suit and she didn't want him to try coaxing the truth out of her. Nora and Bernard led them off of the train, after the rest of the horde had disembarked. Despite the fact that they had changed trains three times already, Murial did not feel it was safe enough to say that the wanderer was not still tracking them. She had kept mostly to herself the entire time and used her "concentration" needed to sketch as her excuse for not talking.

Jack remained at the back of their small group in order to oversee the removal of their luggage while Bernard took care of purchasing the tickets for the next leg of their journey, leaving Murial and her mother alone. Standing amidst the massive crowd boarding and exiting within the larger station, a sense of panic rose within Murial's mind. The person, or persons, who was trying to scare her, could be watching her that very minute without her knowing it. All of a sudden, it felt far safer in the comfort of the train car where she had been able to keep an eye on everyone coming and going around her. *I think I must be going mad.*

"Far be it for me to pry Murial, but I overheard part of your conversation with Jack hours ago; the small part of our trip that you actually talked on. When are you going to learn from the past?" Nora fixated her motherly gaze on her daughter.

"Mother, I have, and I can take care of myself." Murial's thumb twitched the way it always had when her stress was intensifying. She hid her hand behind her back so her mother could not spot it.

"Yes, you certainly can." Nora's eyes scanned Murial from top to bottom. "But can you allow someone else to take care of you?"

"What do you mean?"

"For being an artist, you are not very observant when examining neither yourself nor the people around you."

"Thank you, Mother. That was as ambiguous as ever."

"Murial, your past experiences have given you cause to fortify yourself with…how should I put this…rock hard walls to shield yourself. Now, they have done a good job at that, and that is not necessarily a bad thing, but sometimes those walls work in reverse as well." Their conversation was cut short when Bernard rejoined the two women from the train ticket booth.

"Ladies, our next train will be arriving tomorrow morning. Might I suggest that we locate the closest hotel for the night and then find a delectable restaurant for dinner? My treat." Bernard boasted the tickets in his hands. A suspicious thought crept into Murial's head. Walter had told her that Mr. Shetron was one of his father's closest friends, and would stake everything he had on a bet that Mr. Shetron was on the up and up with her mother. However, she couldn't help but think for a split second that he might be the one trying to mess with her head. Shannon was with the Drouthers, who could care less what happened to the rest of the Robertson family, and with Murial out of the way, Bernard was able to take her mother without much resistance. *How can I think that low of him? On the other hand, there was no one following me before he came along.*

"That sounds lovely." Nora dipped her head and allowed Bernard to escort her out to the street while Murial waited behind to locate Jack. She found him talking with the porters at the baggage car and took note of how he abruptly broke off his conversation with them as she approached. "Did Bernard obtain the tickets?"

"He did and the train is not due until tomorrow morning. We are heading over to a hotel for the night." Murial glanced over at some of the crates displaying a logo stenciled in black ink on their sides. It appeared to be the letter 'C' with a triangle inside of it and two vertical lines striking through them both. "What are those?"

"They are from Mr. Shetron's old shipping company. A couple of last items that he is transporting to his ranch." Jack and Murial left just as one of the ticket agents came over to instruct the porters on where to take the crates. One of the porters followed them out with the rest of their luggage as they exited the brick building to discover that Nora and Bernard were already waiting for them beside a carriage.

"The driver knows of an excellent hotel that is a stone's throw from the station." Bernard opened the door for the women while the porter loaded their bags into the following wagon. Murial stepped up onto the carriage step, following her mother into the cramped quarters, but faltered miserably when the bottom hem of her dress became caught. Jack helped her by removing the snagged cloth and Murial's cheeks turned red with embarrassment. She had not been so clumsy since she was nine years old and suddenly found herself wanting to jump out the other side of the carriage to hide.

After they piled in, the driver whisked them down the street and toward the Royal Gardens Hotel. Traffic was heavy at that time of day, so Mr. Shetron took the opportunity to tell them all about some of the more interesting points to owning a shipping company. "Oh, there had been some times when I caught a few of my captains trying to smuggle my own goods out from underneath my nose. They thought that they could earn some extra money on the side if they claimed that the missing boxes fell overboard during some rough seas. Even had to track down a hidden cavern where one of my captains had stashed a few boxes off the coast of Nova Scotia. Apparently he had a buyer already lined up to take the goods off his hands in that region."

"Sounds like it was far from a dull life." Jack commented. "Almost reminds me of some stories I had while living in Arizona. Found a man hiding in a cave up in the mountains who was wanted for murder." His face graced a warm smile from the memories that had surfaced. "We eventually learned that he was innocent and was being framed by his brother."

"By his own brother? Wow. I would like to hear more about your experiences in…what was the name of the town again?" Bernard was encouraging Jack to share more details.

"Conestone, and perhaps later. We still have a lot of traveling to do." He respectfully pushed the idea aside and changed the subject by asking Bernard how far his ranch was from Los Angeles.

"About a six hours ride south east. Braken has fabulous weather and the town is still growing. My daughter has been tending to my home spread with the help of my foreman, Gregory Franklin. But when I get back, she is going to run the dress shop we built together. Charlene has always wanted to run a shop, and since the town didn't have one, we decided to open it up under her mother's name. It's almost ready now and she has been so excited for the opening day." Bernard's face lit up with fatherly pride and Murial suddenly felt envious of a woman she had never met and knew less about.

Chicago was filled with so much excitement that Nora tried to take it all in at once: the smells wafting from the restaurants, the sounds of the people walking to and from their destinations, and the pronounced heartbeat of a different city. For most of the ride, she found herself staring outside the open windows at the variety of wagons and carts sharing the road until the hotel came into view and the carriage slowed down at the front entrance. Murial's focus had remained at her hands during the trip while Jack stared mindlessly at the street rolling by. Bernard stroked his beard in thought, shifting his gaze between Murial and Jack.

"We're here." The driver announced in a courteous manner. Although Murial had been to Chicago once before, the hotel she had stayed in was not as nice as the Royal Gardens. The lavishly decorated lobby was large enough to fit three hundred people and was carpeted wall to wall. A magnificent staircase ran up on the left side of the room while a parlor sat to the right. The entrance to the restaurant was beside the stairs and led into a ballroom-style eating room.

"Mr. Shetron, this hotel must cost a fortune. I'm sure we could find some much more affordable accommodations elsewhere." Murial's mind could not settle down. All the people coming and going were rattling her nerves. Chicago held some bad memories for her and she did not wish to repeat them.

"Nonsense. I only use the best. Besides, what good is money if one cannot spend it?" Bernard strode up to the front counter and asked for two rooms relatively close to one another. "Two beds in each room please, My Good Man." A bellhop led them up to the third floor and showed them two rooms across the hall; one for the ladies and one for the gentlemen.

The room was more spacious and fancier than Murial could have imagined. She had been around rich people before, however, Mr. Shetron was more carefree with his money than the others she had known. Despite the fact that her father had held a prominent job while he was still alive, his earnings were either spent haphazardly gambling or being carelessly invested in failed ventures. The result was that of a charade their family had to partake in almost constantly to keep up their image for the community. Another reminder of why she had despised her father. "Bernard must really like you, Mother."

"It would appear so." Her mother's eyes were blinking back some tears of happiness. "I never thought that I would be treated so nice by anyone since..." Trailing away in her voice, Nora stopped herself short and clutched the pendant around her neck. It was a small round piece of silver that most people would overlook. It held no design, say for the artisan's initials on the back: SR. She always wore it around her neck and never told anyone where it truly came from. Each time someone inquired, her story would vary depending on who was asking the question. "No more of that." Nora straightened her upper lip. "Now, we need to freshen up and head down stairs in time to meet up with the gentlemen for dinner. By the way, what did have you so tight lipped on the train?"

"Nothing. Walter had sent a joke." Murial sat down upon the padded stool in front of the vanity and inspected the condition of her hair. Her fingers pulled and combed through the messy tangles in an attempt to tidy up the frizzy nest that had once looked pristine.

"Murial Jayne Robertson!" Her mother's voice snapped her to attention. "You may be able to get Jack Fulton to lean your way, but I am your mother and I don't bend when you bat your eyelashes at me." Nora demanded. "What is going on?" Mrs. Robertson squinted her eyes at Murial. "For some reason, or another, every time Conestone is mentioned, Jack has been brushing it under the rug. Does that person in the wagon, Mr. Smith, have something to do with Conestone?"

"Your curiosity is going to kill you, isn't it?" Murial jabbed back. She had been wondering the same thing after they left Pennsylvania. It was the only thing that was making any sense, but that didn't mean that she wanted it to be true. Quite the opposite in fact. "I just want to forget all about it, Mother." While Murial had told her mother a great deal of what happened in the small town in Arizona, killing the stout man had not been one of them. The right time had never seemed to come for her to reveal her secret, and pretty soon, too much time had passed to the point where it became more of dredging up an unpleasant memory than anything else.

A knock at the door brought the two women to a halt in their argument. A different bellhop produced a note addressed to Nora and she read it aloud so that Murial could also hear the message.

"It's from Bernard. He says that dinner is to be at the downstairs restaurant at 8:30 sharp."

It seemed to both ladies that they could have bathed in the river and still looked worn out by their trip after half an hour of tidying up. Their dresses appeared old and tired, not nearly fanciful enough for the clientele the restaurant normally served. But the gentlemen were classy as ever and commented on their beautiful looks as they escorted them into the dining room.

"Where did you get that suit?" Murial marveled at how handsome Jack appeared.

"Mr. Shetron saw it across the street and purchased it."

"Does it not seem rather odd that he is constantly spending so much money on us?" Murial lowered her voice to a whisper.

"It's not for me to judge on what other people spend their money on, but yes."

Jack and Murial were interrupted by the host presenting their group to a table dressed in a white table cloth and with plates that had gold edging inlay within the porcelain. Golden chandeliers draped downward from a tall ceiling that had been dressed with hand-carved wood fitted around paintings done by a local artist. Murial couldn't help but stare at the magnificent work above them. Only when her neck was cramped beyond all help, did she bring her attention back to the table.

"Now then, I would like to hear some of your stories from your time in Conestone, Mr. Fulton." Bernard began.

"Perhaps I overstretched how interesting it was out there, Mr. Shetron. The ladies have already heard those tales and I do not wish to bore them by telling an overtold story past its prime."

"On the contrary, Jack has wonderful tales from the West." Nora interjected and turned her focus onto the young man. "Go ahead, Jack."

Hesitating at first, Jack reluctantly began with a story that entailed a robbery at Walter's bank in which he, and Deputy Sheriff Curt, had tracked the robbers down against all odds. Jack's eyes lit up as he reached the part where they had almost lost the convicts to coyotes, after trying to keep ahead of an incoming thunderstorm whose lightning was the cause of a few wildfires engulfing half a mountain range. Murial was relieved to see Jack more like his old self in the midst of talking about the western town. However, at the conclusion of his story, she noticed his demeanor revert back. *Maybe Mother is right. There is something about Conestone that has him so…* Bernard had become so engrossed in the tale, that he hadn't even noticed that two waiters had already placed their food upon the table in front of them.

"Wow, you certainly have had an adventure out there. I'm afraid that life at my ranch is rather dull in comparison." Bernard dove into his pheasant. "If you have more stories like that one, you should be a character in one of those Dime Novels."

"He is." Nora beamed. "Written by one of the masters of the Dime Novels himself." Bernard looked over at the cowboy in astonishment.

"I must have a copy of that novel. And I would consider it a huge favor if you would sign it for me."

"It would be my pleasure." Jack tried to hide his embarrassment at being the center of so much fuss. He was thankful that their attention switched onto the delicious meals cooked by a chef brought in from Europe. The chef's mastery of skills was reflected in the wonderful food and Murial finished her plate faster than ever before. She asked the waiter to pass her compliments onto the chef once the last drop of sauce had been devoured.

The evening was dwindling before they knew it and the time for bed was approaching faster than expected.

Murial had been fighting a sheepish feeling of shame and guilt all throughout dinner and approached Jack with an offer of a moonlit walk in the hotel's garden as a type of peace offering. Nora gave her daughter a stern look of warning against doing anything that would appear unseemly, to which Murial replied with a nasty look of her own.

Exiting through the side doors of the hotel, Jack and Murial walked past the freshly trimmed bushes and the red roses in full bloom. She studiously watched the ground as they continued along the stone pathway. Above their heads, the moon shone brightly and the air was calm. If it were not for the surrounding buildings, one would have thought they were walking in the countryside as opposed to inside a bustling city. "I must apologize for the way I behaved on the train."

"Are you referring to not telling anyone what was really written on that piece of paper or shutting everyone out and blaming it on your need to concentrate on your sketching?"

"I guess it was kind of pointless to hope that you would be fooled by such an amateur's attempt at a lie." Jack remained silent. "It was nice to hear you talking about Arizona again."

"Murial, stop beating around the bush." He stopped for a moment and looked at all of the bushes surrounding them, shaking his head at the unintended pun. "There is something you are not telling me and I don't care for it. You have been nervous since we stepped off of the train and I know it has to do with the note as well as Mr. Smith."

"It's being in Chicago again. That's all, Jack." Murial didn't like to lie to him again, but this time it was not a complete lie. "I was here once before and it did not end well for the city." She glanced up at him, seeing his eyes in a distant fog.

"Jack, is there something I did? You seem distracted as of late." Murial was growing concerned over how absent his mind was becoming. She had her suspicions that it dealt with his parents but she couldn't be sure. *Like I am in a position to say anything.* Lying was all she had been doing to him since they boarded the train near Philadelphia.

"Murial…I…" A sigh escaped into the night. "Forget about it." Jack held out his arm and Murial silently accepted his offer with her's in return. As they stepped along the path, a rustling sound came from behind a nearby hedge, causing a shiver to run up Murial's spine. She whipped around in the direction of the sound. Within a few seconds, a little brown rabbit jumped out from under the greenery and scampered away across the gardens. "Just being in Chicago, huh?" Jack knew she was still holding back from him. Murial forced a smile. For the rest of their walk, neither one spoke a word.

Breakfast arrived at the ladies' room early the following morning. A slight knock against the door's stained surface alerted Nora and she opened it up to find a food cart left in the hall without anyone attending to it. The eggs and bacon wafted into the air, tantalizing their noses. Murial's stomach grumbled and she crawled out from under her covers to get a better picture of what awaited them. Her eyes were heavy from weariness and although the bed had cradled her body, it was her mind that could not have been lured into slumber. She awoke numerous times during the night because of it, to her great dismay. "Did you order the food?"

"No." Her mother smiled. "But I believe we can guess who did." She excitedly picked up the envelope and gave a baffled expression when she saw Murial's name written on the front instead of her own. "It is addressed to you."

Inhaling a deep breath, Murial warned her mother not to eat the food until she had read the message within the white envelope. She slowly flipped the flap open, pulled the card out and read over the words with a newfound horror in

85

her eyes. Nora immediately yanked the note from her daughter's icy grip and read it aloud. "Your cowboy goes first." Confused, her mother demanded that Murial give her an explanation as her daughter ran over to the hotel door, throwing it wide open, and peered down both sides of the hall in the hopes of seeing whoever had delivered the cart. Unfortunately the hallway was empty.

"Murial, get back in this room at once! You don't even have a housecoat on!" Nora pulled her daughter back into the room just as the sound of opening doors projected down the sterile hall. Her eyes seared into Murial's. "You will tell me this instant what this is all about!"

Murial shut the door with a dreaded sigh. *Pretending that everything is going to be okay is not going to work anymore.* She informed her mother of the man's voice at the train station and the note she received aboard the first class car near Philadelphia. Nora's face was unreadable. It held a blank expression that gave Murial no clue as to what her mother was thinking. The silence was growing unbearable for her daughter. "Say something. Please."

"Did you tell Jack about any of this?"

"No." Murial could now see her mother's frustration mounting.

"I cannot believe you didn't tell him about this! I am so disappointed in you Murial." Nora rested the note on the food tray, staring at its words. Not even a smudge of ink flawed its perfect appearance. "But why would someone come after you and Jack? Whose blood is supposed to be on your hands?" Her eyes squinted in remembrance of something. "Does it have to do with Arizona?" Murial's face casted a look at the floor. "I always suspected that you hadn't told me the whole truth."

Now is the time to tell her, I guess. "Well, you could be right. I did not want to believe it, still don't in all actuality, but the man I killed might be the reason behind the person hunting us." With reluctance, Murial revealed the rest of what had occurred a year ago. She told her mother of the stout man and the trial of the mustache man named Brewer. She watched her mother's eyes widened with disbelief. "I'm sorry, Mother."

"Murial…"

"I know what you are going to say…" Murial stopped herself when Nora held her left hand up in the air, asking for silence. Her mother's composure was poised.

"I can't believe you didn't tell me all of this until now." Murial was taken aback by her statement.

"Wait, what?"

"Have we grown so far apart that you would not tell me something as monumental as that? I know we were never as close as you would have liked…"

"That is an understatement and we have been over all of that before."

"Yes, but, really?" Nora's hands flew to her hips. "Killing someone is not a small detail to leave out. Not to mention the warning that any relatives might be out to get us for revenge."

"To Jack's and my's knowledge, there were no other relatives."

"Well that's comforting." Mrs. Robertson held up the note to her daughter's face. "You two still think you are right about that?"

"You want me to say that we were wrong? Is that what you want me to say?" Murial angrily struck the note away with her hand. "Okay, fine, I was wrong. Are you happy now?"

"Overjoyed." Nora's sarcasm was thick. "Now, the first thing you are going to do is to finish dressing and then walk across the hall to tell Jack everything you just told me." Murial rolled her eyes. She was not looking forward to that conversation. Being scolded by her mother was one thing, but she didn't want to have to deal with Jack's temper as well. Studying the hot breakfast on the cart, Murial picked up one of the plates and brought it closer to her face. "You are not going to eat that?"

"I am not that stupid, Mother." Murial took the plate over to the window and rested it on the sill's ledge while she popped the window open. Using a fork and spoon to swipe it clean of all the food, Murial took her anger out on the eggs and ham with bacon. She began to go for the other plate, to do the same, when a shout from the sidewalk below caused her to stop.

"HEY!" Murial cautiously peered over the sill to see a man pointing up at her with an outraged woman at his side. Her hat oddly enough resembled the plate she had just unloaded out the window. "YOU'll PAY FOR THAT!" The man straightened up his jacket, turned on his heels, and stormed into the hotel's front entrance. Humiliation was painted all over Murial's face.

"What was that about you not being stupid?" Nora watched her daughter through the reflection of the mirror as she brushed her hair. Murial shrugged her shoulders in response.

"Oops." Running over to get her skirt and corset on, Murial finished getting into her day outfit as fast as she could. Her goal was to get down the stairs as quickly as possible, not wanting Mr. Shetron to be bothered by the hotel staff in regards to her mistake. However, a quick knock on the door moments later told her that she was too late to sneak down first. A hotel porter greeted her at the door. *Phew! At least Mr. Shetron is not there with him.*

"Pardon me Miss, but a man wishes to speak with you downstairs." The young man informed her. His hair was trimmed short for the ease of hiding it under his hat and a short mustache rested under his wider nose.

"Thank you. I will be along presently." Murial finished tidying up her hair and left her mother to do likewise. Looking out into the hallway, she couldn't help but feel reluctant to venture away from the room. With the porter almost out of sight, no one else appeared to be around.

"Murial, you should not keep the gentleman waiting. Especially after you just dropped food on him from the third floor." Nora stuck the last pin into her hair bun. "And I would rather think that no one will make an attempt on either your's or Jack's life in this hotel. Too many witnesses at this hour of the morning."

"That is not a guarantee that they won't try."

"It doesn't make any sense to do it at eight in the morning. If I were them, I would wait for a spot where you were alone or secluded from the others, or close to dark perhaps. Say…when we continue our trip out to California."

"While I am heart-warmed by your show of concern for my welfare, our jails are not filled with clever criminals. If they were smart, they would not be behind bars." Murial gently closed the door behind her, swallowing her anxiety in a single gulp and began her descent to the lobby of the hotel. Mr. Shetron practically ran into her on his way back up the stairs. "Mr. Shetron, I'm terribly sorry. I should have paid more attention to where I was going."

"Bernard, please. And it is I who should be apologizing. I must confess that I was preoccupied with watching a highly irate man fuming over by the check-in desk. Never seen a man so hot over a hat before. Good thing you are not involved with that mess." Bernard stroked his beard as he pondered in thought.

"Yeah, you are probably right." Murial smiled and continued her way down the remaining stairs. Suddenly, a strange feeling washed over her, as if she was being watched. Stopping dead in her tracks, Murial scanned the room for anyone acting peculiar. People were coming and going in no specific pattern, making it hard to distinguish any one person from the crowd. Making sure to check every possible direction, her eyes glanced back at the staircase she had just left to find Mr. Shetron still standing where they had chatted; his focus trained on her. Instantly his eyes enlarged and his body became shifty with unease. Fiddling with his hat, Bernard cleared his throat before turning abruptly around and vanished up the steps.

Murial thought that the whole thing was extremely unsettling. Although she couldn't be sure that it was her he had been staring at, given that there were so many people milling about, the idea made her shake from disgust. *Maybe he was watching someone else.* Flipping her gaze to the opposite side of the enormous lobby, Murial looked straight past her position and tried to eyeball the location that Bernard could have been studying. An empty chair rested against the far wall, with a lamp seated upon a table to its right.

Using the crowd to avoid the angry couple at the counter, still fuming over the egg speckled hat, Murial remained in the shadows of the taller men in the lobby to keep out of sight. Fear rose in her chest when she accidentally found herself visible behind a shorter woman. Quickly, Murial dodged behind a bellhop before the irate man had located her. Still, she managed to inch her way over to the parlor and stopped a gentleman from sitting down in the empty wingback seat in the nick of time. There was a recent divot in the cushion, and the faint aroma of burnt tobacco filled the air. Her hands reached toward the table and touched what appeared to be some ashes from a recently smoked cigar or cigarette. *How odd. There are not enough ashes, but there is not a tray here either.*

Turning to leave, a small reflection caught her eye by the floor. Murial bent over to take a glimpse under the table. She was surprised to find that an ashtray had been stowed underneath with the remaining butt of a cigar. Smoke was still barely rising from its dulled end that had not been completely snuffed out. "Hmm." The sound of a man clearing his throat came from behind her and Murial looked up to see who it was. His brown hair was aligned perfectly on his head, matching his impeccably sharp appearance. Slowly, Murial got to her feet with the ashtray in her hands and managed to keep the cigar butt from dropping onto the floor. Her eye level only came up to the man's chin.

"May I help you?" She smiled nervously.

"I believe you are the one who dumped this vile food onto my wife's imported peacock feathered hat." He produced a dark blue hat with three protruding peacock feathers and the most recent addition of eggs dripping from its threads. "Are you one of the maids at this hotel?" Murial looked down at the ashtray she was still holding in her hands and a thought dawned in her mind.

"Yes, Sir." Murial quickly placed the tray back onto the table. "It's my first day, Sir. I am terribly sorry for what happened. I had gotten my directions all mixed up and thought I was on the east side of the hotel. There, I am allowed to throw any leftover food out the window. It is the alley, you see." She made sure to throw in a little curtsy for good measure. "I'm truly sorry. I can try to fix it as best I can." The gentleman eyed her suspiciously, sizing her up to see if what she had said was the truth. *Now I've done it,* Murial told herself. It was the biggest lie she had come up with thus far and she had a bad feeling he could read right through it.

"Well, then I suggest you had better get a better grasp of your directions for tomorrow or elsewise I will make sure you will have to get another job. Good day." Tipping his hat snobbishly, the man half turned to leave when he paused instead. Holding the hat out over the floor, the man shook off all of the eggs he could muster and with a final turn, along with a smug smile of satisfaction, he walked away with determination in every step as Murial watched after him.

"Thanks." She mumbled under her breath. Murial stooped to pick up the egg and located a garbage can with the help of a real staff member. Smacking her hands clean of the wretched food, Murial decided that it would be best to return upstairs with the rest of her party.

"WHY DID YOU NOT TELL ME THIS SOONER?!" Jack shouted. Murial's eyes winced against the outburst she had been dreading. It was worse than she had imagined it would be. Taking a step backwards, Jack tried to restrain his annoyance before continuing onward. "You should have given me the note on the train in the first place." He took a look around the space and noticed that one of the windows was open in Nora and Murial's hotel room. Hastily, Jack walked over and slammed it closed. "I don't think we want to announce this to everyone on the street."

"Are you going to pull the drapes too?" Murial jabbed back. She crisscrossed her arms across the front of her chest and shifted most of her weight onto her left leg. Jack flipped around, locked eyes with Murial, and used his right hand to pull the velvet drapes closed in a single motion. Tense silence engulfed the room after the fabric completely covered the view of building tops. A sigh escaped Murial's lips and she rolled her eyes. "What difference does that make? Nothing has happened thus far and I'm telling you before one of us gets killed, am I not?" Her defensive eyes narrowed in on his. "Besides, none of the buildings across the street are tall enough for someone to get a clear shot at us."

"Oh, and I am supposed to be grateful that you informed me about this after my life was specifically threatened? Thanks for the consideration." His grip strengthened on the note, causing it to crease and wrinkle from the pressure.

"You didn't seem all that concerned about me keeping it from you on the train or last night." She rocked her weight back and forth on her foot's heel. "I had a hunch you could see through my lies but you failed to push me harder for the answers. So why are you so outraged now?" Deep down, Murial fought against the knowledge that it was mostly her fault for keeping the truth from Jack. A bad habit she had learned from her father was placing partial blame on the accuser to ease one's own guilty conscience. It was a destructive tactic that was hard to break and harder still to admit.

"Because this person has no face, no name, and no real evidence of existing to speak of. He or she has tracked us all the way from Philadelphia, telling me that this individual is determined and driven to get whatever they want." He waved the note in the air. "And apparently what they want is my head on a stake."

"Mother, leave us." Nora exited the room without a word, using her hand to guide the door softly shut behind her. Murial closed her eyes to steady herself, recollecting her attitude for a slight adjustment. "I am sorry Jack." She reopened her eyes to see the darkened room that felt lonely and betraying by the cloaked sunlight. The gap between them felt wider than ever. "I should have told you on the train but…" Words failed her as more lies were the only thing presenting themselves for her to say. *When did I become so prone to lying? It is not like that is a favorite skillset of mine.* Truth had always been Murial's backbone, one of the things they shared in common, but it seemed too hard to deal with at the present moment for a reason she did not think he would understand.

Jack and Murial stood still in the room. Their faces turned opposite ways in an effort to avoid further conflict. "Do you think it is Brewer?"

"I do not know what to think, or believe anymore." Jack crumpled up the note and threw it at the food cart situated along the far wall. Murial didn't want to say anything to that remark, knowing full well what he was referring to in the latter part of his statement. She waited and watched as Jack sat on the end of one of the beds. Neither one said anything for a spell until Murial broke the ice.

"I have been keeping an eye on the people around us and have not seen him anywhere."

"And what makes you so sure that it is Brewer doing this? Last time we saw him was at the trial and he was on his way to prison."

"He could have escaped or busted out before arriving at the jail."

"Curt would have sent us a telegram if that had happened."

"Who else could it be then? I am not an assassin, you know. I haven't killed anyone else."

"Why not Mr. Smith?"

"You yourself said that he was bought. Just an errand boy doing a job for someone higher up."

"I might have been wrong about that. Maybe he is the brother of the man you killed. Regardless though, you should remain within sight of one of us for the remainder of the trip." Jack instructed her. "Or have you forgotten what your old job used to be?"

"Fine." Murial's lips were tight but she tried to see past her pride. She would have offered the same advice to anyone in her situation. "I will do as you ask, but I am not going to cower in fear and let them get exactly what they want." Grasping her twitching thumb, Murial observed that Jack was keeping quiet and decided to take the opportunity to help smooth things out between them. "Jack, I was going to tell you right away about this morning's note. That was until the man came bursting into the hotel all fiery mad about his wife's…"

"You don't seem to get it. I did not pressure you into telling me because I knew it would only make you more hostile towards me." Jack picked himself up from the edge of the bed and looked into her eyes. "I trusted you to tell me on your own." He started walking over to the door when Murial stopped him by calling his name.

"Jack, there is something else I need to tell you."

"What?"

"Earlier, when I was down in the lobby to apologize for the egg mishap…"

"The what?"

"Never mind. Anyways, I was down in the lobby when I bumped into Bernard and I felt him watching me from the base of the stairs. When I looked back, he seemed startled and rushed up the steps. I thought he might have been looking past me, rather than at me, so I followed his line of sight and found an empty chair by the far wall of the parlor. Below the chair's side table, someone had tried to hide a tray with fresh tobacco ashes along with the leftover stub of a cigar."

"Your point?" Murial took a step forward, trying to close the gap between.

"My point is that someone had just left the table and I think that person was the one who spooked Mr. Shetron."

"Are you saying that he is the one behind all of this? Murial, anyone could have spooked him for a number of reasons that have no bearing on our prowler at all." Jack continued to the door and turned the knob, about to leave. "I have to go and ask the kitchen staff about this note. Perhaps they will have a lead that does not involve running around in circles." She couldn't help the fact that her temper was returning and unleashed her frustrations at him.

"I don't get this. You have tracked down bank robbers and abductors in Arizona before. You have stared into the face of killers and have watched men hang from the gallows. Why are you so rattled by this…this…phantom?" The look in his eyes scared her, ripping a terrible lightning strike through her core. For a split moment, Murial saw through his facade and the look of fear was something she had never seen in his stare before. Then he straightened himself up, shutting her out of his thoughts.

"Because there is more going on here than you realize."

"I truly am sorry, Jack." Without another word, Jack shut the door behind him and left Murial standing by herself in the empty room, shrouded in darkness.

When Murial finally decided on opening the door, she was met by her mother chatting away with Mr. Shetron in the hall. She waited to catch her mother's eye and tilted her head as a signal for her mother to rejoin her in their hotel room. Nora politely excused herself and slipped in as Bernard proceeded down the hall.

"Is everything okay? Where is Jack going? I saw him leave about five minutes ago." She looked at her upset daughter and patted her shoulders in an effort to comfort Murial.

"I'm fine. Jack went to question the kitchen staff to see if they have any information on the bearer of the note. But the real reason I called you in here was to ask you not to tell Bernard about any of this."

"I was not going to." Nora held back a smirk in delight at the confusion on Murial's face. As she was growing up, her daughter never truly saw the other side of her mother that wasn't dancing with the right political people for her husband's career or catering to the social prim and proper for luncheons that were full of shallow talk. *Then again, that's not on her,* Mrs. Robertson told herself.

That one is on me.

"You weren't?"

"No."

"Why?"

"Murial, are you so dimwitted as to not have figured that out already? I thought you would have more brains for that sort of thing. Obviously he could be the one behind everything. It would make sense. He has been everywhere we have been, owns land close to Arizona, and we would be less likely to suspect him due to the fact that he is our host."

"Mother…your own friend!"

"Do not try to shame me, Daughter. What kind of a fool do you take me for?" Nora narrowed her eyes. "Besides, you suspect him as well or else you wouldn't be wanting me to keep him in the dark." She glanced around the subdued room. "Which is evidently where we are right now."

"Where is Bernard?"

"He said he had to telephone a friend before we headed back to the train station. He was going to utilize the phone in the lobby." Nora's mind drifted into her imagination. "Electricity is wonderful, don't you think? You might be able to have it on the farm one day. I am sure Katy would love that."

"Getting back to the subject at hand, he is worth pursuing as a suspect, but he could not have been the one that whispered in my ear at the train station back home. He was already on the train with you and Jack the whole time."

"Jack had said that Nicholas Smith, or whatever his real name is, could have been hired to follow us. So why could Bernard not have done the same by hiring a man, or Mr. Smith himself, to do the job?"

"And I do not know how the man I killed and Bernard are connected." Murial gave it some thought. "If they even are." Her fingers massaged her forehead as an ache was beginning to take shape. "My brain is starting to hurt from this running around. I wish we had more to go on."

"Bernard used to manage a shipping company and has met various sorts of people in his position. It could be that the connection lies there or maybe it worked out differently? " Nora shook her head. "I see what you mean, Murial. There isn't much to go on except for a lot of unanswered questions."

Just then, Jack returned to the room with a grim expression on his face. "Well, what did you find out?" Murial excitedly asked. Peering into the hall behind himself, Jack made sure there was no one in the vicinity before closing the door.

"The food was ordered from our room, room 309." His words settled in the silence.

"Then, it was Bernard." Nora gravely stated.

"At first glance, yes, but I am not so sure. The kitchen staff only received a telephone call from the front desk by a man claiming to be stationed in our room."

"But the hotel switchboard operator would be able to corroborate that."

"She did. But both also state that there was no mention of a note to be placed on the cart."

"He could have slipped it onto the cart between the

time that the porter left the food and the time that Mother opened the door."

"That is possible because I was not watching him all the time this morning. But, the worst part is, that the porter who brought the food up does not work here."

"WHAT?!" Both women exclaimed their shock in unison.

"When I checked with the kitchen staff, the manager only told me that there was no mention of note to be delivered with the food. Then I happened to take notice of a young man who was trying hard to hide his face from me. But I managed to catch a glimpse of him anyways. His eye had a light bruise and there was a cut on his eyebrow. I cornered him, asked about the injury, and that's when he confessed to being knocked out before he could deliver the cart."

Murial gulped. "What did he look like? The man who attacked him."

"He could not remember. Says that the man came up from behind. But that isn't consistent with his injuries. Chances are that he is keeping quiet about it. I was going to pressure him for more information when the manager booted me out before I could."

"When I pulled the food cart into our room, there was no one in the hallway." Nora's hand clasped the old necklace laying against her fair skin, her fingers toying with its small chain.

"Then we are back to where we started, again. It could be Bernard or this 'fake' porter. Or they could be in cahoots with each other." Murial sighed. Saying it aloud did not make the statement sound any better than the jumbled mess spinning around in her brain. "The only thing we can be certain of is that there is someone following us."

Nora looked down at a small pocket watch she carried whenever she left the house. "Oh my goodness! We have to run to make the train in time. Bernard was already telling me about how he might have to switch the tickets to a later train because we were running behind. I better go and see where he is." Turning to her daughter, Mrs. Robertson asked Murial to take care of their luggage and left the room for the final time.

Murial double checked that their suitcases were all packed before bending over to pick them up just as Jack beat her to it. "I can get those on my own, thank you." She reached her hand over, trying to snatch her bag from his grip unsuccessfully.

"And so can I." He motioned for her to get the door and walked into the hall with a bag hanging on either side.

"Do you think we should return home?"

"I know what I would do. But what about you?" Her stomach turned with fear that bubbled up like a spring. She had a chance to turn back now, to return to ground she knew and would have a home field advantage should her prowler try to do anything. *Land that I was already being watched and hunted in. How much safer would it be to head home?* Murial shook her head. It was better to confront the danger than to keep pretending it didn't exist. That option she had already tried and the result turned out to be a quarrel with Jack, the one ally she had grown to lean on for strength. And the way she had repaid him for his kindness was to be deceitful. What started out as fear consuming her mind changed into shame stealing her confidence.

"I want to continue onward and find out who is behind this." She reached out to grab Jack's arm. He looked over at her with a puzzled expression.

"What is it? Can we not talk on the train? We are going to be late if…"

"I understand. But, please, just hear me out. I did not tell you about the note and all because I wanted to pretend that it wasn't really happening. That it is all just coincidence or random events that have no connection to one another."

"Is that not the same thing?"

"The point is…that I messed up." *There is no way I am going to tell him the whole reason,* Murial told herself.

"You could say that again." She slapped his shoulder as he chuckled, and walked down the stairs whilst a family of four began the search for their room going the opposite direction.

"I am being serious here. A minute ago you weren't all laughs and jokes. I just want the past to be past and it seems like every turn or step I make brings me back to it."

"Maybe it feels like that now, but it will not always be that way."

"How do you know?"

"You just have to have a little faith." Jack swung the bags around in order to talk to Murial face to face, rather than over his shoulder on the stairs. "I thank you for the apology, and I apologize for the way I overreacted. However, you should have known that pretending there was nothing wrong was a sure road to disaster. It did not end too well for your father when he tried that and you were the one pointing that out to him. Now, if you don't mind, we do have a train to catch."

"Finally! You two walk slower than turtles." Nora rushed over to her daughter standing in the lobby, pushed her through the door, and into the carriage.

13

After confirming with the porter that all their luggage had been loaded onto the baggage car, the foursome boarded for what would be their home away from home for the next couple of days before changing over to yet another train in Nebraska. Bernard was pleased with their awed faces at the grand splendor that was awaiting for the first class passengers taking the fashionable Pullman cars out West.

The walls of the car were ornately covered with a flower print outlined by hand carved wooden molding. Gilted golden frames held replicas of famous paintings from the old European masters and the chairs were plush covered with fabric imported from London, seated to face one another at slightly different angles to house private conversations. Forest green was splashed everywhere to accent the brick red color scheme through the use of pillows, drapes, and lamp shades. Murial's hand ran down the side of a plush chair, her fingers remembering the smooth velvet from the first time she rode in one at the age of twelve. Her father had to take a trip for work and invited both his daughters along to gain the favor of an older senator who had a fondness for children and not for power greedy men. This was a much more preferable mode of transportation over riding in a stagecoach on any given day of the week. Unfortunately, the railroad didn't extend to every town yet, so stagecoaches were still the way to travel in the more rural parts of the country.

"I had only ever heard about these cars through newspaper articles and friends, but my husband had always downplayed them to me. He never described them as being so grand." Nora soaked in the ambiance. The sculpted ceiling had been shaped into an elongated scalloped edge design with hanging lights illuminating the car adequately. Windows provided additional natural light and allowed the passengers to wave farewell to friends and family before departing from the station.

"Oh, my dear Nora, this is only one car." His eyebrows shot upward, extending his hand out for her's and taking her away to tour the rest. Murial stood awkwardly beside Jack and decided to sit down out of the way of the oncoming passengers after a woman in a red hat pardoned herself, walking between them. Jack took the seat across from her.

"Murial…"

"Shall we agree to stop keeping information from one another?" She stared out the window, not making eye contact with him.

"What?" Jack was thrown a little off guard by her question.

"You said that you trusted me to tell you about certain things and felt betrayed when I didn't."

"Yes…"

"Then what are you not telling me?"

"Murial, I cannot discuss it. That is all I can say."
Murial smoothed out a wrinkle in her tan pleated skirt with
her left hand. Its matching top, buttoned up to the neck, sat
squarely on her shoulders and gave her an authoritative
stature. "I'm being honest with you. Really, I am." Her head
remained pointed toward the window as her eyes rolled to
their corners, giving him a sideways glare.

"Alright." She smiled to let him know that she
trusted him just as the sun streamed through the glass.

"Jack? Jack Fulton?" A slender woman gracefully
strolled over to where they were seated. She was dressed in
purple from head to toe. Cream bows accented the draping
folds down the front of her skirt and matched the ruffles
along the edge of a triangle cut out over her chest. A button
at the base of the neck kept the collar closed. "Wow. It has
been so long. Small world, isn't it?"

"Getting smaller by the looks of it." Jack grinned,
tugging at his shirt which was suddenly feeling a little
tighter around his neck. "What are you doing in Chicago,
Georgina?"

"Having lunch with my fiancé's family. I'm actually
staying here for the summer with his parents and sisters, but
Martin, my fiancé, is taking me out to Springsvale Valley
today to introduce me to his aunt and uncle. They own a
factory out there." Her pink lips spread out wide, allowing
her teeth to show in perfect rows. Blonde curls framed out
her unblemished face under a beautifully handmade hat.
"Say, were you not supposed to be having lunch with your

mother and Jocelyn the week before last? Or whichever day that was. I am terrible with dates."

"Yeah…" Jack shot a nervous glance Murial's way.

"I still write to her every week. Remember how we used to be inseparable back as children? Of course life has sent us down different paths, me with Martin and Jocelyn with you, but we do not let that stop us from keeping in touch." She took a breath just long enough to sigh. "It will not be the same after I move here permanently, you know. I mean, Chicago is nice and all, with fabulous meat houses that make great steak, not like that Crancin butchery back home, and they have wonderful shops and…the list goes on. But Jocelyn will not be here with me." Her eyes perked up. "Oh, but did I mention, she is going to come here for the wedding. My whole family is. Are you going to come with Jocelyn?"

"Ah…Georgina, I have not actually had lunch with her yet. I had to postpone because of…" Jack's hand started to gesture in Murial's direction, who's eyes were like gun barrels ready to fire him down at will.

"Jack…" The bouncing blonde curls almost had a doll effect on her perfect appearance. She placed a gloved hand on his shoulder. "When are you going to be a man and see that Jocelyn is right for you? Your mother was ecstatic when you came home, practically telling everyone like a church bell. She loves Jocelyn and knows, same as I do, that you two were made for each other." Georgina removed her hand, re-clutching her purse dangling from her wrist. "Unlike that no-good, money-grubbing Senator's daughter you have been leading around on a string of pure fantasy. To think that your parents would even consider approving such an unrefined creature as she is beyond all reason. There is no way your family is going to allow scum like that into their good name. You should leave her with the cows where she belongs." Her smile returned with relief. "There. That made me feel so much better. I had wanted to talk with you about that for some time now. Jocelyn has been upset with recent events and your avoidance has been distressing her ever so."

Jack was utterly speechless. He wasn't sure what to say to Georgina. Luckily, he didn't have to when the young woman noticed his female companion seated across from him for the first time. "Oh, where are my manners? My name is Georgina Rapstead and you are?" Murial smirked in the window's reflection. She had it figured out exactly how she wanted to handle the snobby doll. Gathering her composure, so as to not show her disgust at the woman prematurely, Murial presented herself as a graceful lady by standing up to match Ms. Rapstead's height. The difference was a solid three inches, with Georgina being the shorter.

"Not at all, my dear lady. Allow me to introduce myself since my shocked conversationalist is at a loss for words. I am the no-good, money-grubbing Senator's daughter who is at the end of the fantasy string." Inside, Murial could feel the satisfaction of payback warming her heart as she watched the cheeks of Ms. Rapstead change from baby pink to embarrassing red. "Oh, did I offend you? My apologies for being so unrefined. I do not get out of the cow stalls much, you know, and am not used to being around people other than the scum of my cousins, the

Crancins." She sniffed the air on purpose near Georgina's shoulder. "I must say, though, that that smell of manure is simply refreshing. Tell me, do you bathe in it or does it just happen naturally?"

Georgina's chin shot into the air with repulsion. She gave a little huff, glared murderously at Jack from over her high nose, and spun around on her heels before marching toward the next car in a state of her own disgust. A satisfying grin spread over Murial's face as she watched after the angry doll. "So…" She turned around to look at Jack who was still in a state of shock. "Is that the real reason you decided to cancel the lunch I was to have with your mother?"

"Part of it." He coughed up the invisible blockage that made his words hoarse in sound.

"Unbelievable." Murial resituated herself back onto the chair. Her butt sinking into the impression she had just recently vacated. "I did not realize your mother held that much disdain for me. I knew she held little fondness for me, sure, but to deliberately conspire against us in that fashion takes real determination." All at once, the worrying she had been trying to suppress came up to the surface. She had seen what her father had done to tear their family apart and she didn't want to see another family go through the same pain and hurt that she had endured. "I don't want to be the knife in your family, Jack." A warming, small breeze came in with the next passenger from the entranceway. Closing her eyes, Murial breathed in the sunshine scented with fresh ground coffee beans from the nearby stand, layered with fresh shoe polish wafting from the shoeshiner's current customer.

"Every Christmas, your family would go around the street and sing carols to our neighbors, and I used to wish that my family was more like yours. My parents mostly argued and would put on a fake smile around my Father's friends to keep our "image" looking right." She reopened her eyes just as the smell of burning coal was beginning to fill the station. The whistle blew loud enough to be heard across the country, let alone for the station itself. "At the time, I did not realize that your mother was so shallow. We all have our double sides though, do we not?" Jack moved closer to the edge of his seat, grabbing a hold of both of Murial's hands. She wasn't sure if he caught onto her soft jab at him or not. He still hadn't told her everything and normally she wouldn't be so nosy, but the circumstances were far from mundane.

"Murial, listen to me. Every family has their issues, none are immune. My grandfather used to beat my grandmother over petty things. That is why when my brothers and I were born, she moved in with us to help my mother raise us. It was a way she could escape my grandfather's abusiveness without disgracing the family's name. Her father had picked my grandfather for her, telling her that he would be a good match and give her everything she wanted in life. But he could not give her what she truly longed for. Leaving home the way I did four years ago should tell you enough that I do not hold my family's opinions on a pedestal."

"Then what's changed?"

A sharp sound cut through the air, shattering glass all

around their heads and littering the ground with fragments. Murial put an arm up to shield her eyes from the shards and looked through the broken window to see the barrel of a revolver aimed directly at her. Both Jack and Murial ducked below the window's sill while the other passengers were dodging behind anything big enough to hide their bodies. Screams echoed into the air from a few of the women in the car as the men pulled them down behind the chairs and tables. Pandemonium had also been brewing on the platform, causing everyone to start running around in a chaotic frenzy. Another shot fired into the car from the same gun. The bullet embedded into the opposite wall of the train car after soaring well over their heads. *What was that one aimed at?*

Jack and Murial remained pinned down below the chairs with no weapon to use between them. *Great! I am getting tired of this. Face me already you coward!* Murial began moving the heavy chair she had been sitting on by banging the side of her body against the wooden feet. Glass had cut some of the fabric where the underlying cushions were now protruding. "What are you going to do? My gun is back in my luggage."

"How convenient for it. I am going to get behind that segment of wall separating this window and that one over there." She pointed her finger up at the space separating the two. BANG! Murial removed her hand quickly from view. "I want to get a look at the attacker this time." Suddenly, a man in a blue suit made a flying leap onto the car. He landed on his stomach, pulled a gun out from a hip holster, and jumped up to return fire against the shooter. One shot was all it took to spook the man on the platform, who ran off through the remnants of a crowd in the midst of scurrying out of his path of escape.

"Are you two alright?" The man looked down at them from where he stood, a tall gentleman that didn't need a hat to add any extra height to his stature. His hair was charcoal black, freshly trimmed, and matched the color of his newly shined black shoes.

"Yes. Thank you…" Murial stopped herself short of saying his name aloud. Although she hadn't seen him in over a year, there was no mistaking that it was Reginald Green. If he was still in the same line of work from when she had last met him in the spring of 1886, then there would be no telling what he was in the vicinity for and it was best to find out before speaking his name. "It is nice to know that some people do not sleep." She silently took note of the man's wink. *Same Reginald.*

Jack picked himself off of the ground, shaking himself free of any glass fragments, and reached for the back of his neck, wincing as he touched open skin. "Were you hit?" His hand came forward with blood matching the color of his stained collar.

"It appears so." Jack watched the blood ooze down his fingers. "Looks like it grazed me." Two of the porters arrived to see what all the commotion was about and fetched the conductor when they saw the damage sustained in the attack. Murial was about to send someone to fetch a doctor when the conductor appeared and instructed a porter to alert the police officers he saw down near the ticket office earlier.

"I'd say you're getting close by the look of things.

Glad I was able to come in on all the excitement." Reginald lowered his head to Jack's ear and whispered so no prying ears could listen in.

"Maybe and maybe not. I will brief you later." Jack applied some pressure to his wound. "Ouch. Why is it that the shallow ones hurt the most?"

"Where's your gun, Deputy? Do you not have any weapons on you?" Just then, Murial came back, ending their hushed conversation hastily.

"The doctor is on his way and the police are being notified."

"It's only a scratch. I will be fine." Jack insisted at the same time that Nora and Bernard materialized at the connecting door adjoining the neighboring train car. Mrs. Robertson raced over to Murial, scooping her daughter up in her arms.

"Are you hurt at all?" Nora asked shakingly. "We heard the gun fire and tried to weave through the mass of passengers to…" Some tears were beginning to form in the corners of her eyes. "What happened?"

"I am alright, Mother. Really. And Jack is too." Nora looked over Murial's shoulder at him.

"Oh, I am glad you are alright as well Jack."

"Thank you for your concern Mrs. Robertson."

"Did you see the shooter?" Bernard inquired. His eyes were darting around in a nervous manner. Murial curiously studied his antsy behavior while she remained within her mother's arms. *Curious way to be acting since the bullets were not fired at him.*

"He had a large hat and a long trench coat that

mostly covered him up. Elsewise, we were hunched on the floor to stay out of his sight." Jack kept his hand pressing down on his neck between the fourth and fifth vertebrae from the base of his skull. Within a short timeframe, Dr. Toleman arrived to patch Jack's wound up and instructed Murial on how to change the bandage out the following day, keeping an eye out for any possible infection.

"Any further to the right and the bullet would have nicked the spine. You are a pretty lucky man that it did not." The ladies thanked him for his work and Bernard paid the doctor a little more than what was required for his services for handling the matter so quickly. By now, two police officers had shown up to start collecting statements from everyone who witnessed the incident, causing the train to be delayed by over two hours.

"We are never going to make it to California at this rate." Nora fanned herself in one of the chairs, having already given her statement of not seeing anything to the officer twenty minutes beforehand. Her boredom was hitting its peak and all she wanted to do was to retire to the private area that Mr. Shetron had arranged for their group.

"I do not think it will be much longer, Mother. They have questioned most of the people here by now." Murial watched Reginald from her peripheral vision by the far side of the car. She was wondering how the police were going to handle his role in the situation. His wink had most likely been a signal that he was on an assignment and getting questioned by the police might blow his cover.

"Are you hungry?" Jack walked over to where the two ladies were sitting. Bernard had understandably fallen asleep on the chair beside Nora.

"Positively starved." Murial could feel her right thumb beginning to twitch again. She grabbed it quickly with her other hand, steading it from becoming a nuisance.

"How can you think about food at this hour?"

"With all due respect, Mrs. Robertson, it is past noon

at this point."

"But Jack, perhaps it would be best if you headed back to the sleeper car that Bernard showed me earlier. It looks restful in those berths and you were just shot at." Nora laid her head against the palm of her hand. "I can feel the disgruntlement growing in the air around us."

"Thank you for the suggestion, but I assure you that I am quite alright. It was just a graze and I have been through worse than that. It just hurts like a bee sting." Jack turned his attention over to Murial. "But I could go for some food. How about it?" She took a gander at his popped up collar, concealing the bandage as if it were not even there. The only visible evidence to the whole mess was the dark stains against his medium blue shirt.

"Sure." Murial looked back to where Reginald was still having a conversation with the same policeman who had questioned her on the shooting. It vexed her to see Reginald moving his head slightly upward in some sort of an acknowledgement while his eyes were pinned in her direction. Looking over at Jack, Murial's gut got the hidden feeling that the two men knew each other, or at least were on the same thought process for an unknown reason. *No sense in asking either one about it.* Jack was as bullheaded as she was when his mind had already been made up; not to mention that Reginald was not going to divulge more than what was necessary.

Following Jack into the dining car, Murial felt the last of her adrenaline beginning to fade from their recent scare. Her nerves had taken a while to simmer down from the faceless man's attack. Thoughts were ricocheting off the sides of her brain like a ball against a brick wall. There was not one idea that sat still long enough to look over before another one ended up on the forefront of her mind.

"That is alright with you, isn't it Murial?" Jack swung around to make sure everything was okay when he heard no reply from her. "Murial?"

"Huh?" Blinking her eyes in an attempt to wake herself up from a bout of absentmindedness, she stared blankly at Jack. It took her a few seconds to realize that he had been talking to her without her even noticing. "Sorry. My thoughts were running away with me. What now?"

"This gentleman said that the kitchen is a little backed up, so the wait is longer than normal. But we are not in any rush, are we?"

"No, that is fine." She forced a smile on her face. The waiter, clearly not convinced by her false expression, led them over to a booth table by a window facing the platform. Murial slid into the seat across from Jack and pulled the drapes closed immediately. Two menus were placed in front of them by the man dressed in white, along with their order checks to mark their choices with a provided pencil.

"Now look who is closing the drapes." Their waiter gave the two of them a funny look. "Just a little humor." Jack glanced up at him from the food selections he was skim reading.

"As a gentle reminder, due to having some issues with this prior in the day, you must fill out your order check if you wish to eat. We cannot fill it out for you nor can we accept any verbal orders." The man left them to examine the options listed on the single-folded book of paper to pour more water into the empty glasses of a nearby table.

Jack watched Murial above the brim of his menu. He could see her paper book shaking and surmised as to what it meant. "Your thumb is twitching again, huh?"

"It is not!" Murial huffed. She tried holding the menu up with one hand to prevent the paper from shivering. Perusing through the listed entrees, Murial's stomach rumbled when she read over an option comprised of the Table D'Hote American vegetable soup with broiled fish, rissole potatoes, succotash, salad with orange and French dressing. Marking her choices on the paper, she made sure to add a slice of pie and milk before finishing her order as Jack circled the A La Carte special consisting of pot roast with noodles and vegetables along with bread and a pot of coffee.

Jack laid his menu down first. "We are all right, Murial."

"I am calm. But did you see the way that Bernard was shifting around nervously after asking us if we saw the shooter?"

"Yes, before he fell asleep from pure boredom. Maybe he does not like guns and the scene brought back some painful memories. I cannot read his mind." Murial just stared at him from over her paper menu.

"You believe that as much as I like radishes. Don't you remember him telling us about his gun collection he has back on the farm?" They handed their completed check orders to the waiter and sipped on some wine he poured into their glasses.

"Face it. We are still nowhere in trying to narrow down who is behind all of this. It could be Brewer. He did have a conniving grin on his face at the trial, saying how he was going to repay us for what happened, but the last I heard from Curt was that Brewer had made it to jail and I have not received any other word from him since."

"I did not think that he and the stout man were truly brothers." Murial pondered.

"Does not matter if they were blood related or not. Sometimes out in the desert, there are bonds created stronger than what mere blood can form. But he is definitely raising the stakes by firing shots at us in the middle of the day with all sorts of people around. This is not the western front, it is Chicago."

"If it was him, then it stands to reason that he is not on the train since we witnessed him running away after that man…returned fire." Murial saw a shadow fall over their table, from behind, in mid-sentence. She gazed up against the strong lighting pouring in from the other side of the car to see Reginald looming over the two of them.

"May I join you?" His voice was deeper than Jack's, with a smoothness that could charm a panther.

"Sure thing, Reg." Murial was shocked to hear Jack say his name. *So I didn't imagine it. They are already acquainted with one another after all.* Reginald slid into the elongated seat next to Jack, taking note of the pulled drapes. "Murial, this here is…"

"Reginald." She smiled at Jack's stunned face. "I am guessing your last name is different from whence we last met."

"Reginald Vermen, Miss Murial. Time has stood still for you, if I may be so bold in mentioning."

"Always the flatterer." A little blush warmed her cheeks. Jack flipped his attention from one to the other, clearing his throat. "Oh, pardon me. Reginald and I met last year, in the spring, when I accompanied my father on a business trip. He hired Mister…Vermen for the duration of our stay in the city."

"Cannot say I am sorry about your father's passing, Murial."

"Not many can. So what brings you aboard this lovely train headed for ultimate destruction?" Their guest raised his eyebrows in interest.

"I have a feeling that Jack is going to brief me on the situation at hand?" Reginald waited for his seat partner's response.

"After we go somewhere more private." Jack surveyed the crowded dining area. "Too many ears for my comfort." Within five minutes, their waiter brought over the first of their food orders and handed Reginald an order check.

"This food certainly smells very good." Reginald's mouth watered as he filled out his order with a Table D'Hote roast leg of lamb with mint jelly, chilled tomato soup, pickles, potatoes and succotash paired nicely with a salad, fresh fruit, and tea. "So, Jack. You didn't tell me that the cannon-tempered spitfire your parents didn't approve of was Ms. Murial Robertson."

"You told him?" She was becoming a master at the death stares. At this rate, Murial estimated that Jack would have been dead twenty times over since they left home if looks could kill. "How many know? Wait a second. On second thought, I think I would rather know how many do not know. It is starting to sound like that is the shorter list."

"Hey, easy there Murial. Just having some fun with my man, Venom, here." Reginald jabbed Jack in the arm with his elbow.

"Venom?"

"Sure. He used to work with a man nicknamed The Serpent out in the Arizona Territory. Never knew The Serpent's real name, though, but he acted like a ghost. I was on a case with them for a time, I'd say about two years back, and that is when I gave him the nickname of Venom. Because of how he could kill with one strike."

"The Serpent was my uncle." Murial waited for Reginald's food to be placed on the table before continuing. "His name was Sebastion Robertson."

"Robertson? You mean, he was your father's brother?" Murial nodded in agreement. She stared down at the delicious food; missing the look that Reginald shared with Jack. The trio ate in silence while the train finally began to lurch forward along the steel rails.

By the time they were finished with lunch, the train station had disappeared from view and the rhythmic sound of the train wheels clickity-clacking against the tracks kept the other conversations on beat. At last, they were on their way to Nebraska for the final train switchover into California. "Shall we go?" Murial padded her lips with the napkin. She was eager to find out what was going on, if the boys club would let her in on the deal.

Murial insisted on paying for her portion of the lunch, but Reginald wasn't having it. "It is the least I can do for you after what you did for me." With that statement, she stopped arguing, figuring that it would appear rude to continue refusing his offer, and allowed Reginald to pay the $4.75 bill. Jack led them out of the dining car and asked a porter where the private section was located while Reginald took a sweeping look behind them as they walked on through to the next car. Once they left the dining car, the same waiter approached a quiet man sitting alone at a corner table to inform him of the news from the kitchen.

"The cook would like me to notify everyone that we are in the midst of making more of the American Vegetable Soup and it will take a few minutes to prep. Also, that our stock of Italian bread is being refilled and will be ready in time for the dinner service this evening." When the man didn't respond, however, the waiter tried asking a few more questions so he could keep his tables moving. "Did someone give you a check order? Are you ready to hand it over yet?"

The man's appearance was that of a cowhand foreman, with a black vest over his red shirt and a properly shined belt buckle situated around his waist. Through a well-groomed mustache, his gruff voice calmly replied, "Yes, I am now ready to order."

15

"Your reasoning makes sense, but just the same, I do not think you want to underestimate this Brewer fellow. He could have hired someone to fire at you from the platform as a distraction for him to slip aboard unnoticed or to throw you off his scent entirely." Reginald pulled a cigar from the inner pocket of his blue jacket. Murial sat across from the two men in the private room that Bernard had purchased for him and Jack to use on the trip. It was a small space with two long benches nestled against opposite walls with shelves protruding out over their heads to hold luggage.

"I am most interested in what you are doing here, Reginald. Or is it so secret you are not allowed to talk about it?" She watched him pull a box of matches from his pants pocket.

"I am here to follow a certain package that is being transported on this train." He tilted the cigar at her. "And you know that is all I am allowed to say." A knock sounded at the door, causing the trio to stop talking altogether.

"Murial, are you in there?" Murial opened the door to see her mother standing in the hallway. Nora looked past her daughter to see Reginald sitting next to Jack. "Were you not the one who fired back at the shooter earlier?”

“Yes, ma’am. And you must be Murial’s beautiful mother.” Nora could see through his charm potion.

“I wanted to thank you for coming in when you did. Please excuse us, gentlemen.” She pulled Murial into the hall, pushing the door shut behind her daughter and almost catching Murial’s skirt in the threshhold.

“Mother, what do you need?” Nora was notorious for coming in at the wrong time. Murial’s curiosity was killing her on the inside to find out what Jack and Reginald would be talking about once she was out of the room.

***

“Talman gave me your telegram. Are you sure she does not know anything?” Reginald pulled a pearl handled pocket knife from the same pants pocket his match box had been in.

“I am positive: I checked the house before her mother sold it, I rifled through her mother’s things at the farmhouse and you visited his office in Washington.” Jack removed his jacket, tossing it over to the now vacant seat across from Reginald. By now, a long lit match was slowly burning the ends of Reginald’s freshly cut cigar. That was one thing the man cherished, his cigar ‘ritual’ he performed before taking the first inhaling breath of the only brand he would ever smoke. With all of the uncertainty Reginald’s job brought him, late nights and long trips with little rest in between, enjoying a peaceful minute or two lighting his cigar was the time he could use to just relax and think.

"I already cleared Nora Robertson as a possible accomplice a while ago." Reginald watched the end of the cigar beginning to whiten as the yellow flame warmed the end. He slowly rolled the brown tube around, so as to not overburn any one spot. A gradual, even burn was the secret to such a wonderful inhaling experience. "I was referring to Murial Robertson. Or did you forget what your boss instructed you to do?"

"No, I did not forget."

"She went along on almost all of his business trips. And her astute observations make her the most likely person that would know anything about what is going on." Reginald wore out the match and struck another one to keep toasting his cigar.

"And I also mentioned in my report that Clive was my pick for having any information for us to glean from. He was the one double-dealing with Drouther behind the Senator's back. It is more probable that he could have been in this mess just as deep as his boss was."

"Great! Let me go out to Arizona and ask his dead corpse if he knows where the secret lair is located."

"That was not my fault. Seb killed him. I told him to wait for me, but he did not listen. Not that I blame him for what he did. Murial…"

"Is just one woman and we are talking about the country here. What do you think will happen when Drouther's plan is unleashed? Huh? Don't let your feelings toward her skew your judgment here. You already told us that Clive's papers did not reveal anything and time is dwindling." Reginald let the match go out, deeming that his indulgence was readied, and took in the first breath of his new cigar. A smile formed on his face. "That is pure heaven."

"Then it looks like they assigned the wrong two men for this task, considering that you seem to know her so well also." Reginald pulled the cigar from his mouth.

"Jack, sorry I am being so testy but I just got yelled at by Talman at headquarters before getting onto this train. A right ol' scolding that one was."

"For what?"

"Standing up for you." The cigar popped back into Reginald's mouth, his eyes staring down at the floor as he spoke. "Now, I like Murial too, but Talman and your boss seem to have it in their heads that you are too close to her to complete your job accurately and should be kept out of the loop from now on." Reginald slid up to the edge of the seat, smoke rising from the burnt end of his cigar. "But they also have not been through what we have, and I trust your assessment." He returned the matchbox and knife to his pants pocket. "Do you want to see this thing to the end?" Jack moved his eyes up from the notch in the ground he had been staring at for the past few minutes.

"Yes."

"Then tell me, right here and right now, do you think Murial knows anything about her father's involvement with Drouther's scheme?"

"No." Jack's eyes were rigid and fixed on Reginald's. Having worked with the cigar enthusiast for some time now, Jack knew that the only way Reginald would believe him was to stare him down as if in a gun fight. Reginald studied his face for a moment, nodding his head that he was satisfied with Jack's answer.

"Alright. Talman put me on this train not only to make contact with you, but also to track a shipment out to California. I was wondering if you could help me."

"Who is the owner of the merchandise?"

"Goes by the name of Bernard Shetron. Do you know him?"

"You already know the answer to that question." Reginald smirked. He missed working with Jack.

"He used to have a shipping company with another person, a silent partner in the business."

"He never mentioned he had a business partner."

"They were good at disguising it, but we heard from a couple of their past employees that there was a second man that ran the shadier side of the legitimate business. We do not know how much Mr. Shetron was involved, if he knew anything at all, mind you. All we know is that there was an arrest made one night when some cargo was being smuggled in on the docks about two years ago. After that, Bernard Shetron began selling off his interests, dissolving the shipping company, and uprooting his life completely in order to move out to California."

"He did have a few crates put into the baggage car for his ranch." Jack ran his hand through his hair, going over everything he could remember about the crates in his mind. "What do you want me to do?" Reginald shook his head.

"You are still the lead on this thing in my book. This time around, you are the one who knows most of what is going on and is closest to the situation at hand."

"Are you saying that Shetron's shipping company was helping Drouther ship supplies out to Conestone?"

"That is what we believe. I need to obtain the name of his silent partner to confirm our suspicions. Talman wants me to see if I can get anywhere from that angle."

"Didn't the police have a record of his arrest? I know that the concept of a police department was newer around those docks at the time, but surely there is evidence of it somewhere."

"We sent a man out to check into the matter and strangely enough, the record is missing. Smells like Drouther might have a hand in it, if you ask me."

"Government men, you mean. You fellows are contracted for government work from time to time, why not try your connections?"

"I'm merely a Pinkerton Detective, but you are a Deputy U.S. Marshall. Figured you might have some idea of who to contact. I was told that their badges were the same as your's." Reginald watched Jack's face squint up.

"Like they are going to tell me anything." Jack pulled at his collar. His wound was beginning to sting from sweating underneath the bandage. "Let's talk some more about this at dinner." Reginald respectfully rose from his seat and placed his hand on his friend's shoulder.

"Meet you in the dining car around six?" Jack silently answered with a nod of his head, trying to resist the urge to ask a question that had been nagging at him throughout the whole conversation.

"You did not stand up for me, did you? Talman's shouting fit wasn't because of me."

"What are you talking about?" Reginald shrugged. "I owed you a favor and now its paid." He shifted uncomfortably where he stood, slowly reaching for the door knob.

"No, you did not owe me anything. That debt was paid and you know that." Jack stood up to meet Reginald eye to eye. He studied the man's face, the cogs of his mind working it out. "You did it for Murial. You stood up against their thinking that Murial is involved." Reginald's gaze remained steadfast on Jack's.

"I would do anything for her."

16

"Murial, have you been listening to me?"

"Huh? What? Of course I have." Murial didn't want to admit to her mother that she had not been listening to most of her words for the last five minutes or so. Instead, she had been trying to unsuccessfully listen in on Reginald and Jack's conversation through the door. Of what she had heard of her mother's ramblings, she was missing something from one of her bags.

"Then, answer my question."

"I already have. Yes, I was listening." Murial leaned her head closer to the wall, straining her ear for any piece of information she could gather. Her interest piqued when she overheard Reginald say Bernard's name. As if it could improve her listening, Murial's eyes squinted, willing her ears to pick up on more details. Jack was answering Reginald's question when Murial heard a female voice coming up the hall behind her back.

"Excuse me, pardon me." Georgina Rapstead's look was pleasant enough towards Nora, but as soon as she saw that Murial was the other woman standing in the hall, her chin shot up in the sky and she quickened the tempo of her feet to rush by her. A young man was in tow of Ms. Rapstead with beady eyes and a tall hat placed over his dirty blonde hair that peeked out under the back of its wide brim. Murial guessed that the man must have been Ms. Rapstead's fiancee. *Not bad looking, but a little uptight if you ask me.*

"Is that Georgina Rapstead?" Nora's gaze followed after the snobby couple.

"Yep, in all her glory." Murial casted a look at her mother in curiosity. "How did you know? I did not think that the Rapsteads were still talking to you."

"Oh, they are not. But she has the same blonde curls and chin like her mother." Nora abruptly changed the subject line again. "So, Murial, since you are so keen…" Her voice trailed off when she saw that the back end of Murial's dress was not protruding enough. With all the commotion going on, Nora had not noticed the missing clothing garment until Georgina had rushed past them. She lowered her voice, looking around to make sure no other person was in sight. "Where is your bustle?"

"Mother, do you really think I would have been able to move as quickly as I had if I was wearing one earlier today? There is a reason some of those women could not move very fast when the bullets went flying. Some of their bustles were on the older side and thus, more restrictive in movement ability." Murial decided to give up on trying to listen in on the men's discussion. At this point, anything she could possibly overhear would be so far out of context that she would not have all the facts to understand it correctly.

"You are not properly dressed, Murial."

"Properly dressed? I read in a paper about an

anonymous letter that was sent in with details regarding health concerns for women, that could be attributed to wearing a bustle. Remember how Mrs. Frederick developed back pain that worsened with age?”

“Yes, but…”

“You are not able to sit correctly on any seat due to their construction, no matter what new material or design they come up with.”

“Murial, please.” Nora saw a man’s shadow at the far corner of the train car. “Come inside.” She shoved her daughter into their private room. “Why do you always have to work against me?”

“What?”

“Never mind. Do you know what happened to the photograph you gave me?”

“You packed it in one of your bags. That is all I know. Is it not there now?”

“No. That’s what I had been explaining to you…anyway, I cannot seem to find it.”

“I will just get you a new one.” Murial heard Reginald opening the door across the hall and bolted up to their own, placing her ear against the wooden surface, She listened for the receding sound of the man’s footsteps, but not a peep creaked from the floor, causing Murial’s eyes to widen with realization just before the door was pulled out from underneath her.

“Figured I might find an ear there.” Reginald looked down at Murial, who had fallen to the floor due to becoming unbalanced. “My, my. Looky there. It is a whole female attached to that ear.”

"Ha-ha. Very funny, Reginald." Murial picked herself up, dusting off her dress and straightening out her shirt. "So what were you and Jack talking about?" She had a feeling it would get her nowhere, but it didn't hurt to try at least. Reginald held up his index finger, waving it teasingly in the air at her.

"Unh uh. No. You know better than that with me. See you later, Miss Robertson." With a tip of his head, Reginald bid his farewell and headed down the hall to their left. As soon as his body moved away from blocking their doorway, Jack became visible standing within the room from across the hall. Seeing him there, Murial got the sense that there was something bothering him until Jack took note of her studious eyes and turned around. Part of her wanted to inquire into the matter, but she thought better of it. *I'll ask tomorrow.*

"There you are!" Bernard's voice carried down from the end of the car. Murial looked to her right and saw the older gentleman striding over to meet up with the rest of them. "How was lunch? I was about to venture over that way myself, but wanted to first ask you to pick." His nose sniffed the air quizzically, pulling his attention from his current train of thought. The aroma was starting to reach Murial's own nose and caused her mind to start spinning with questions. It puzzled her as to why she had not picked up on the scent before, because it was becoming all too familiar in a frightening sort of way.

Mr. Shetron's gaze fell onto the partly used cigar still smoking on the table. "Jack, I did not know you smoked that North Carolina stuff." Bernard smacked him on the arm.

"Fine choice, my boy. Only the best is what I say."

Knock. Knock. "Who' there?" A husky voice asked the blackened dead air. He was slumped against the back of the private compartment located at the end of the row within the car. It was the perfect place to hide. With an escape route only three feet to his immediate left, there would be no one to stand in his way if the plan didn't go accordingly.

"Your mother." Came the reply from outside the locked door. The man, slumped in the seat, strained his right arm up towards the lock and clicked the latch over to open. Shortly thereafter, the man with a well-groomed mustache cracked it open and quickly shut the door behind him. "We may have a bump in the road."

"You always' did like to 'tir up trouble. What did you do thi' time?"

"I didn't do anything, Boss." Brewer stuck the cigarette into his mouth that had been hand rolled in the second class passenger car, with rows of seats far more accommodating than that of third class. There, he had been in the midst of talking with a porter when the conductor came down the aisle. The porter, scared to get into trouble for neglecting his duties for too long, had led Brewer into the end of the private compartment cars to continue their well-paid conversation.

"You like to 'ay that line whenever trouble is around. Look, I let you do it your way when it came to 'neaking me aboard this here train, but your dramatic' are going to cau'e more 'ttention than I care for."

"You reached out to me, remember? You are the one that hired me again."

"I have few other option' currently." In the darkness of the room, Brewer couldn't see the man's scarred face but he could hear the injury in his voice. A gun had jammed and backfired a few years ago, leaving his vocal cords partly damaged. It was a miracle that he had healed as well as he had, growing a beard to help cover over the wound. When he was approached by the man for a job, Brewer had not even recognized him at first.

"You wanted to get on board without anyone seeing you right? Did you not do that?"

"Yeah. Before cop' were crawling all over the place and nearly di'covered me."

"You have a pardon don't you? A signed piece of paper from the government?"

"That wouldn't mean a thing to them there blue jacket'. By the time they would of made 'ure it was good, thi' train would have been long gone. And I do not have forever to complete my ta'k."

"Don't give me that one." Brewer struck a match on the bottom of his boot and used the flame to light up his new cigarette. "You could vanish if you wanted too." He deeply inhaled the first puff of the North Carolina tobacco mix.

"Oh, I plan on that. But I don't need any interruption' until I complete what I came to do." He pulled his knife from a sheath tied at his side. The point was sharp and lethal, the way the scarred man like it. His finger ran along the flat side of the blade. "What happened to that wandering feller?" In the darkness, the man couldn't see Brewer's shoulders shrug with indifference.

"Left him back in Chicago."

"You took care of it?."

"He won't talk." Brewer moved his cigarette to the other side of his mouth. There was no reason he could think of for telling his boss that he actually spared the man's life.

"Good. Now we just wait." The scarred man flipped his knife over to the other side. "Now, what was thi' here trouble you were talking about?"

"We got a Pinkerton Detective on board." He watched his boss's reaction in the dim lighting coming from under the pulled drapes to the hall. The tip of the man's knife reached up and shined in the light, glinting like a dangerous beauty. "He was meeting up with Jack Fulton, the sheriff from Conestone."

"Intere'ting." The scarred man replaced the hunting blade into his sheath. "You know what you need to do." Brewer wasn't scared of much in life, except for maybe his own death. His boss didn't invoke the sense of fear or desperation in him that he did for others. He had killed far too many men to care any longer, but there was a determination brewing inside of him. It was to such a degree, that Brewer agreed to do the job for mere peanuts in pay with a promise of more after completion.

At the time that the scarred man had asked Brewer if he was up for the task, he hadn't cared that his old accomplice was willing to come along for meager dollars, until now. He was safely on the train, traveling to California almost on schedule, but there were too many cops and detectives around for comfort. Was Brewer trying to entrap him just like someone else had done before?

"Brewer, you've done well." He waited a breath. Trying to get a feeling for what his companion was thinking. "I didn't que'tion about your loyalty back in Fairfax, but I have to know why now. Why are you willing to do it all for a fiver?"

"Because I have my own score to settle with someone." Brewer gathered what the man was driving at. "It's not with you, Boss. Have no worry. I just figured that I might as well get paid while going after the person I was hunting down anyway."

"Jack Fulton, you after? Remember, as long as…"

"I know. 'Don't touch Shetron and all is good.' No, it is not him. I am after the woman, Ms. Murial Roberston." His voice oozed disdain and contempt between his lips. He had been dreaming about how to wreak his vengeance upon her since his boss busted him out of jail precisely 283 days ago. Even before then, if he were to be honest.

"And what did that girl do to you?"

"She killed Thomas." His eyes filled with hatred.

"That woman did Thoma' in?" A low whistle escaped his boss's mouth. "One tough cookie that one."

"It was a…since when do you care?" His boss leaned over to him.

"Because I want to know what the enemy' like. Bernard ain't alone. I need to know who we are going up again't."

"Then why not just go after them here and now? Plenty of stops along the way to jump off at and enough wilderness to loose anyone come searching." Brewer saw his boss's crooked teeth in a wide, sinister grin.

"Leverage, Brewer. Leverage."

The scenery of the mountainside, and sloping landscapes of the mid-western terrain, was a sight to be treasured. Soil untouched by any European footprint had a certain purity that caused the passenger's faces to marvel at the exquisite wonder of God's creation. Snowcapped mountains stood rigid and strong in stark contrast to the soft fields spotted amidst the deciduous forests below. It was serene and calming, the wind pushing fresh pine scent through the open windows of the train cars.

Murial sketched some of the landscape in a small journal she kept in her personal bag, sitting atop the overhead rack along with one of her mother's own bags. Although she felt that the seats were not as comfortable in their private compartment, compared to the cushioned chairs situated in the parlor car, the area had become too congested of people for Murial's liking. She worked best in a quiet space where she could focus and not allow other people's voices to cloud her head. Looking over the forest she was trying to grasp a good likeness of, Murial took some artistic liberty by adding in longer shadows to the scenery in her work for greater contrast and more dimension than what the afternoon sun was currently providing.

Her mind was lost in the detail of the beautiful countryside when the door slid open to the suite and her mother stepped into the room. Nora looked over her daughter's shoulder to see how her drawing was coming along. "That looks very nice, Murial. Are you going to turn it into one of your paintings?"

"I would like to eventually." Murial stopped the motion of her pencil to look up at her mother. "Did you have a pleasant lunch with Bernard?"

"Yes, I did. Thank you." Nora sat herself across from Murial. "Did you have lunch with Jack today?"

"No. Reginald accompanied me." Nora looked out the window, seemingly lost in thought.

"How do you know Mr. Vermen?" Murial figured her mother would ask sooner or later. She was surprised it took as long as did, since it had been two days since the shooting. They were on their last night of their current train until changing over at Sun Valley Station.

"His actual name is Reginald Green. Vermen is just his cover for his current assignment." She gathered her sketchbook and pencils, closing them up in a tin box, and sat them on the seat next to her. "It is a long story. You really want to know?" Nora nodded and Murial obliged after making sure the door was securely shut; the memory being played in her mind's eye as if she was still there.

"It happened in the spring of last year when Father and I traveled to Chicago for work. He was to meet up with a business owner and another senator on talks regarding the eight hour work day laws. We arrived on the evening of

May 3rd with just enough time to check into a hotel for the night. See, we had scheduled to be there a day earlier but complications due to labor protests and marching riots kept impeding our travel. Anyway, the next morning was when Father had been told to meet with Senator Hemperstein and we showed up about ten minutes before nine o'clock.

But that was not a very good morning to be in the city. The night we arrived, protestors had been killed at a strike occurring outside a factory. It had been reported by eyewitnesses that police officers fired into the crowd and the city was in a uproar. Senator Hemperstein's office was encased in panic, rushing around in preparations for a disastrous scenario. It was then that Father was advised to hire on another bodyguard in case things were to get rough. Hemperstein's secretary suggested the Pinkertons, their home office was in the city, but Father refused. They all thought it was because he was tough." Murial took a breath. "It had more to do with not having to pay out the money more than anything, if you ask me."

"Is that how Mr. Green fits into all of this?"

"Senator Hemperstein had arranged to meet up with a business owner who owned a wholesale warehouse near Haymarket Square, located on Desplaines Street. The businessman was supposed to gather some of the other shoddyocracy owners with him. It was after dark when we went to the warehouse and I sensed that someone was tracking us. He kept his distance, hiding in the shadows and staying out of sight, but I caught a glimpse of his own dark reflection in the light of the torches along the street. No one was on the roads at that hour, so we met up as per the plans.

I waited outside of the room where the three men talked. During the meeting, I chatted with the man's secretary about various things until shouting sounded on the street from below us. We ran over to the window, overlooking the square, to see a man giving a speech to hundreds of people from a hay wagon.

Rebecca Townser was her name, the secretary at the warehouse. She informed me of the riots that had been increasing throughout the city. Many of the business owners, such as her boss, did not comply with the eight hour work day law that had been signed back in the 1860s. That was what Father and the other two men were discussing. Hemperstein was trying to…well, enough with the politics. I watched on with Rebecca as another man climbed onto the hay wagon with a speech of his own. We were up too far to hear their words, but the excitement of the crowd was all we needed to figure out what was going on. Suddenly, people's heads began turning around to see a number of police officers approaching to break them up.

I tore myself away from the windowsill and rushed into the meeting. I shouted to them to remain within the building and fetched Senator's Hemperstein's two security men to check out what was taking place. They did not want to listen to a woman giving them orders, so I went out alone. That is when it all went crazy. Men were shouting at the police who were shouting right back. I maneuvered around the side of the crowd, keeping to the buildings as much as humanly possible. Then something was launched at the officers by a person in the middle of the mob, causing the start of gunfire shooting off in all directions. It was not until later, that I had learned it was a bomb the person threw.

Everything was pure chaos. I dodged out of the way, trying to help a few people to not become pummeled by others, when I saw Reginald pulling apart a man-to-man fight between a cop and an immigrant worker. Once he broke them up, the cop aimed his gun at Reginald, who had fallen to the ground from a woman backing up into him. I located a rock by my foot and used it to knock the weapon free from the officer's hand, pulling Reginald over to the outskirts of the crowd by the buildings. Only after we made it back to the warehouse, did he tell me that he was a detective with the Pinkertons." Murial had been looking at the seat with her mind lost down memory lane. Looking over at her mother, she was taken aback to see Nora's face scolding her with her face.

"Your Father, nor you, never told me about any of this! I even asked you if you had seen what happened after I read an article about it in the newspaper when you returned home." Her fists rested on her hips. "Why did you lie to me?"

"I was not the one who lied. Father told you that there was nothing interesting to report. He figured you would be able to read through any story I was to come up with, so he took care of it, and told me to keep my mouth shut. I was the one who wanted to tell you the truth." Murial shoved her drawing supplies into her bag. A knocking at the door startled both ladies and Nora opened it up to see Jack standing there in a sullen manner.

"Bernard says that we will be arriving at Sun Valley Station around ten tomorrow morning."

"Thank you Jack." Nora dipped her head in appreciation and reclosed the door. She waited till she heard his footsteps leave in order to continue their talk. "That man has been so depressed as of late." Turning to Murial, she saw her daughter looking out the window in a daze. "Have you told him about any of this?"

"No. I saw no reason to. It is best left as a memory." Murial touched the glass with her fingers, outlining the shape of the trees passing by on the glass pane. "Besides, Reginald and Jack are acquaintances. If Reginald had wanted to tell him, then he would of himself. Maybe he has for as far as I know."

"Do you not see it?"

"See what?"

"The way Jack is acting? He is not himself Murial. Did you not just witness the melancholy attitude he just had at our doorway?"

"How should I know? He has been avoiding me ever since that meeting with Reginald that you pulled me out of." Murial's nostrils were flaring. "If you wouldn't have taken me from that room then maybe I would be able to figure out whatever is going on."

"Maybe they would not have said whatever they did in front of you? Did you ever think about that?"

Another knock at the door prompted Murial to open it this time, her hand gripping strongly onto the handle out of frustration. Bernard stood confused and uncertain with the two ladies poised across from one another, their eyes sharing a glare. "Is now a bad time?"

"Nope. It is actually perfect timing." Nora forced a

smile on her face.

"Okay…well I was wondering if I could steal your mother away for a little bit, Murial."

"Be my guest." Murial swung her hand out, gesturing her mother to leave the compartment with the man.

"On the contrary, Murial was just about to leave to find Jack." Nora smirked as Murial stomped her foot. Fists held at her sides, she stormed out of the compartment and turned to watch Bernard step in. *Take a deep breath. Everything is going to be alright. Lord above, give me strength.* She felt her anger lessening as she watched the scenery drift by at a steady pace. *Maybe she, however irritatingly, is right.* With the turn of her heels, Murial set off in search of Jack to see is she could get some answers out of him.

"This train is not big enough for you to hide forever." Murial said as she approached the two men having a drink. "Reginald, can you give us a moment?"

"Sure thing. I will see you later." Murial waited for the detective to disappear amidst the wandering passengers before sitting down across from Jack; a glass of whiskey being cradled in his hand.

"Talking to me instead of Reginald? That is a new one." His bitter and distant voice sliced her like a knife. *Me? He is the one who has been staying away.*

"What are you referring to?" Her eyes caught sight of his army colt hanging by his side. "You retrieved it from the baggage car?"

"Thought it would be nice to have around in case someone takes another shot at us. Picked it out the last time we stopped to have the train cooled down." He sipped the golden brown liquor. "So that way Reginald does not have to come in and save us again."

"Jack, I did not think you were the kind of person who would run to the bottle." Murial pointed to the half empty, clear glass bottle sitting near his hand.

"I'm not." He slammed the shot glass down on the table, causing others in the lounge car to give curious stares and dirty looks in their direction. "A man is allowed to have one drink."

"If you have a question on your mind, you best speak it plainly."

"I am wondering why you and Reginald have been so close."

"Jack, really, I thought he was your friend." Her eyebrows squinched. "Wait, are you jealous of him?" Jack backed up a bit. He gazed around the car at all the onlookers, clearing his throat. To everyone there, it looked as though he was drunk, but the truth was far from it. It was Reginald who had consumed almost half the bottle.

"No."

"Then what is it that is bothering you so much? My mother is consistently badgering me about it."

"I just…" Murial smirked at his loss for words. Her mother had been right.

"Jack, Reginald and I are just friends and nothing more." She gave him a hushed and shortened version of the tale she had just briefed her mother with, leaving out certain details for possible prying ears that Jack could mentally fill in at his leisure. "He is still too much in love with Betty anyway." He gave her a peculiar stare.

"Who is Betty?"

"He didn't tell you?"

"No." By now, the other passengers on the train had resumed their own conversations, deeming that their abrupt interruption was uneventful. Murial leaned over the table to explain.

"Like I said, I met Reginald at the Haymarket Incident. His girl was working late in a building along the street, taking counts for inventory, when a stray bullet came soaring through a window and killed her. Her name was Betty Longstring."

"He never told me that. I saw the photograph of a woman he carried with him in Arizona, but he talked about her as if she were still alive."

"To him, she still is alive. I helped him with the funeral arrangements and all. She had no other family in Chicago. Her parents lived in the countryside and the city was as untamable as a wild stallion in the days that followed."

"So, that is all?"

Murial nodded. "That is all there is to it. We are just good friends. I helped him with a real difficult time in his life. She was his soul mate, that Betty. Took a while to get him back on his feet. We kept in touch through letters for the months that followed. Have not seen him since, until now." She eyed the whiskey glass. "And he is too partial to the drink for my interests. Now, that I answered your question, you need to answer mine."

"Okay."

"What is…Brewer?!" Murial froze in panic. Her muscles locked up with no intention of moving, starring over at the far window seat. Jack flung around to look just as a porter walked across their view, revealing no one there after he passed by.

"Hey, Jack...I need to talk to you." Reginald slid into the compartment that Jack and Bernard had for the duration of the train ride. With his back to the man sitting on the seat, he peered down the hallway to make sure he wasn't being followed by anyone. "I received word from the police officers in Chicago." As soon as he turned around, Reginald's face went white as a bed sheet. Sitting in the corner was Brewer. His well-groomed mustache partially covering the smirk he bore.

A revolver was perched atop his knee, aimed directly at Reginald. "Good-bye Detective." Brewer pulled the trigger and a bullet penetrated Reginald in the stomach. Two more shots went straight through his gut as he fell to the ground, grimaced with pain.

"Reginald!" Murial sprung up and smacked her head into the bed above her. "Oww." Her hand immediately went for the instant throbbing that ensued within her skull.

"Murial, are you alright?" Jack's hushed voice came from outside her sleeping berth. Wincing again, Murial wriggled her way over to the opening and popped her hurting head through the drawn curtains constructed out of green fabric.

"Jack, what is it?" Her eyes continued to blink in an attempt to remove some sleep from their corners. She had no idea what time it was, but it certainly felt as though she had just laid down to rest.

"I was saying that Reginald received word from the police officers in Chicago." Murial stared at him for a heartbeat. *So that's where my dream came from.*

"How did he get that?"

"We passed through a smaller station about five minutes ago, and dropped a few passengers off. There was a telegraph waiting for him."

"Excuse me." A female voice came from the bed above Murial's. They both watched a blonde haired lady look over the ledge through their own set of curtains. "Would you mind taking your conversation elsewhere?" The woman parted her hair to see them more clearly. Her cheeks were as doll painted as Georgina's had been but her eyes were smaller and she bore a saddle nose.

"Pardon us." After Jack gave Murial a few minutes to get re-dressed, they quickly made their way toward the baggage car and met Reginald just inside the entrance.

"I thought you both should hear this. The police tracked down the man who fired a shot at you in Chicago. He had dirty blonde hair and was wearing a blue cardigan. According to what they could dig up, his last name was Smith." Reginald handed Murial the telegraph to read over with her own eyes. "Are they not always named Smith?"

"It says here that they shot him when he resisted

arrest." Murial gave Reginald a perplexed look. "Do you believe this?" She waved the paper at him.

"I trust the officer that sent it. I asked him to let us know once they learned anything about the shooter."

"I am not talking about that." She gave him an apologetic glance, realizing that he had no idea as to what she was referring to. "Oh…sorry, Reginald. If you trust the man who sent this, then that is good enough for me. Unfortunately, however, they cannot acquire any more information from Nicholas Smith. Another dead end and literally this time."

"What? You know this man?"

"He was watching us at my farm back home near Philadelphia." Murial handed the telegraph to Jack. "Then he tried stealing a ride into town, or more likely following us, by hiding in the back of our wagon. Jack was the one to smell the…" Jack tapped her shoulder.

"Murial, I just remembered that your mother wanted to speak to you before we arrive at the station." She was perplexed by the odd request and his off topic announcement. "Something to do with a painting about a sun over the hill." A light dinged at the back of her head as soon as she heard the phrase they had picked for when things were not quite right. It was their own code that no else knew, not even Walter or Nora.

"Okay. Do you know where she is?" Murial and Jack thanked Reginald for the information and then proceeded back up the line of cars. They passed through the berthing car, Murial's previous area already being occupied by another passenger, and continued their trek into the dining car. At two in the morning, no one was awaiting for any food orders and the place was dark. The bar area had closed up only minutes beforehand, so a few kitchen staffers were all that was looming in the shadows.

"What is it?" Murial whispered.

"You are not the only one I have been aloof with."

"Reginald? You cannot honestly suspect him."

"He smokes the same company as what Nicholas Smith did."

"So? That could only be a coincidence. Reginald likes his cigars and Bernard said they are the best."

"Think about it, though, Murial. He would have known how to locate you and could have easily picked up that Nicholas Smith character to do his dirty work because he would be too recognizable should one of us have spotted him at the farm."

"You are crazy, Jack. Reginald was the one that shot back at Smith in the station."

"Yes, but that could have been their plan all along. That dramatic entrance was so that we would have his trust and not suspect him." Jack shook his head. "Earlier, I had asked him a question, and when he answered it, I thought he had been talking in regards to you. But he could have meant Betty."

"Any time you feel the need to clue me in, feel free to oblige."

"He told me that his boss gave him a good yelling for standing up for me as a person not of interest to the case he is working on." He watched his words, making sure to keep his secret hidden; not sure on how she was going to take to the fact that he had been lying to her about the other reason he left Conestone. Jack didn't want her to miss his point if she were to get sore at him once everything came to light. "The more I thought about it, the more I had a hunch that he had meant you instead of me but wanted to hide the fact that he liked you from me."

"Okay…"

"Except, when I asked him about it, he replied with 'I would do anything for her.' Reginald could have been referring to Betty, since he talks about her in the present and feels the survivor guilt that you saved him and she did not make it."

Murial was shocked beyond the capability of her words. Everything Jack said was quite plausible, no matter how desperately she wanted it not to be true and wished that she could shake the very notion from her mind. In lieu of any evidence, the argument was still weak because it all came down to a singular object, the smell of a tobacco brand that was only circumstantial at best.

"For you to be right, we need more proof than what we have." She did not care for what she was saying. *I feel the need to wash my mouth out.* "But Jack, I know Reginald and so do you. This is ludicrous. To think that he would strike now is plain…"

"Likely. Come on, Murial. Look past sentiment. Before your father's death, you would not have even allowed a personal connection to cloud your judgement." Murial stared right through him.

"Do not be going off on me, Jack." She stormed off toward the private compartments and found her mother reading a book in the ladies' room.

"I couldn't sleep." Nora looked up and saw Murial's troubled expression. "What is the matter?"

"Nothing. Something I wish to forget in its entirety." Murial angrily sat down across from her mother, noting the glint in her eyes. "What has you all gitty? I hardly remember a time when you could not sleep. Unless it is being on this train. Which, in that case, I can agree with."

"I do not know what you mean." Nora straightened her stance and began reading her book once more. There was a pleasant smile spread under her nose.

"You are about to burst to tell me. So why don't you just do so?" Murial challenged. She was far too tired to try reading between the lines.

"Murial, I do not have to put up with your sarcasm." Nora turned her gaze out to the wilderness beyond the glass, too dark to see anything more than a sheet of black. She had not wanted to tell her daughter at this time, perhaps when they were alone together in California and it was not in the wee hours of the morning. But then again, there were no other ears in their compartment and she had asked. It was not ideal, but then again, when did life's biggest moments ever happen at a convenient time? "Bernard has asked me to marry him."

Her daughter's eyes blinked. She was mixed in how she wanted to react to such an out of place remark. "That is definitely not what I thought you were going to say." Nora had only known Mr. Shetron for less than a year and they hadn't even reached California yet to see his ranch. Walter's father had vouched for Bernard, but as Jack had just so

bluntly pointed out, people change over time. The Crancins
had not seen their dear friend in quite a while and there was
no telling what his intentions were at the moment. Murial
was so caught up in her thoughts that she failed to hide her
reservations on her face and it betrayed her skepticism.

"What did you think I was going to say?"

"I have no idea. Perhaps that you figured out who the
murderer was in that mystery book you are reading? Or
maybe that you discovered that a famous singer was riding
on the same train as us. Essentially, anything else but that."

"I know. I'm not entirely sure either. I really do like
him, a lot in fact," Nora beamed, "but he did say that he did
not expect an answer until after we stayed at his ranch for a
couple of weeks." She moved over to the seat beside Murial.
"This is kind of sudden, given that your father passed only a
year ago. And then there is this whole business with him
possibly being behind the person following you."

"Mother, if you want to marry him, that is your
choice. I do not care how long it's been since Father died.
We both know it was not a paradise when he was around."
Nora gripped onto Murial's shoulders, forcing her daughter
to look her square in the face.

"Now see here, Murial, I realize that he was a
difficult man and you did not understand his decisions on
numerous occasions, but you were not always the easiest to
live with either. He provided a roof over your head and gave
you a life much easier than most. You don't know the whole
story when it comes down to it. While I did not love him
like a fairytale story would have me to, I do remember the
good times we had as a family. They may not have been as

frequent as you would have cared them to be, but they still happened and were beautiful in their own way."

"He arranged me to marry a pompous, and mind you also brainless, man who..."

"I also agreed to it."

"After you promised to stay out of my relationships from the way your last attempt ended? Why am I not surprised?"

"I thought he would be good for you, Murial. It was when you returned from California and informed me on the situation that I had learned how wrong I had been. For that, I apologize." Nora picked herself up from the bench seat and left the room, leaving Murial to herself again.

The train pulled into Sun Valley Station in Nebraska right on time. Nora poked Murial awake as the engine stopped next to the platform, smoke billowing like fog from its stack. "We are here." From that point onward, the morning flew by in a clouded daze for Murial. She had barely acquired any sleep the previous night, and none that was actually solidly restful. Her neck was cramped, shoulders sore, and her back was stiff from the uncomfortable position she had been in for hours on the bench seat. Many of the passengers were disembarking, including Reginald who accompanied Murial and Jack off the train behind Nora and Bernard.

Birds flew overhead, extending their wings over the air lows and highs. Their feathers flapped against the invisible forces as the sun shone down upon the platform below them. The sounds of everyone's shoes clicking against the wooden floorboards was to a beat all its own and the trees danced around them. Murial tried to take a welcomed breath of fresh forest air into her longing lungs, but she was too close to the train for that just yet. Instead, the smell of burnt coal and warmed ashes caused her to cough and partially choke while cinders latched onto her hair.

"Are you alright?" Jack grabbed ahold of her arm, noticing the reddish tint to her face.

"I'll be fine." Murial sputtered out. She quickly wove her way over to the edge of the station's building in order to escape from the overwhelming smoke.

"I have to send word back to headquarters. See you on board the next train." Reginald flashed a flirty smile over at Murial, making sure she was doing well before dashing off to locate the telegraph office. Bernard lead the rest of their group inside the building and over to the ticket counter in order to handle making the next set of arrangements, as he had done from the journey's inception, while Nora and Murial waited beside Jack in the corner of the small waiting room. Watching out of the train station's only window, Murial noticed Mr. Shetron's crates being unloaded from the baggage car. There were about eight of them in total, all with the same stenciled insignia she had seen back in Chicago; the letter 'C' with a triangle in the middle and two lines slashed through them.

She was about to return her focus onto the commotion within the train station when Murial took a double take at a man snooping around the crates wearing a blue suit and hat that covered over his short hair. Inching closer, over to the windowsill, she squinted her eyes in an attempt to see the person clearer. It was Reginald! *He said that he was sending a message back to the office. What is he doing trying to look inside Bernard's crates?* "Jack, over here." He matched her gaze to witness the same scene.

"What is Reginald doing? Is that what he is on the train for? To follow Mr. Shetron?"

"Here are our tickets." Bernard announced. Murial and Jack hurried over to Nora's side. "We are in that train right over there," he pointed to the other side of the platform, "and then off to Los Angeles."

"I feel like we could have crossed the Atlantic Ocean faster." Nora jokingly replied. Bernard escorted her out of the station, arms interlocked, while Murial and Jack brought up the rear once more.

"Oh, Jack, by the way," Bernard cleared his throat. "I have been meaning to ask you what your friend, Mr. Vermount...I believe, does for a living?"

"Mr. Vermen. And he is in land dealings."

"Really? How fascinating." Bernard looked over their shoulders, studying the activity behind them. "Could have fooled me. I would have betted that he was into shipping. Elsewise, why would he be inspecting my crates so thoroughly?" Jack and Murial glanced at one another. They had to come up with a good story, and fast.

"Because we told him that you used to own a shipping company and he has experienced many bad dealings with the shippers he has used in the past. See, he doesn't just do land deals for other people, but also for himself." Murial hooked her arm through Jack's. "I told him that he could take a look to see how well everything was packed when we reached California but I guess he decided to take a gander before then." She batted her eyes sweetly. "I hope that is alright with you, Bernard."

"I will go get him." Jack pulled himself away from

Murial. "He needs to still purchase a ticket most likely and I do not want him to miss out."

"You are right there Jack. The next train isn't due for another day." Bernard gazed over at Murial with a twinkle in his eye. "And I am glad that he is interested in the finer aspects of shipping. Maybe if you could introduce us this evening, over dinner, I would be glad to give him some pointers."

"I would be delighted." She smiled, trying to hide the fear in her eyes. *Lord help us.*

Reginald undid his tie. It was the first thing he always took off when undressing for bed. A hard bench may not have been the same as sleeping in a berth, but he had a mild case of claustrophobia and those cramped holes in the wall were out of the question for him. Starring at the mirror he had attached within the lining of his suitcase, he smirked in thought to himself. The very same principle he used to capture crooks and thieves also applied to him: being a creature of habit. Patting his pants pocket, Reginald's face showed his surprise as he discovered his box of matches was missing. *Shoot! I must have left them back in the dining room after meeting up with Mr. Shetron.*

For a brief second, he thought about placing his tie back on in order to relocate his matches, but ultimately decided against it. Exhaustion was seeping into his muscles and he could always purchase another box in the morning. His eyes grew heavy from the constant traveling he had endured over the past five months. Against Talman's explicit orders, Reginald declined to take a break. "Get some rest and find a hobby to occupy that never-ending brain of your's," he had said. It was far easier for one to suggest such a thing, than it was for it to actually work.

The bags under his eyes were increasing in sag, aging him a few years beyond his real birthday. No matter what he did, his mind would eventually end up thinking about her. *Betty.* Warmness filled his heart at the mere mentioning of her name. She had been the light in his life, bringing him hope when his job left him with only the crueler side of human nature at times. He worked for whoever paid his bill and they were not ideal clients on some occasions. A war between workers and employers was reaching new heights in not just Chicago and he found himself trapped in the middle more than once.

Standing between a warehouse, only property valued in dollar signs to the owners, and the workers, trying to stand up for themselves against tyrannical oppression, slowly ate away at him. If the employers would treat people as human beings, lives would not be ruined as much as they were. Eight hour work days. Was that such a hard task to accomplish? Was that asking too much of the employers who paid little for jobs no matter how difficult or dangerous they may be? Betty had been a victim of that. She was an innocent bystander doing a job, working the twelve hours she was required to do, when her life was tragically lost unnecessarily.

A tear rolled down his cheek. He pictured Betty's beautiful smile, eyes like the ocean's, and…Reginald shook his head. The memories were growing thicker with time, not fading like other's promised they would. That was why he took on so many assignments. Maybe, just maybe, he would be able to push them away by working so much. All her face brought him anymore was pain beyond all reason and the anger he had been suppressing towards Murial. *If only she hadn't saved me from that officer's bullet. If only...*

Ifs were a never-ending whirlpool sucking a person's mind into further depression and misery. He had already gone down that road before and Murial had been there to help get him out of it. *I really would do anything for her.* Reginald sighed. She implored her father to hire him, helped him with the funeral for his precious Betty, and really tried to pull him from the pit he was wallowing within. Even after all of that, he still harbored a desire to hurt her; for her to feel the torment that he was going through, the guilt of surviving when Betty had not. Many people, civilians and police alike, perished that night or later from injuries they had sustained from the Haymarket Incident. Why did he live?

Seeing her on the train, though, cowering under the window sill as the bullets flew into the car, Reginald felt nothing more than the need to protect her as his job demanded. He felt freedom surrounding his soul as he talked with her, ate dinner with her, and chatted like old friends. Her eyes brought back all the struggles she shared with him about her nasty father and the choices in her life that had become her own set of bars. He was never a churchgoing man, but there was a special light in her eyes that gave him a new rekindling of hope.

"Ah yes." Reginald neatly folded his jacket into his suitcase, his mind changing the subject entirely. It had been a foolish newborn mistake to allow Bernard to catch him looking around the crates. Jack and Murial covered nicely for him, even getting him invited to talk to Mr. Shetron himself. His observations onboard the train out of Chicago had not proved to be of great help, but his conversation that evening had. Before retiring to his private compartment, traveling in style on the government's tab, Reginald slipped a note to Jack. They needed to talk the next morning on what he suspected.

"Good night my sweet." Reginald kissed his fingers, placing them against a photograph of Betty he perched in his suitcase. He was never without that photograph. Placing his shoes under the bench, Reginald saw a note slide across the floor from being shoved through the crack under the door. He wondered if it was from Jack or Murial. Instinctively, he reached over to pick it up and BANG! The door to his compartment smashed into his head as Brewer plowed his way in.

"Thanks for the hospitality, Mr. Vermen, or whoever you really are."

23

"Murial!" A hand appeared through the closed curtains of her berth, shaking her arm vigorously. Her eyes flashed open with disappointment.

"I am just destined to be sleepless." She yawned as wide as her jaw would allow before poking her head out of the berth to see Jack standing there. "Is it just me, or did we already read this part of the book already?"

"The train has stopped."

"Why? What happened?" Growing panic helped to waken her up.

"We just passed over the North Platte River, at least that is what the conductor called it, where one of the engineers saw a body fall over the bridge." Murial's nerves were on fire.

"Who was it? Do we know who?" The look on Jack's face was her answer. Her stomach was twisting in knots, desperately wishing for him to say "no, we do not."

"They think it was Reginald." Murial didn't waste any time. She redressed, smacking her head on the bottom of the berth above her just as before, and shimmied her way out of the crawl space. Racing behind Jack, she came upon their friend's empty compartment where she froze at the doorway. The once tidy and neat space was ransacked with clothing strewn on the ground and a pearl handled knife lay on the bench.

"No, no!" She shook her head in disbelief. "It cannot be." Murial looked pleadingly up at Jack. "Maybe it is like what happened to Walter. Maybe he is still alive and someone else went into the river."

"I'm sorry Murial, but the porters and I checked everywhere. We cannot find him."

"It can't be true." She looked down at the torn photo of Betty resting helplessly beside Reginald's black shoes. "It can't be true." Murial walked into the room, careful not to step on any of the evidence thrown about. *Where are his cigars?* "Did the engineer hear a yell? A shout? A scream? Anything?"

"He did not. Just saw a lifeless body tumbling through the air. It could be that he was dead before someone launched his body out the window." Murial examined the broken glass, painted with blood from being smashed into the dark red pool under the sill. Panic and fear churned into anger.

"It was him."

"Who are we talking about?"

"Brewer. I know it was him." Her eyes flared. "He has to be stopped. Enough is enough." She stormed out to the hall where Jack caught her with an outstretched reach.

"Whoa, there. What are you planning on doing?"

"I am tired of being left to hang out like drying fish." She pointed back into the room. "No one else is going to die because of me."

"What if he didn't die because of you?" Jack tried calming her down. "Reginald was working on a case of his own, and whoever it was could have gone after him for a different purpose entirely."

"I am assuming you are referring to Mr. Shetron then." Her hardened stare would not budge. "It was his crates that Reginald was looking at and Bernard caught him snooping around them."

"Reginald would not like me discussing his case with you."

"Reginald is dead, Jack. I do not think he has a choice in the matter." He placed his hands on Murial's shoulders.

"Can you trust me just a little bit longer?" She wriggled out from under his grasp.

"Trusting you has only gotten a man killed. One that apparently was working on something with you." She took a step back from him. "You must think me blind. The secrecy between you two, your avoidance of me, all of it is pointing to something you still cannot seem to talk to me about." Murial gathered up her courage. "Tell me right now what is going on or I am heading home the minute we reach the next train station. And you lose the bait for whatever prey you hope to entrap."

"Sir, is there something we can do?" A porter bravely asked behind Jack's back. He turned to see the shorter man's uncertain reaction, not sure if he did the right thing by interjecting into their argument.

"We are fine, thank you." Jack snatched up Murial's

right hand, leading her back to the ladies' private accommodations. Nora was asleep in a berth, providing them with an empty space to clear the air. "I was going to wait until the right moment to tell you this."

"When? At my funeral?"

"Stop it with the sarcasm already." Jack sighed. "But I guess I do deserve some of it because I should have come clean back in Philadelphia. Murial, I am a Deputy U.S. Marshall who was assigned to a case investigating you and your father."

Murial's face was emotionless to match what she was thinking. Jack waited a breath to see if she was going to verbally respond before continuing. "When I was out in Conestone with Walter, there were some questions that came up in regards to some counterfeit money at the bank. I reported it to the treasury department and they assigned it to the local US Marshal, who deputized me in order to give me the proper authority to help him track down the head of the operation."

"And they suspected myself and my father because of…what?"

"We have an idea as to who the top man is, but we need evidence to convict him by the book. Especially since he has such a high social profile and is an influential member of the government. There is only one chance at taking him down for this and it has to go right."

Murial's mind turned, deciphering as to which one of her father's former colleagues he could be referring to. "You think Senator Drouther is behind the counterfeit bills?" She observed Jack's uneasy expression. "Look, I have nothing to do with any of this. I personally despise the man more than anything else, you know that. But since you are talking about the person as if they are alive, that eliminates my father and Conestone has to be the connection. Geographically, Arizona is next to California and…" Her eyes lit up like the imaginary light that clicked on over her head. "My artwork. They think that I was helping to create the fakes with my art skills."

"Well, that possible avenue had come up. But…regardless." Jack shook his head clean of what he was about to say, changing onto a different branch of the conversation. "That is why Conestone had telegraph wires leading up to the town despite it not being reachable by train, only by stagecoach if you recall. The one thing I was able to uncover there was an established messenger system being shared between at least half a dozen men. Every week was a different set of two men rushing a message to the telegraph officer with no specified schedule that would be too noticeable to pick up on."

"You were never able to catch any of them?" The whole thing sounded like something out of a novel or someone's fantasy. Murial could not believe it.

"We managed to apprehend a couple of the men, however there was one distinct trait they all shared, making it impossible to obtain any useful information." Murial tilted her head in anticipation for the answer. "They could not read. We did intercept a runner before he could deliver his message on a Tuesday night though. Unfortunately, it had been written in code as a precaution." Jack's brow furrowed in frustration. "No matter how we watched, who we asked, or where we managed to locate bits of clues, everything turned into a dead end."

"Perhaps Conestone is only for the messenger side of the operation and there is nothing else to be found?" Murial shrugged her shoulders in passive thought. Still, the mysterious nature of it all did intrigue her. "Thinking back on it now, I never saw anything out of the ordinary about the telegraph system being there. I am so used to seeing the wires almost everywhere anymore."

"You did have other things on your mind at the time as well." Jack looked her in the eye, squarely in front of where she stood. "Murial, your father was becoming increasingly more involved with the Senator."

"Yes, but that was because his political career was failing drastically, and he needed all the support he could get to keep in office."

"But what if it was more than that?" She cast a puzzling glance at him, growing cautious of the speculations that were sure to follow. "Among Clive's belongings, I found one of the counterfeit bills with a note attached. It read 'SD – July 25th.' And we already know that he was double-dealing with the Senator behind your father's back."

"It was probably Clive then." Murial began to fume as another idea was beginning to dawn on her, perhaps delayed, but it was not lost. Jack dismissed the notion.

"The handwriting was your father's and not Clive's. Clive could have been attempting to blackmail someone, but that is irrelevant at this stage since he died. That note was the first lead we had been able to dig up with a promising outlook." Jack's voice lowered. "So naturally, you being his daughter…someone who was close to him…it was the logical step to think that you were a possible accomplice in their scheme." He watched her slow simmer turn into a full boil, hastily rushing another idea out before she was going to blow her top. "Or have some information that would lead the case into another direction." Murial's stare hardened. The irises of her eyes were blacker than night, roaring with flames.

"So all this time…for the last twelve months…you have being leading me on with false pretenses, that you were actually interested in me, in order to investigate my family?!" Her blood was hot. She was disgusted by his play of deceit. "All for a few counterfeit bills? That is what you have been after? So that you what? Can solve the case and get a pat on the back?!"

"The problem is not as simple as a few dollar bills. Walter's bank was not the only one with the forgeries. Other banks, all across the country were seeing the bills pop up. Each area has an investigator on it, but they have all have come to the conclusion that the head of operations is in Arizona. Being held in a territory, and not in a state, it would be easier to fly under the radar with such a scheme." Jack witnessed the look of being betrayed flashed at him.

Instantly, he wanted to take back every word he told her about the case. It was the very moment he had been dreading since she showed up in Conestone. He truly cared for her and it hollowed his heart knowing that she might never be able to see that. *Better me than someone else.* That was the sentiment he reverberated to himself every time his guilt was winning the wrestling match. It's lasting effect had ebbed over time. Now, those words were mere shadows of their meaning compared to the heartache Murial was showcasing. She was not without her wits, deducing that she would be able to see through the facts rather quickly no matter how he broke the news to her, and Murial did not disappoint.

"Well, I guess it is safe to assume that my father's papers did not provide you with any sort of lead because you have stayed at the farm all this time. Is that right?" Murial crossed her arms. "You would have told me some made-up excuse before leaving for good if you had located anything useful. Is that why you were so eager to help my mother move into the farmhouse? It was your cover so you could rummage your way through my father's items before the debt collectors grabbed everything they could carry?!" Her voice was rising in volume. Normally, she would not try to attract attention, but there was no stopping her from speaking her mind on this matter. Hopefully, the walls of the cabin would keep her anger from reaching the ears of the other occupants. "And I suppose that someone also checked his office in Washington for you. After all, I do not seem to recall you leaving on long trips except to go to your parents and that friend from school. Oh, I am sorry, was all of that a lie as well?"

"Murial, stop it. I really did go to see my parents that trip and I did tell you what happened. Most of it anyway." Jack's mouth slid into a half smile, causing the left corner to rise his cheek upward as Murial rolled her eyes in exasperation. She walked over to the window, watching the passing scenery that was much more serene than what was happening within the train. "Reginald and I are in the dumps for protecting you. Both our bosses wanted you to be brought in for questioning long ago. We have been persuading them that it would be better if…"

"Both of you turned your back on me, instead." She flipped her head around to size up his words. She wasn't sure whether to believe him or not. It could just be another lie to get back into her good graces. Her lips were tight, pressed into a thin line. "Now we are even, I guess. I do thank you for telling me, Jack. At least I know who I cannot trust anymore."

"It is the truth, Murial, I swear it. Reginald endured a fresh shouting match with his boss, Talman, just before boarding the train. It was because he was sticking his neck out for you. I am on my last string with my supervisors as well. They believe that my judgement is skewed due to how close we are."

"Obviously you have not spoken to them recently." She narrowed in on Jack's shame-filled eyes. "Why target me? Surely it was no secret that my relationship with my father was rocky at best. Why not go after Senator Drouther and see if you can find any evidence from the so-called head of whatever operation is being ran?"

"He is extremely cautious on those he brings into his confidence. It is too risky that someone would be discovered and the whole thing would be all for naught." Jack slowly approached her, still standing by the window. He could see how physically tired she was; her energy drained from a combination of traveling, little rest, and his most recent addition of revealing his secret. Keeping his job from her was the last thing in the world he had wanted to do with its burden growing worse day by day. It twisted his soul in all directions, and sickened his stomach over the realization that she would eventually find out no matter what he did. Quietly, he wished for nothing more than just one more minute with Murial on the farm like they used to be. *A falsehood I had helplessly tried to keep alive for myself. What greed.* Placing his hands on her shoulders, he was relieved to see that she didn't fight him.

"The bottom fact is, I am not still here for my lousy job, which does nothing but get me shot at by the way, but because you are in danger and..." His words broke off. "I can hand in my resignation if that means anything to you."

"Sounds like a feeble attempt at saving your hide with me." She rolled her right shoulder out of his grip. "I do not know if I can trust you Jack. Not after this."

"Give me a second chance, please Murial." Jack didn't believe his own words. *Really, after what you did to her and you still think there is a chance?* They felt empty as he spoke. It was pointless to ask, and yet, he could not stop himself from doing that very thing. If there was even the tiniest glimmer of a chance with her, he would not hesitate to jump at it with both hands.

"I will remain on this trip to flush out whoever is following me, once and for all, so I can get my life back. I honestly don't know about after that, Jack." Murial looked away as he tried to move in to give her a kiss on the cheek. "Leave me alone, please. Just…leave me alone." Reluctantly, he obliged and shut the door behind him.

Murial's hands rubbed up and down her arms, as if she had a shawl or blanket wrapped around her shoulders. It was a comforting tactic that had proven to help in the past; however, it was worthless at present. Uncontrollably, her thumb twitched against the brown fabric of her outfit while rain began to pelt upon the window. Mindlessly, she watched the drops stream down the glass before landing on the ever-moving ground, only to be absorbed into the soil below the green grass. Everything in her world was shaken to its very core. She could feel it collapsing faster than words could rebuild, deeper than a hug could mend, and more painful than all the medicine could heal. Tears welled up in her eyes, threatening to mirror the rainfall outside. *Oh Uncle Seb, what do I do?*

The conductor notified the local sheriff about their missing passenger over the telegraph wires once they reached the next station along the tracks. Murial managed to sneak her way into Reginald's compartment before they arrived, taking the torn photograph of Betty from the scene. As far as she knew, Reginald still had a brother living on the outskirts of Chicago and wanted to make sure that the photograph reached him. No telling how long it was going to take for the investigation to be completed and the rest of his belongings shipped back. Jack and the porters gave their statements to the deputy and the process of waiting commenced yet again.

"I will be dead by the time we grace California." Nora placed her head in the palm of her hand. She had finished the book she had brought along with her and was in no mood to begin another one.

"That just might happen the way this is going." Murial flatly stated. "We are just glad that two Deputy U.S. Marshalls were out this way to help with a prisoner transfer for the local sheriff. It might go faster with four men as opposed to just two." Surprisingly enough, the group was informed that the train would be continuing on as scheduled sooner than what was first anticipated. Most of the search was going to be around the river to see if Reginald's body had made it to shore with the current. That suited the passengers just fine if it meant they did not have to be delayed any longer.

Within an hour, the train was up and roaring; its wheels rolling down the tracks at a faster speed than before. The engineer had already been late twice in the past month and did not wish to make it a habit for fear of being reprimanded by his boss. Trees and mountains whisked by their view in a never-ending array of vast beauty. Bernard was pleased to finally announce that they were in California after about ten hours of travel.

"Hallelujah!" Nora clapped her hands in the air. "We made it at last. Finally!" Murial kept her mouth shut, so as to not rain on her mother's jubilee. She knew the journey was not over yet, as they were to switch over to a stagecoach to reach Bracken after unloading from the train. It was going to be an arduous trip over hard rocks and curvy trails weaving in and out with the natural landscape. Going anywhere through the desert in a stagecoach was one attribute of her previous job that Murial did not miss.

"Oh my!" Nora held unto the side of the stagecoach, bouncing up and down on the wooden seats. The rocks were too numerous to count and too hard to ignore going down Raven's Trail. Thin bunches of deergrass and sagebrush dotted the tan landscape stretching out farther than their eyes could see. Sunlight bathed the countryside in a glowing hue of light yellow, brightening the peaks of protruding rock shelves. Evening was painting the sky in a darkening blue and elongating the shadows sprouting out from the base of cacti and palo verde trees.

"It shall not be long now." Bernard grimaced a smile as a shot of pain went up his back.

"Looks like you are going to get a train out here soon." Jack tipped his head in the direction of a group of men pounding hammers against steel tracks. Their sound echoed through the stagecoach only to drown out in the expansiveness of the desert. For two hours Murial had felt the road through the large wheels, bringing up memories that were both good and bad. Traveling around was a breath of fresh air with the new people she met and the experiences that came with it. Of course, however, there were also times of bitter pills to swallow with those fond outings. *Seems like to get the good, we must endure the bad.*

"Yes, we are in fact." Bernard stroked his beard. "I had some influence with that, if I might so proudly boast, and am quite excited to get Bracken on the map as if were. The town is growing at a steady rate, all kinds of ranchers and shopkeepers moving into the area. It is where I fell in love with the land." He pointed down at the floor. "I had decided right then and there that I was going to plant my roots on that very soil."

"How did you happen to find Bracken?"

"It was a mere two building outpost when I first laid eyes upon it with a man that owed me a few favors in the past. Senator Drouther is the name." The other three's eyes widened. "Do you know him by chance?"

"Um…" Murial coughed from the dust rolling into the cabin by way of the open window. "As a matter of fact, we do. His son, Samuel, married my sister, Shannon, not long ago."

"You don't say? I helped him with his election and as a thank-you, he helped me acquire the land for my ranch." He straightened up as soon as he said it. "I did not do anything illegal, mind you. Just helped with a donation or two, and didn't want anything in return. But he said that he felt indebted to me and wanted to repay my kindness."

"Sounds reasonable." Nora smiled over at Murial. "He certainly does have a reach in the political realm."

"More than I thought. He had the price lowered to more than a fair offer. So I decided to put some of my savings into helping Bracken grow into a full-sized town."

"What a wonderful idea. Will your daughter be there to greet us when we arrive?"

"If she did not grow bored of waiting from all of these delays." He joked. "I am delighted that you three could come with me, truly I am. Traveling alone is not nearly as much fun."

"I am surprised you would be still saying that considering all of the issues that have arisen since we agreed to come along on this trip." Murial eyed Jack as she said it. A cloud of dust caught her attention out of the corner of her eye. It was small and considerably distant from their current location, but the cloud was moving at a considerable rate of speed. At the front of the miniature dust devil, was a black spot that enlarged slightly when one of the two horses gained the lead. *Must be two lone travelers.*

"Not at all. I have not had such an interesting train ride in all of my life." Bernard's face took on a more sullen demeanor. "I do hope that they find out what happened to Mr. Vermen. I had only but one chat with him, however he seemed to be a fine young man. Were you friends with him long?"

"For a few years." Jack spoke up for the first time since climbing into the stage back in Los Angeles. Awkward silence overtook the wriggling air until Mr. Shetron pointed to a small dot of buildings nestled against a rising hillside.

"There it is. Bracken." A prideful smile filled his face. Murial looked over at the twenty or so manmade structures that appeared less out of place compared to other towns she had visited near deserts. The town was located on the south side of the hill that marked the halfway point between two valleys.

"Are those towers for mines?" Murial asked in reference to the three dark towers shooting up along the hillside. They were spaced evenly apart and encompassed a semicircle around the town. Jack also took special note of their unique presence. The closer the stagecoach came toward the buildings, the more details they could see of the tall metal structures. One person stood guard on each of their points, holding onto a rifle, and training their attention onto the incoming stage.

"They are lookout towers. Just in case an ambush occurs. I should not have to explain what an unpleasant sight that would be to you two." Bernard tipped his head in the direction of Jack and then Murial as he spoke. "Just as a precaution, is all."

"I have not seen that used for a town. Mostly only for prisons." Bernard laughed at Jack's statement.

"I promise you, Jack Fulton, that you are not under arrest. Lookout towers are most effective for such places, so why not use them to protect civilians as well?" Bracken came rushing past their view as the stage hit main street. Storefronts were being built and for sale signs were hanging in the windows.

"Is business that bad?" Murial observed.

"Heavens no. These are being built to attract new owners and to bring more folks to our town."

"Here we are." The driver called down, pulling up on the reins for the horses to stop in front of the ticket office. Murial's gut was feeling full with skepticism. *Did my mother gain the affections of an outlaw?* Dust billowed around the large wheels of the stage, giving all the passengers a reason to cough. Bernard opened the door, climbed down first, and then extended his hand out for the ladies. Nora glanced around at the town, trying to look it over without judgement. It was definitely not anything she was used too.

"How unpleasant for you to have survived your long journey, My Friend." A man brimming with ego approached the group just as Jack stepped out. "And I see that you have brought back some wonderful companions with you." The man picked up Murial's gloved hand and kissed the top of it. "They bring a new life to this eyesore of a town."

"Richard Thompson. I might as well have known you would be here to greet me. The answer is still no, before you rudely bombard me with your tiresome questions, and the answer will always be no. Now leave us alone." Bernard looked up to see the driver handing down their luggage to them from the top rack.

"Not before you introduce me to these lovely ladies." A smile brimmed on the pudgy man's face as he stuffed two fingers of his left hand into a small vest pocket where a pocket watch used to call home. His light brown suit jacket and pants pared nicely with his dark green vest resting over a white shirt and black tie. Bernard reluctantly introduced them to the annoying man, making sure to add that they were his guests staying at his ranch. "In other words, Thompson, hands off."

"Well, if any of you should find yourself wanting some more pleasurable companionship, please feel welcomed to visit my ranch anytime." Mr. Thompson walked away with a tip of his hat. Murial inched over to Jack, lowering her voice to a whisper.

"Do you find the towers a little odd?"

"Yeah. We will have to keep our eyes open." Jack gave Murial a little nudge with his hand to move away from the back of the stagecoach so that he could reach the rest of their luggage. A couple of women walked past them, dressed in clothing more plain in pattern and design than what Nora wore on a daily basis. They voiced their welcomes to the two ladies before continuing along the sidewalk in the direction of the general store.

"Daddy!" Charlene shouted into the afternoon warmth, running up to her father from the bank. Bernard spread his arms wide like the wings of an eagle and wrapped his daughter up in a bear hug.

"My little dumpling, oh how I have missed you." Bernard hastily pulled his daughter away from his embrace so he could get a good look at her. "I think you have grown taller since I left." Charlene smacked her father's shoulder playfully.

"Nonsense, I stopped growing years ago. Glad to see you back and safe after what happened."

"You already know about the incidents?" Nora inquired.

"Only the samplings Daddy sent me in his telegrams." She dusted off her dress when she saw Nora's fancier attire. "You must be Mrs. Robertson." Charlene walked up to Murial's mother with poise. "My, it is very nice to meet you ma'am. Daddy told me that he was held up East due to a stunning beauty, but you are a much prettier picture than I had imagined." Her cheeks blushed with embarrassment. "I apologize if that was too forward of me. I am afraid that my speech has grown accustomed to the western style and has adopted a much more bolder approach in such regards."

"You are not too bold, my dear, please call me Nora. This is my daughter Murial Robertson and that gentleman over there is Jack Fulton." Jack dipped his head in respect as Charlene's eyelashes flittered a little. She was a young woman, Murial surmised no more than eighteen, and had fiery red hair twisted into a bun at the back of her head. A skirt of blue and a top of white adorned her slim figure, pointing all attention to her sparkling green eyes.

"My goodness, it will be a splendid change to have the house full after it has been so eerily quiet. Greg is over at the general store for some more tobacco. We can meet him over there, Daddy. Ruggard and Darryl were sent to collect the rest of your supplies back in Los Angeles. Knowing those two water snakes, they will most likely make it back to the ranch tomorrow."

"Excellent." Bernard showed his guests over to the general store, where his ranch's wagon was awaiting their presence. Greg stepped out of Hawkin's General Store, jaws already chewing away on his freshly purchased tobacco. He had hazel eyes and wore a plain green shirt over his brown pants. A double gun belt rested on his hips, holstering two Smith and Wesson Schofields. Mud and dirt were caked onto his boots from not being cleaned in some time and were starting to look like a rock formation in their own right. Above his upper lip, a small mustache was growing.

The sight of it flashed Murial's mind back to Brewer and his well-groomed larger version.

"Wow." Gary stopped when he saw Murial absentmindedly gawking at him. "And what brings a lady such as yourself out here?" His tongue moved the chewing tobacco to the other side of his mouth. Quickly pulling the strings of the tobacco pouch closed, the farmhand shoved his supply into a saddle bag draped over his right shoulder. When he pulled his hat off in a show of respect to the three woman standing in his presence, he revealed a duller shade of chestnut brown hair in need of a good washing. Charlene stormed over and stomped her heeled boot on top of his foot. "Hey!" He replaced his hat and looked over at her, puzzled as to her reaction. "What was that for?" Murial couldn't keep her laughter at bay as she witnessed the two partake in a comic bantering.

"Charlene. Is that any way to treat your fiancé?" Bernard gave his daughter a look.

"It is when he is looking at another woman." Charlene folded her arms in front of her chest, a small pout on her face.

"I cannot give a decent lady a compliment?" Greg countered.

"Of course not." Nora joked. She could see it in Charlene's face that the act was nothing more than a spat of good-natured fun, something Greg himself had come to understand. He poked her in the back, throwing his saddle bag onto the wagon, and dodging away as she tried to return his jab. Bernard shook his head.

"You two act like children."

"You both remind me a lot of those two." Nora pointed back at Murial and Jack, who were working on putting the luggage into the wagon. Charlene's face lit up with a big smile.

"Are you two getting married?"

"Oh, um…no. Just old friends." Murial was not sure what to say. She didn't want Charlene to feel embarrassed for asking the question.

"When is the big day going to be?" Jack interjected and switched the topic back onto the happy couple.

"We were waiting for Daddy to return home before setting the date. But now that he is here, it will be the first thing on our agenda." Charlene was enlightened with joy and Murial found herself feeling happy for the young woman. Her bright eyes seemed to have only hope for the future ahead.

The group set off for the ranch while the sun drooped low in the sky as twilight was rapidly approaching. With every step of the horse's hooves, Murial longed to see the ranch even more so. She felt dirty from head to toe and could feel her sweat soaked collar itching against the back of her neck. Greg had the wagon moving at a faster pace, trying to reach the ranch before complete nightfall. When Jack looked over to see Murial, she seemed a little dehydrated and he collected a canteen from atop their luggage to hand over to her. Her parched throat gratefully welcomed the water, reviving her voice. The oppressive heat in the west was a beast all its own, sucking the life out of a person one degree at a time. It may have been dry, as opposed to the humid climate of the east, but that did not mean it was not hot.

According to Charlene, the higher temperature had just arrived that day and would most likely require a thunderstorm to clear out. "We are overdue for some rain. Our area has been suffering a slight drought and we have been rationing out what water we have to keep it from becoming worse." Murial's mind drifted away from the conversation taking place in the back of the wagon as the terrain caused her to drift into her memories of her father's last campaign trip along the trails.

Taking the train was the preferred method of travel for senators and for high members of society alike. Not just for the obviously more luxurious accommodations, but also for the reasoning that their destinations were the most populous cities. The cost of a ticket might have been higher, but it would ensure a gathering of people at larger proportions to fill the venues for their speeches. On the complete opposite of logic, Senator Robertson had chosen the stagecoach more often than not and towns that were smaller in numbers. Strategically, and economically, her father's campaign route did not make any sense. At that time, she could have cared less, having grown accustomed to his bizarre decisions in the past. But now that more information had come forth, her father's choices bothered her.

Jack's comments back on the train made more sense the longer she dwelled on them. Her father's money problems were extensive when he passed and that would have made him desperate. *He was a man trying to cling to the last of a collapsing political career and trying to find the money he needed to keep the façade of dignity afloat. Maybe Jack is right that Father was in deeper than I realized.* Before she could go any further with her present thought, Bernard announced their arrival at the entrance to his ranch with still a small amount of natural sun to lead the way. An enlarged gate was opened by two armed guards with rifles in their hands. "Welcome back Boss." The left guard grunted.

"Are those Winchester Yellow Boys?" Jack inquired with intrigue while they passed through. The brass frame of the .44 caliber rifle had been engraved into his mind ever since he had been knocked unconscious from being struck in the head with the barrel of one last year.

"Each one of my hands carries what he likes, but yep, they are. To which gun do you prefer by your side, Jack?"

"Single Action Army Colt. My Grandfather bought it for me when I turned eighteen." He patted the holster at his side with fondness.

"Nice choice, My Boy. I'm more of a Remington man myself, but I have collected a few Colts over the years. When we reach the house, I must show you my collection." Bernard grinned with joy at the thought of showing off his lovely "trophies." It was his hobby in life, something that he thoroughly enjoyed talking about.

Murial felt the lure of sleep drift over her. She looked up to see the moon rising in the sky and the stars beginning to twinkle. Charlene noticed her about to doze off and quickly nudged her in the shoulder. Turning her head sharply around, Murial noticed a kindness in the woman's eyes reminiscent of a fawn in the forest. "I had hoped that you and your mother would help me with some wedding arrangements. My father's job had us moving around a lot when I was younger, and as a result, I do not have many friends."

The pronounced innocence and loneliness in her statement tugged at Murial's heart strings. There were moments that she took for granted the friends and family she had acquired over the years without a single thought about it. Being caught up in her own miseries had sometimes blocked her mind from everything else, say for the sorrow she was accustomed to dealing in. Smiling with genuine compassion painted on her face, Murial expressed how happy she would be in helping her. Charlene's eyes lit up brighter than the Northern star. "How terrific! The day after tomorrow we must go back into the city for a wedding dress. I am sure that you will want tomorrow to rest up from your long journey."

"Home, sweet home." Bernard exclaimed when the house had finally come into view. Fires flamed on torches around the porch for the incoming group's return against the dark bleakness of the horizon line. In the flickering light, Murial could not believe her eyes when she saw the spread that he had built. A massive barn was situated to their left and the two story house lay to their right. The porch curved around both levels and the cowhand bunks were located in between the two large structures. Greg pulled the horses to a halt, allowing three cowhands to grab their reins and assist the travelers down from the wagon. The luggage was the last thing unloaded.

"Wow, you sure do have a lot of help around here."

Nora commented. She took a mental count of the number of men she could visually see in the dim lighting; eighteen to be precise.

"A spread this big needs an army to keep it in tip-top shape, ain't that right boys?" Bernard joined in on the whooping and hollering with his men as their agreement sounded throughout the group. Murial wasn't too sure about the whole situation. Uneasiness festered in her gut, creating a panic that set into her mind. If anything bad should happen, there was no way out. They were cornered in a nest of armed men with no way of knowing who to trust.

"You have an all metal windmill?" Nora pointed up to the tall, metal structure with curved blades being pushed round and round by the wind's forceful energy.

"You bet. They are the wave of the future when it comes to pumping water up from under the ground. Does the work better in lighter winds than the wooden models."

Charlene led their guests inside the house. Nora kept glancing over her shoulder at Murial with an apprehensive look. The beautifully carved door opened to reveal a lavishly decorated interior. "Are you ready for the grand tour?" Bernard's daughter was elated with the fact that she was going to be able to showcase their home to a couple of outsiders.

The parlor was impeccable with couches and chairs and a grand piano in the corner of a room with wallpaper that would have made the Drouther's envious. Frames with prints of artworks, ranging from old masters to newer sensations, hung on the walls lining every hall and room. The beds were adorned like fanciful desserts, with ornate pillows and blankets that one could become lost in if they sunk below the surface. Mahogany banisters led the way up the stairs, crafted on the east coast by the same gentleman who had created the Robertson's old banisters. It felt good to have something familiar under Nora's hands, ascending up the stairs to where Charlene was about to show them where their rooms would be for the duration of their stay.

"The hotel in town is not finished yet, so we have everything set up for you ladies down this hall." Charlene's hands gestured to the two bedrooms facing one another to the right of the staircase. "Mr. Fulton will be down the other hall." She left them to unpack their belongings and headed over to her room at the hall's end.

"Murial?" Nora looked over at her daughter. "What do you think about all of this?"

"Honestly, I am not sure what to think. We are either on the safest ranch in the country or the deadliest."

"Brewer, what took you so long?" A pair of cowhands sipped some weak coffee from their tin cups as flames flickered up from the fire at their feet while two guns rested at their sides. Empty plates sat still on a nearby flat rock, waiting to be rinsed off with a cup of water from the nearby stream. "Thompson gave you a vacation, not retirement." The blonde-haired young man laughed while poking his friend in the shoulder with an index finger. "Ain't that the truth, huh Martin?"

"I got delayed." Brewer's body was coated in a layer of dust. A line of dirt running horizontally across his face indicated exactly where his handkerchief had been during his ride. It was a hard run for his horse, and his boss's, as they raced across the rocky terrain off the beaten trail that afternoon.

"Sure. Stick to that flimsy excuse. See what Thompson says about it." The blonde man flung his cup around wildly in the air. "Three days. That's how much you are late, Brewer. THREE DAYS." He shook his head in a mocking of shame. "Not good Brewer. Not good at all. You almost got replaced with Martin here." Pointing at his comrade once more, the man about fell over under his own swaying power. Brewer kept his temper in check the best he knew how around the kid known to all as Mitchum. There was no show of respect to anyone from him, especially not to his foreman Brewer. Mitchum always picked at him for trite matters to seem bigger than the mouse he truly was.

"I'm surprised he hasn't belted you yet for the trouble you are always causing." Martin whispered into Mitchum's ear. The boy brushed the warning off as if it were a fly.

"It's because he secretly likes me taking him on." Mitchum picked himself up from the broken log he utilized as a seat. "I have guts while the rest of you are yellow-bellied swine." His balance was horribly off, forcing him to stumble and fall approximately two inches away from the ashes of the burning fire. "Whoa." Martin sighed in disappointment.

"How much has he had this time?" Brewer played with a piece of straw coming out from under his mustache.

"A whole bottle." Martin moved his leg to reveal an empty glass jug he had been hiding. Then the other. "Or two. He is a little 'how came you so,' if you know what I mean." Brewer heavily placed his hand on Martin's shoulder. He had not heard that term since his father passed away eleven years prior. Nowadays, many folks just called a man drunk when he was that far gone.

"I like the way you talk, Martin. It is old thinking, but sure is right. And 'little' is an understatement." Picking the glass jug up from the ground, Brewer tossed it into the fire. Tiny sparks rose in the air against the flow of gravity after the glass landed in the middle of the burning timber. Out of the spout, a few remaining drops rolled over the edge and created a blue flame that flickered for a second. "The good stuff from Clad's still?"

"You called it. Thompson gave us a bonus for doing a side job for him. Half now and half later. Mitchum all but spent his first half already. Darn saphead." The fifty year old man stared into his tin cup, barely filled half way with water flavored coffee beans in it. His right hand slightly shook while he brought the liquid to his scabbed mouth. Sunlight had peeled parts of his skin off of his lips from the previous week and it was beginning to finally heal over.

BANG! Both Brewer and Martin flashed eyes over at Mitchum. Snorts erupted from the horses as they pulled on their reins tied to a fallen tree, trying to escape the raucous. His gun rested in his right hand while his left poured the remaining liquor down his gullet. "Oh, yeah!" Brewer flew over to block the young man's path.

"Better give me your piece, Mitchum."

"Sure thing…" Mitchum pretended to re-holster his weapon before pointing it straight into Brewer's stomach instead. "Not on your life, Grandpa." Brewer punched Mitchum unconscious and watched his limp body fall backwards onto the ground.

"My horse hates loud sounds." Brewer spit at a rock next to Mitchum's face as he walked over him on his way back to the campfire and sat down next to Martin.

"What's the job?" Brewer inspected the pitcher lying on top of the hard soil by his feet. The idea of food and drink was slowly taking over his brain. It had been awhile since his last meal. Not to mention the extra handkerchief he stowed in his pocket for the boss.

"A beating."

"Who is the target?" Brewer moved his head to the right. Martin's hair aged since he left. The dirty blonde streaks slowly losing out to the gray running wild all over.

"Bernard Shetron."

Murial's eyes struggled to remain closed against the morning sunlight strobing through the pulled curtains and landing across her face. It was already the second day she had been at Bernard's ranch and the trip's toll still lingered in her muscles and bones. Much of the previous day had been devoted to reading a book she had borrowed from the shelves in Bernard's study or joining in on the polite conversations around meal times in the eating room. Jack kept Murial in his sights most of the day, even over Murial's objections by stating there was no real danger within the house. Bernard was not cleared of all suspicions just yet, but she found it rather hard to believe he would attempt something in front of Charlene.

Jack is trying to protect you. That is all. She tried reminding herself. *He is doing this because he cares, or so he says.* No matter what words she consoled herself with, the answer stuck out like a sore thumb to her. He had a year to come clean about his secret and failed to do so. Inside, Murial was a jumble of nerves and fear mixed with a newly found loneliness she hadn't felt before. Even when her father was still alive, tormenting as only he knew how, she had felt all sorts of animosity and numerous versions of hopelessness, but never actual loneliness.

Her mother had gone on a picnic with Bernard the prior afternoon. Two hours later, Murial was astonished to see her mother trying her best to navigate the horses back to the ranch. She called out to Charlene and Greg, alerting everyone else in the process, and they all fled to reach the weaving wagon. Bernard's face was bleeding at his right eye and his chest was bruised. Nora explained that a man with a handkerchief, hiding the bottom half of his face, had sneaked up on them and gave him a beating with a little help from his friends. They threatened to do worse the next time if he didn't sell his land to Mr. Thompson by the end of the month.

"Is there a sheriff in town to report this to?" Jack had asked. Greg informed him that there was and they convinced Mr. Shetron to go into town the following day. By morning, Bernard's bruising had darkened and Charlene insisted that he visit the doctor, trying to get through to him as he worried about a missing crate one of his men had just informed him about. From what Murial could gather, the crate disappeared in Los Angeles during the night when Ruggard and Darryl were playing cards with a few dock workers.

Nora was already waiting outside the door to her room when Murial entered the hall from her's. Charlene was practically bouncing with excitement over their scheduled adventure into the big city. *That makes one of us,* Murial mumbled in her head. She didn't mind helping Charlene pick out a wedding dress, but the thought of traveling back to Los Angeles so soon caused her to ache all over without stepping a foot outside the house.

Bernard was showing off one of his prized possessions to Jack in his study when the ladies came down the stairs. It was a .44 caliber New Model Percussion Rifle with an engraved patchbox in the wooden butt of the gun. Murial had never seen a hybrid of a rifle with a revolver's rotating multi-chamber before, combined with an octagonal barrel. She overheard it's proud owner boastfully declaring that there were only a thousand of them ever made before he noticed the three women standing by the front door.

Murial avoided making eye contact with Jack for the ride into Bracken. She had discussed the trip with him the previous night and knew his unwavering opinion on the matter, He tried persuading her to stay where he was as a precaution, but she disagreed. If she backed out of going with Charlene and her mother, not only would it hurt the young woman's feelings but it would also raise questions for Bernard. *"It is still best to play along for the time being."* Her words danced in her mind.

"That is a big risk. Charlene could be putting on a innocent front."

"What? Like how you did to me? You got us into this mess in the first place. If she is lying, then what is one more knife going to do to my already scared back?" Murial winced from the memory of instant regret that flooded her heart as soon as she said that dreadful line. Jack had a job to do and she would have done the same thing if she were in his shoes. *It just feels so raw right now.* She could feel the divide between them growing deeper and wondered if the life she had grown fond of was slipping through her fingers like a leaky sieve, despite her own lies in trying to preserve what she had. *Maybe I can mend this a bit.* Murial came back to the present and asked Bernard if he knew the man who would be the armed guard on the stage to Los Angeles.

"Man by the name of Burdette will be escorting the stage. He was not on your trip coming in because he was on call for his other job." Greg answered.

"And what is his other job?"

"Gravedigger." Bernard called back over his shoulder. Charlene sat between the two men on the front seat while the rest were in the back of the wagon, a choice Nora was glad to make after her ride on the front bench seat at home. "He is a good man and a great shot." Murial glanced at Jack to see if he noticed her small step toward peace, but he was as hard to read as ever.

The ladies split ways with the gentlemen once they arrived into Bracken. Greg gave Charlene a kiss for safe travels while Bernard gave each of the ladies a hug along with a similar blessing. Murial stayed by her mother's side, watching Jack already making a beeline to a brick building displaying a sign that read "Sheriff's Office." Charlene was about to purchase the tickets when Murial offered to pay for them.

"I cannot let you do that. You are our guests and I asked you to come with me."

"Charlene, your father paid for our entire passage out here. It is the least I can do." Murial joined the two ladies on a wooden bench outside the white building. She handed a ticket to each one of them, saving the last for herself.

Charlene caught her staring in the direction that the gentleman had left, empty say for a swirl of dust and a lone tumbleweed. "Forgive me if I am prying into a sensitive matter, but what is your relationship with Mr. Fulton?"

"He is a family friend of my Father's." Murial managed to squeeze out a response before her mother had a chance to open her mouth.

"Oh, you are lucky to have such a good friend come all this way with you."

"He is a very good friend indeed." Nora didn't look over at her daughter as the words spilled from her lips. Charlene got the hint that there was more to it than met the eye, so she changed the subject to what she was looking for in her wedding dress. That particular conversation was more in Nora's field of interest and the two were non-stop chatterboxes for some time.

"I am just glad that I am getting married in California. It was passed a few years ago that any of my belongings remain mine even after I'm married. Does Pennsylvania have laws in place to protect your ownership?" Charlene shifted her gaze between the two women.

"Yes. Quite a while ago our state had those laws put in place." Nora attempted to get her daughter into their talk. "At least the politicians did something right, huh Murial?"

"The stage is here." Murial pointed to the brown mobile box being dragged by four black horses.

"Brewer, where is he?" A worn eyepatch was draped over the man's right eye. He was a talkative man, which would normally not be a welcomed trait, but his lips were sealed when money was involved. His back was aching from riding on his horse for so long and he reached for the base of his spine with a grimace. "My back is killing me. You do realize I finished the night shift just three hours ago?"

"Quite your moaning. We are almost there." Time was wasting if they were supposed to hit the stage. Their informant from town was scheduled to meet me at Spirit Cave right as the sun rose above Talon's Rock. *Three other men. Three, he said. Well, I got the three.* Brewer didn't understand why he needed witnesses and possible loose ends to accompany him. All it would take was a well-chosen position to take out the driver and armed guard. Sure, the horses could run off like mad. But he would have that fixed. A barricade of brush and logs would box the horses in with nowhere to escape. The land was nothing but stacked rocks at the one section of the trail. *Unless he doesn't trust me.*

"I 'ee you've brought the men, Brewer." The scarred

man appeared before them from behind a rocky outcropping in front of the hidden Spirit Cave. With the sun at almost peak, the shadows in that area were harsh and almost blinding in the night and day difference. All three men held their hands over their eyes, shielding the light out so they could see the man standing amidst the large shadow. "They what I a'ked for?"

"Down to the boots." Brewer threw a sack of food at the man's feet. "Last one. Cook knows I have been taking extra food and put a stop to it."

"You afraid of a cook? Lo'ing your courage on me?" The man tilted his head, studying Brewer. His nose sniffed the air, smelling the ham that was wrapped up in the fabric. With a toss of his hand, the man threw a hat at Brewer. A satisfied smirk peeked out from under Brewer's mustache, grateful to be having his lifelong friend upon his head once more. It was beginning to get a little too toasty on his hair for his liking. "Your hat. It came in handy."

"Men," Brewer twisted his hands atop his saddle horn as the sound of another horse approached. The group did a collective turn of their attentions and looked straight at the third new hire who arrived from town. "This here is Angle. He is the man I was telling you about." His tongue toyed with a new piece of straw. "Yes, sir. Angle is a man working for the federal government now. Once a prisoner, now turned rat." A grin spread wide under his snickering eyes. "Why he was the one who…"

"Enough." Angle kicked the food aside, drawing a Belgium Texas-Type Revolver from his side in a blink. "You want to die?" His eyes scanned between the other three men who's revolvers were all aimed directly at him. Brewer threw the straw on the ground. "What' this?"

"Just a mutual understanding, Angle. See, I do not trust you, as you obviously do not trust me, elsewise you would not have wanted three other men to assist me. Protecting myself is all." Brewer shrugged his shoulders. "These men are loyal to me, not to you. I know you are just using me, as you knew I was using you." He disembarked from his brown horse and strode up the rocks to where his old boss was standing frozen still. "Now that I've got your complete attention, let me tell you something."

"I could shoot you right now if I wanted too." Angle spat out through clenched teeth. He was not used to being betrayed, and did not wish to start. Once was one too many for him.

"You can. But you won't. You need me to get the girl for you so you can do your bit." Brewer zeroed in on him, eyes set on one another in locked concentration. "I have my own plans for revenge too though. And you are not going to kill me before I get that one sweet notch on my gun handle. Got it?" They starred long and hard at each other, a silent agreement being exchanged.

"You men up for robbing a coach?" Angle holstered his gun and flicked the tails of his trench coat up from behind his legs. Brewer's men raised up their revolvers and did likewise before whooping and hollering with delight.

"What's the deal?" The thin man asked. Angle could see he was reserved in his celebration until he heard the rest of the proposition.

"I have a little unfini'hed job with a friend of mine.

By the name of Bernard 'hetron. Any of you know him?" A silent murmur was shared by the group. "Figured you would have, con'idering your employer, Thomp'on, want' to buy the ranch for pennie' from him. Brewer informed me about the little land war raging between the two and that' fine by me becau'e we are going to help him get that land."

"Is there something you are after?" The man with the eyepatch spoke up again. A devilish grin broadening above his square-shaped chin.

"A young woman by the name of Charlene, the daughter. You can keep everything else you lay your dirty hand' on. All I want is the woman." The men were turning to leave when Angle called for Brewer to wait. "Don't foul thi' up for me, Brewer. I do not care if that Murial woman' on board or not. I will come after you if you defy me now. Do you hear me?"

"Loud and clear."

Bouncing along in the stagecoach, Nora's body was protesting after the first three miles. She stared out the window and hoped that the younger ladies, and a gentleman named Mr. Windgate, could not see the strain she was desperately trying to hide. Her teeth grimaced as the wheel plowed over a large rock in the trail. The gentleman seemed to be oblivious to the rough travel as he continued to engage them in a conversation detailing the launch of Bracken's hotel within the next month. He was the primary investor in the endeavor and was pleased with how things were progressing for his fifth hotel.

Continuing onward for the next mile or so, Murial found herself longing to be back on her farm. She missed Firestorm and all the animals, Walter's humorous side and playful antics, and most of all, the way her life had been before all of this had started. It was so unfamiliar to her, wanting to go home instead of wishing to stay on the road. *If only*...BANG! A bullet shot into the air and caused the driver to quicken the pace of the horses. Air raced by the windows as the driver used his whip to encourage the horses to run faster than the wind itself. Burdette fired back at the three horsemen chasing after them when another shot rang out.

Nora shoved herself into the middle of the small bench after the driver's dead arm appeared slouched over the left front window. Another shot rang out, this time from the side of the stage rather than from behind, and a loud thud stilled the chaotic scene. Their armed guard's body flopped along the side of the trail, kicking up small debris into the heat drenched afternoon.

Charlene tried steadying herself by placing her hands against the back of the bench and the side wall of the stage. "Should someone climb out and take over?" Her voice sounded as bumpy as the outside terrain.

"Be my guest." Murial suggested. All the passengers shared looks of helplessness between them. "What about you, Mr. Windgate? Got a gun?" Their stage was gaining in speed as the horses continued to run with no one at the helm.

"I only use it in emergencies."

"Right now would most certainly count as one." Nora kicked the balding man in the knee. "If you don't use it, I will." One of the horsemen finally caught up to the runaway stage and forced the horses to do an all-out stop, causing the passengers to fall forward into the front wall of the coach. The pounding sound of their hooves might have silenced, but they were still doing a dancing number inside Murial's head. Staring up at the maroon colored ceiling, Charlene could not keep it from spinning as Nora and Mr. Windgate were untangling themselves from one another.

"Get off the stage, NOW!" A man barked out an order from underneath a wide brimmed hat and a blue handkerchief pulled over the tip of his nose. He came riding up to the side of the coach on a brown stallion and waited for the other three men to climb down from their horses. Holding the group at gun point, the man Murial gathered to be their boss, shouted out his order again along with a final warning of a gunshot fired into the air over their heads. Murial turned to see her mother's scared face and they clasped their hands together just before one of the bandits flew the door open to the cramped space.

In single file, the four passengers stepped out of the stage and were being ushered to stand in front of the back wheel. Nora's eyes widened when she recognized one of the bandits from when Bernard received the beating a day before. "Murial…" She tried whispering in her daughter's ear but was cut off by the man wearing the blue handkerchief.

"Unload all valuables!" He stared them down, over the sight of his .36 caliber Navy Model Revolver. The man with the eye patch shook his gun at Mr. Windgate while their boss kept his focus pinned on Charlene.

"Come on, old man! Faster!" Even with only one eye, the man could easily see that the gentleman was taking his good ole time at empting his pockets. Charlene's gaze kept shifting to the ground nervously. She could feel their boss's stare as hot as the sun, and just as direct. Her body began to shake and she gripped onto Mrs. Robertson's hand in fear.

Making sure that the tall man had everyone covered, their boss jumped down from the horse and strode up to Charlene. His icy glare pierced straight through her. She could hear her heartbeat pounding in her ears while smelling the scent of tobacco on his breath through the cloth over his mouth. Murial surveyed the dry and endless landscape for a possible way out. They were less than five miles outside of Bracken, but it was still a good distance to make with a group of outlaws on their backs, if they could manage to get away in the first place.

"I'll take her." The boss's breath perfumed into Charlene's face.

"No!" She shook her head, remaining rigid to stand her ground and tried to match his stare with terrified eyes. Without another word, he latched his hands onto her arms and drug her away from Nora and Mr. Windgate's sides. "NO!" Charlene screamed, kicking his shins and lowering her body toward the rocks below her feet to use as leverage against him. "LET ME GO!"

"Take me instead." Murial stepped forth, silencing all action around her, her eyes set in firm decision. "Take me instead." She repeated. Her mother frantically tried pulling her daughter back into the line-up. Their boss glanced over his shoulder at Murial. He eyed her suspiciously, mentally calculating whether or not he wanted to take on the risk of defying Angle's explicit instructions. Even with his mouth concealed, Murial could see the smirking satisfaction in his eyes. "Let her go."

"Murial, what are you doing? These are the same men that attacked Bernard yesterday." Nora hissed in her ear. Murial and the man quietly studied one another. She pretended not to hear what her mother had said, keeping her focus on the bandit in front of her. *When it rains, it pours I guess.* This was something she had to do. It was their only chance at escaping. His homely mask didn't hide his true identity from her. They were the same killer eyes that watched her testify at his trial a year ago. They were the same blood sucking, murderous eyes that had threatened to wreak their revenge from the doomed chair he sat in the last time they met. No more pretending, no more looking back. There was no denying it that those eyes belonged to Brewer.

"Boss, remember what Angle said?" The man in a red handkerchief stated in a gravelly voice.

"I know what Angle said!" Brewer snapped at him. The thin man, in a green coat and brown pants, took a few steps backward from their boss's enraged response. Yanking his mask down from his face, Brewer dropped Charlene like a heavy sack of potatoes and stomped his way over to Murial. He extended his hand outward. Nora pulled at her daughter's sleeve in a final, pleading attempt to have her reconsider. Murial didn't give her mother so much as a sideways glance; giving Nora the answer she didn't want to hear. Placing her hand in his, Murial and Brewer turned to walk away from the group.

Suddenly, Mrs. Robertson lunged at Brewer from behind; jamming her fingers into his left eye and applying extreme force into its socket. "Don't you dare harm my daughter!" Brewer cried out as his eye was seeing nothing but black and felt the increasing pressure seeping into the back of his brain. The man with the eyepatch tore her mother from his boss's back just as Murial used the opportunity to kick Brewer in the gut with her foot. The man lost his balance on the uneven ground, falling into a bush of buckwheat. Charlene grabbed onto Murial's arm, trying to pull her away from him.

"Get back, Charlene." Murial broke herself free from her hands. "Stay back." The young woman obeyed, rushing over to the side of the stage where Nora had been flung to by Brewer's accomplice.

"Martin! Get her!" Brewer shouted. The red handkerchiefed man quickly latched onto her arm, awaiting for their boss to pick himself up from the rocks. He was slow to move. Pulling out various needles that had stabbed into his body on the way down, Brewer hauled himself up from the prickly pear hidden behind the buckwheat bush, tiny droplets of blood falling from his fresh cuts. Staring at her with one last needle jutting out from his brow, Brewer grinded his teeth in anger and slapped Murial across the face with the back of his hand.

Her head whipped around. The stinging on her cheek pulsated as it turned red from the contact. She could feel her eyes watering from the pain, but ignored it and pushed them back. He was not going to get any satisfaction from her. Brewer plucked the last needle out before he seized control of her arm, dragging her over the boulders to get to his horse. Murial reached out at the animal with her hand as he thrust her body towards the stallion. His saddle was there, bags and all, right by her hand. *If I could just find something to distract him with and separate him from his men.*

"What do you buffoons think you are doing?" Brewer enjoyed standing mighty and tall on the hill, watching over his straggling group of outlaws. It gave him an addictive thrill just knowing that he was defying Angle,

215

the one who taught him how to kill. Besides, he didn't care about the money, nor his old teacher's petty threats. The reason he was out here was to seek vengeance for his brother and his bloated ego felt confident enough to turn his back on Murial. "Shake them down. Get everything you can. Luggage too." He enjoyed seeing Mrs. Robertson and Ms. Shetron squirm whilst hurriedly taking their jewelry off.

As the gang was preoccupied, the next move was Murial's to make. Taking in a couple of deep breaths, she tried to calm her nerves down so that the gears in her mind could get to work. *Think girl, think!* She knew that a minute was all she had before Brewer would turn around to finish whatever cruel and twisted fate he had created for her. *If only I could get to my gun.*

Murial glanced down at her right side, picturing where the small holster was wrapped around the calf of her leg. Any fast action on her part would be spotted by Brewer's peripheral vision and there was too much fabric to gather up in an instant in the hopes that she could get a shot off before he did. *And he has the quicker draw.* Scanning the horse's gear for a potential weapon, the thought suddenly occurred to her that she had the perfect strategy staring her in the face. Her hand began to undo the front cinch strap, unbuckling it from the girth and making sure that it was good and loose. Then she continued to do the same with the rear cinch by unfastening the buckle as stealthy as possible. At first, the plan seemed well constructed in her mind until she turned horror-stricken by the slipping straps. It was too obvious that she had tampered with them and a skilled horseman would notice it in a heartbeat.

Hastily, she pulled on the horse's reins to lead him up the hill. Brewer looked over to see the turn of his horse's head and shot her a look over his shoulder. "Hmm." Murial quickened her pace in a poor attempt at fleeing. At least, with the animal as a shield, she could reach for her gun without him seeing what she was doing. With his widened stride, however, it was fairly easy for Brewer to catch up to her and regain possession of his horse in a matter of seconds. He spat in her face, leaving a clump of mucus and saliva clinging to her left cheek. She remained unwavering, despite the fact that her insides were screaming at her to run. *If I run, I am dead. But I might be dead already.* Adrenaline was pumping through her veins. This was her one shot and she felt the panic rising in her stomach. "Where do you think you are going?" Brewer ripped the reins from her hands. "You haven't seen the best part yet."

"You are right about that. I have not seen you die with my own eyes."

"And you won't. But, you will see your friends die." He presented her with a dark humored grin filled with revoltingly stained teeth and pulled at a string tied around his neck. "You did this to Ryans. And I am going to do the same thing to you after my men kill your blood as well." Murial zoned in on the off-white, hardened charm that hung from the rope-like cording. She wanted to vomit the moment it sunk in that it was a finger bone from the stout man's dead corpse.

"Boss, we got it all." Martin called up from the stage. He couldn't say that their bounty satisfied him, but they had the strongbox yet to open at a later time. It was sure to dazzle their minds since Bernard's daughter was on board. Mr. Shetron was known to give his daughter large amounts of spending money for whenever she traveled into the big city and he had a gut feeling that it would be quite rewarding since it was normally stowed in the box for safe keeping.

"Excellent." Brewer pushed Murial's shoulder back. "Get on Demon." His eyes shifted in the direction of the stallion. "I wouldn't want you to miss the best view as their heads hit the desert floor." She gulped. The straps were on the side he could not see for the time being, so there still was a chance that it could all work out. It all depended on whether or not she could push his buttons just right.

"No." Murial's hardened voice was growing a bit shaky but she tried to keep it steady. Nothing was certain in life, especially at the given predicament. *This has to work. Please, Lord, let this work.*

"Boss, we have to go. We will be missed if we…"

"Shut-up!" Brewer was becoming boiling mad at all the defiance and interruptions impeding on his long awaited moment. Demon was also starting to become antsy with his owner's increasingly loud outbursts, moving his head and flicking his tail with dislike at the raised tempers. "Any more yelling and you will spook my horse."

"I SAID GET ON!" Brewer returned to Murial and smacked her arm. "GET ON!" At the back of her mind, she had a tickling thought. It was a wild idea; an impossible strategy that could not hurt anything if it did not go well. Her captor's mind was dead set on revenge, so he would not kill her before he did away with the others first. *Here goes…*

Murial allowed herself to fall to the rocks when she took a step toward the saddle, knowing full well that he would not be fooled twice by the same trick she pulled in Arizona. "I am not stupid enough for that one again." With one hand still grasping onto Demon's reins, Brewer reached down with his right to pull her up when she kicked her left foot hard into the bottom of his holster, launching his Colt into the air. Fast as lighting, Murial jumped up to slap Demon's backside while hollering against the rocks to amplify her voice. The horse went bolting down the hill, catching Brewer off guard as the reins were violently jerked clean from his hand.

Everyone below was too busy dodging out of Demon's way to see what was taking place on the hill, giving Mr. Windgate the perfect distraction to flick his wrist up for a small Derringer to shoot out from his spring-loaded concealed sleeve contraption. Murial put Brewer in a daze by hitting him on the head with a nearby rock, giving her ample time to hoist her skirt up and pull an Allen and Thurber Pepperbox from her holster. *I need to switch to an ankle version for the next time. If there is a next time.* Mr. Windgate concentrated his .41 caliber on the man called Martin while she aimed her's directly at Brewer, pointing the barrel at his chest and pulling the trigger with all her might before she was ready. Her eyes widened when it almost missed him completely from shooting it off too soon. *Great.*

The sound of the bullet caused all action to cease from below. "Boss?" The eyepatch man called up the hill. Brewer shook his head awake, feeling the blood slowly oozing from the base of his neck where the rock had sliced his skin. Instinctively, he went to feel for the open wound just as his eyesight cleared to see Murial staring him down. She knew her body was shaking, but hoped that it was not visible to anyone else. It wasn't like she did this on a regular basis.

"Lay down those weapons or your boss is dead." Her voice echoed off the high-crested formations dotting the rough terrain. The three men looked at one another in bafflement, unsure what to do. A few baubles of jewelry and luggage totes of personal effects were not worth their lives, and there was no guarantee that there would be any real money inside the box. Martin took notice of Windgate's two and a half inch barrel pointed at the left temple of his head.

"I'll blast through your eye if you move an inch." Windgate promised. Martin could see that the man's warning was not an empty threat and went rigid in compliance.

"You are a bitch!" Brewer felt the fire burning in his gun arm. The eyepatch man slowly lifted his revolver at Murial who caught sight of his movements.

"You shoot him, and you are dead."

"And so am I." Martin spoke up to the right of his friend. The man with the eyepatch tilted his gun upwards with hesitation. He held no real loyalty to Brewer other than where money was concerned. But Martin was a well-respected man in their circle, even though he did stand up for Brewer from time to time. Whatever remnant of a conscience he had, it would not allow for Martin's death to be on his hands.

"Drop the guns!" Murial demanded. "I am not going to say it again." Her hand steadied the gun at Brewer's crumpled form. She was going to make sure that the next shot would penetrate his heart. *This is for Reginald.* The echoing sound of three revolvers hitting the gravelly soil rang out in the still air. Nora and Charlene didn't move until after Murial instructed the men to kick their weapons away from them and for the ladies to put the guns into the stage. "And anything else you may be hiding, gentlemen!"

"Don't listen to her, you idiots. Take them down!" Brewer shouted. "SHOOT HER!" Murial's internal pride held a hint of satisfaction at the sound of metal blades being thunked onto the ground. "MARTIN!" His voice was muffled through grinding teeth as his darkened blood stained the surrounding vegetation. Charlene stayed clear of the three men while Nora went to gather some rope from one of their horses.

"Forget the rope." Windgate motioned the men to walk up the hill about thirty feet. "Tie their horses onto the back of the stagecoach, Ms. Shetron. They can come back to town for them later, when the sheriff is ready to take them to jail. That is, if they don't want to die of thirst." He pondered a thought. "I do not believe that there is any water from here to Bracken. Leave one canteen for them to fight over or to share. Their choice." Charlene threw a canteen down on the other side of the trail where the landscape was steeper and a maze of prickly pears wove in and out amidst snake chollas.

Murial's face gave a victorious flash of a smile. She watched Mr. Windgate force the men to march their way beyond the front of the stagecoach horses. What seemed like an impossible scenario at first glance had become a miraculous escape in the second. *Don't celebrate just yet.* Her attention had been diverted for a mere minute, but that was all it took for Brewer to slide his hand behind his head, feeling for the soft lump that marked the presence of his knife nestled under the back of his vest. Gripping it with a strength fueled by hatred, his bloody fingers curled around the hilt and he launched the blade into the air, targeted directly at Murial. Nora and Charlene looked up at the hill in fear when they heard a shot cut through the silence.

"A storm is coming. Ya hear? I feel it in me bones that a storm is brewing over that there ridge. It be here in three days' time." An elderly man prophesized along the sidewalk in front of the saloon, telling every passing stranger that came within hearing distance of him. His beard was wispy and scraggily, with a wild presence that set the tone for the rest of the man's wardrobe. Two men passed right on by him as though he did not exist, pushing the swinging doors open to the beginning of their reprieve from work and the heat.

The old man rattled his tin can, staring lovingly at the three coins a Ms. Tillerman had paid him in exchange for some information. She was not known to anyone around those parts, but he knew her alright. Buzz. Buzz. A few pesky little insects wove their way in the air by the man's large nose. His eyes blinked while he brought his hand up to swat them away. "Darn pests." A tooth on the top of his mouth was angled outward in an unusual manner. It was the very reason for his nickname, given to him by the locals. "Storm's a coming. For sure, it is a coming."

Just a block away, Greg stopped Jack and Bernard to

point out a boxing match that was being held by a tree and a fenceline down the avenue to their left. A ring had been constructed from simple rope and sticks, entertaining a crowd growing in size in order to watch the "Amazing Arnie" take on anyone who had two dollars in his hand. The man, an overly exaggerated thirty year old dockworker, was about Jack's height with a slightly pronounced stomach and muscular arms. An old wound was visible on his right shoulder from a stabbing of some kind, adding to the elaborate stories a smaller man was telling. Blood trickled down from a cut on his chin as they watched the most recent challenger being drug from the ring's floor by two bystanders.

"Come on, folks. I know there is another challenger out there. Who wants a chance at earning four times their entry fee. Six dollars! That is right. You heard me say it. Six dollars!" The smaller man bellowed. He was dressed in a well-fitted suit and a new hat that hadn't had the chance to get peppered with a dust storm yet.

"I am guessing that math was not one of his top skills." Jack commented. He gave Bernard a sideways look out of curiosity as to what the man thought of the traveling fight show.

"It is called business arithmetic, Jack. How else could he afford such a well-designed hat." The men stood in awe at the spectacle before them. Bernard elbow-bumped Jack and motioned to Greg with his eyes. A mischievous grin informed him what the older man was thinking about when they looked over and saw how transfixed his future son-in-law was by the whole thing. "Does not matter, anyhow." Jack watched Bernard clear his throat dramatically. "I do not know of anyone who can beat the 'Amazing Arnie' around here. Maybe that man can buy a new pair of shoes to go with his fancy hat after he is done collecting everyone's money for the day." Greg watched with intrigue as a farmhand threw up his arm to signify that he was next.

"Looks like we have another challenger." Jack joined in on the fun.

"That is one of the new men Thompson hired on." Greg looked over at Bernard, with a weary expression painted on his face. "He has hired a lot more men since you left, Boss. I didn't want to tell you in front of Charlene, but the boys were relieved when we had gotten word you were on your way back." Bernard remained silent.

"Are you saying he is preparing for a land war?" Jack asked. "I have seen a few of those before. Waste of life and energy if you ask me."

"Well, we are not sure if he is. But, for some reason he has been after Mr. Shetron's land since he arrived." Greg kicked a rock by his foot. "I just hate feeling like a sitting duck not knowing what is going on behind closed doors."

"One thing we are not going to do with Thompson is to underestimate him. I would not put it past that man to obtain more cattle or improve his spread just to cover up for the fact that he is hiring a private army. No, best we keep our guard up." Bernard checked his pocket watch and rubbed the chain mindlessly. Greg returned his attention onto the fight that had ended badly for the new man in town while Jack kept his focus split between the two.

"Is there something else bothering you?" Jack's interest was piqued. It was the third time Bernard had glanced down at his watch since they left the sheriff's office. *I could swear that it had been barely three minutes since the last time he read his watch,* Jack mentally noted. At first, he wasn't sure if Bernard didn't hear him or was plain ignoring his question since he left the words adrift in the open without a response.

"Huh?" The older gentleman abruptly turned and stared at Jack. "Oh, sorry. I did not hear what you said. The noise of the crowd and all." His fingers snapped the pocket watch shut and stuffed it's silver surface back into the pocket of his vest. Grunting, Bernard walked up to the back of the crowd with Greg in tow. Jack hesitated for a second before continuing after them.

The more time he spent with Mr. Shetron, the more he began questioning his motives and mannerisms. There was a untold weight seemingly applying pressure on the man's shoulders and Jack was not liking the feel of it. Casting his eyes to the sky, he watched the towers standing ominously against the blue backdrop. Were they Bernard's or Thompson's? When would the showdown commence over a land that had been purchased with the help of Senator Drouther? How did he fit into this mess and why was Thompson so desperate to lay his hands on Shetron's property? Too many variables plagued Jack's mind. *So many questions and not enough answers to go around.*

"I'll put up the money if you want to fight him, Greg." Bernard flipped out his wallet to procure the two dollar entry fee.

"Are you sure, Mr. Shetron?" Greg's face took on a large amount of doubt. "You think I could take him on?" A few nearby spectators in the crowd were turning to size up the possible new challenger to assess their bets that were taking place along the sidelines. Bernard patted him on the back.

"You beat that man, Greg, and you can call me Bernard in public."

"Do I spot a new challenger in the audience?" The short, well-dressed man pointed in Greg's direction. "What do you say Mister? Fancy your chance at making some big money?" Greg straightened up his back, handed his hat off to Jack, and unbuttoned his sleeves. Bernard handed the two dollars to the short man and clapped his hands together as Greg finished rolling his shirt sleeves up on his hairy arms.

Strange thing to help encourage him by. As if he could read Jack's thoughts, Bernard answered the unasked question. "I do not like to play favoritism, Jack. He is the foreman of my ranch and therefore, an employee. When we are out in public, he is to address me as such. But, when we are in my house, he can call me Bernard if he wishes." Bernard gave him a sideways peek. "He does not get himself any special privileges in my book, just because he is going to marry my daughter. Quite the opposite, in fact."

"So, is this fight a test?" Jack watched on as Greg received a left jab and right uppercut.

"Nah," Bernard smiled with glee, "this is just fun."

Three rounds later, farther than all prior challengers had survived, Greg was finally counted as down and left the ring drenched in sweat and a few bruises. "I almost had him."

"Sure you did." Bernard and Jack joked, picking on him good-humoredly. The trio walked up the empty street, being as how the sidewalk was far too narrow for them to walk side by side. As soon as they reached the saloon, Mr. Shetron spotted the homeless man sitting by a barrel.

"Hey, Single Tooth." Bernard waved at the man from where he stood on the road. He made a point to bring Jack and Greg over to the strange old timer. "Got a question for you."

"Storm's a coming Mr. Shetron." A coughing fit stopped Single Tooth from saying any more.

"You alright?" Jack asked, studying the man over from his greasy head down to his worn out shoes.

"Sure am, Sonny. Just a touch of TB that rattles me from time to time. Came south for my health. A lot of good it's doing." Single Tooth engaged in a half laugh, half coughing fit. He pounded his chest with a fist and spit some gunk onto the sidewalk in relief. "Better out than in."

"You are right there, My Friend. Say, did you happen to see Thompson today?"

"Not yet. Day's only half over though." Single Tooth pulled his hair back and squinted up at Bernard's face. "He do that?" A bony finger pointed at the blacked marks on Mr. Shetron's cheeks.

"No, but one of his workers did."

Single Tooth raised his nose into the air. "Trouble is brewing between you two." He shook his head with purpose. "Big trouble." Pointing to the clear sky, he gave the man a dire warning. "Storm is coming. A storm that will end this drought."

"I am sure that the rain will come eventually. It always does." Bernard produced a dollar from his pocket and tossed it into Single Tooth's can. "Thanks."

"I saw Mark." Single Tooth eyed Bernard, watching the man question as to what he was driving at. "Saw Mark watching the stagecoach depot when you dropped your daughter off with those two other women." Bernard's left cheek twitched with worry. "Then, like a fox after a hen, he ran away." The older man placed his can on the sidewalk by his side. He titled his head around to see Greg and Jack staring at him in puzzlement; a gathering look of concern developing on each one's face. "I like you, Mr. Shetron. You are nice to a fault, unlike others I have witnessed. What I tell you is truth and we both know it." Silently, an understanding passed between them.

"Thank you, Willy." Bernard tipped his black hat and asked the other two to follow him back the way they came.

"Mr. Shetron, you already filed a report with the Sheriff. What are we going back for?"

"Because something is wrong and we need to alert Sheriff Bernheight." Greg huffed at his boss's sudden change in mood.

"Just because of what Single Tooth told us back there?" He pointed over his shoulder with his thumb. "Everyone in town thinks that Ole Codger is a stone throw away from the crazy bin."

"He may have a different way of talking, sure, but there is something in what he said that I have no care for.

Mark was watching the stage and left to tell someone the news that Charlene and the others were aboard. After what Thompson's men did to me yesterday, there is no telling what other tricks he has in that oversized brain of his." Bernard quickened his pace as Jack and Greg did likewise.

One of the deputies opened the door to the Sheriff's office with a paper, nail, and hammer in his hands. Indifferently, he went to the right of the door and nailed the paper to the side of the building. The top word was big and bold, spelling out the word 'WANTED' and all three men stopped dead in their tracks when they saw the man depicted in the line drawing under the title. It was the mustache that sometimes haunted Jack's dreams, eyes that were engraved in Bernard's mind, and a hat that had recently visited the gate to Shetron's land for Greg. Brewer.

"That is him." Bernard pointed at the image. "That's the man that ordered his men to attack me."

"Are you positive, Mr. Shetron?" The deputy was dubious, internally hoping that he was wrong in his identification of his attacker. "You said that all the guys wore masks over half of their faces."

"I would know those eyes anywhere." Bernard's jaw tightened. "They are hard as stone, those eyes. Merciless and cold, just like someone I used to know a long time ago." His voice drifted, as did his thoughts, into a past unseen to everyone else.

"What about you two? You both are acting like you recognize him as well." The deputy inquired.

"I saw him taking a look at our gate the other night." Greg shyly replied. Bernard gave him a fierce glare.

"Why did you not inform me of this?!"

"Well, the man seemed lost, asked where Bracken was, we politely told him, and then he left. But I recognize the hat more than anything." Greg took a long look at the drawing. "I can't be sure that it was him. See, the fellow that was out at the gate was scarred on his face and he had a weird way of talking." Bernard seemed very intrigued by that fact and questioned him as to what he meant by 'a weird way.' "Well, he did not pronounce the letter 's' correctly. Seemed to skip the letter entirely as he talked." Sheer fear drained Mr. Shetron of all life force, freezing him into a statue painted white from shock.

"Mr. Shetron?" Greg was growing quite concerned for his boss just as Jack plowed through the sheriff's door, slamming it shut behind him, and demanded to be told all the information that the sheriff had on the wanted man.

"And why should I do that?" Sheriff Bernheight was not a man that took kindly to others telling him how to do his job.

"Because I am a Deputy United States Marshal, and I am also the man who arrested Brewer in the first place!"

"We know that Brewer escaped prison with some help from a friend on the outside or on the inside of the prison. Not much to go on at the jail-break, I am afraid. He is dangerous and armed at all times with both guns and knives, likes to keep his mustache well-groomed for an unknown reason. Was put away for being convicted in connection to a kidnapping of a woman and the assassination of a senator, but you should already be fully aware of that last fact if you are telling me the truth."

"But, I do not understand why I was not informed by the sheriff of Conestone when his escape was first discovered."

"Would that have been Sheriff Curt Ruger?" Jack could feel his stomach turning into knots. He picked up the past tense nature of the question.

"Yes, it would be." Sheriff Bernheight told it like it was. He figured it would be the best way to handle it and life was too short for beating around the bush with niceties at certain times.

"Sheriff Curt Ruger was killed in the line of duty by…"

"Brewer." Jack gritted his teeth. His eyes filled with a fire of hatred. Curt didn't deserve a fate like that. He had been much too good of a friend, and an honest man at that.

"Actually, the U.S. Marshals do not believe so. I'm surprised that you were not notified, given that you say you are one of them."

"Every workforce has their own communication issues." The sheriff cast a suspicious look at him until Jack clarified his statement. "Let us just say that I am on the outside looking inward with my bosses as of late. Who did kill him?"

"No suspects as of a week ago. After he was killed, his deputy found the office ransacked as if someone was looking for something. But the deputy said there was nothing missing. An eyewitness saw Brewer leaving the office shortly before the deputy arrived, so it was confirmed that he was the man rifling through the sheriff's paperwork, but there was no evidence that he killed Curt." *Oh, he found what he was looking for alright. Where to find Murial and myself.* Jack kept quiet about being followed at the Robertson farm. There was still no telling how Bernard fit into all of this, especially since he was becoming more and more nervous as time wore on. He did testify that Brewer was the one who was behind his beating, but that could just be a clever way to disguise that Brewer really worked for him. "Do you believe he is coming after you for revenge?"

"Sounds like I have a good reason to be thinking that."

"Those women that came into town traveling with you, either one of them happen to be the woman that was kidnapped?" The sheriff studied Jack's stoic expression. It was best to reveal as little as possible for the time being. "I'm sorry. I know what a good deputy means to you." Sheriff Bernheight rubbed the back of his neck with his hand. "Look…Jack, is it? I do not have any extra men to spare you for protection…"

"That will not be necessary Sheriff. Thank you just the same." A concern wrinkle spread over Bernheight's forehead.

"I get that you are a Deputy Marshal and all, but this is still my town and I do not need, nor want, you to go charging all fired hot and mad around this area looking for this convict."

"That is not my style, Sheriff."

"Good, glad to hear it." Jack could tell it in the man's voice that he was not convinced in the slightest. "Of course, naturally that would be all well if I knew you, which I don't."

"Jack," Greg burst through the door, putting a pause in their conversation. "Bernard and I need to talk to you right away."

"I will be right along if you can kindly tell this sheriff of your's that I am worth my word in gold." Jack shifted most of his weight to one leg.

"I'll vouch for him, Sheriff." Greg grabbed a hold of Jack's arm and hauled him out the door.

"Hey, thanks, but what is the big idea?" Jack suddenly stopped short when he saw Bernard's panicked eyes. "What is going on?" He began scanning the surrounding area and shot up a quick gander at the guards in the towers. Keeping his hand close to his gun that rested on his right hip, Jack fingered the butt of it in case it was going to be needed.

"Not here." Bernard hurried them over to the corner of a building watching over the main street. "We need to get a message to Los Angeles to warn the girls about what we know and to instruct them to remain in the city until further notice."

"If they manage to make it there safely, that is." Jack's frustration was building. "I am guessing that is what Single Tooth was referring to when he mentioned Mark disappearing after the stage left?" Hurriedly, the three men left for the telegraph office. "First things first. We'll send word in case the stage arrives there. Then, we head out after them."

Tapping in rhythmic and purposeful patterns, the message pulsated through the wire as the clerk translated their words into coded sounds. Dread was now replacing the knots Jack had been gaining in his gut earlier. The situation was as messy as a plate of spaghetti, full of twists and turns in what was true or false. No matter how one looked at the noodles, however, one thing was blatantly obvious. Brewer was in this disaster up to his ears. Murial was on that stage and it was becoming increasing likely that an attempt on her life was going to happen outside of his ability to do anything about it.

Jack paid the clerk and turned, about to leave, just as the man said his name and handed him a message that had come in ten minutes before. After thanking the clerk, he led Greg and Bernard in the direction of the stables when a sudden shouting and rapid pounding of horse hooves came up from behind them. They turned around to see the stagecoach weaving wildly as Mr. Windgate was making every effort not to hit any of the walking pedestrians. To his left, the driver's limp and lifeless body was shaking like a tree in a strong wind. The hotel owner pulled the horses to a stop in front of the depot. "GET A DOCTOR! SOMEONE, GET THE DOCTOR!"

"What happened?" Greg yelled up to him as Jack raced to the door of the stage. Charlene reached for the handle at the same moment he flung it open. Nora was cradling her daughter in a bloodstained dress from the warm red liquid seeping out of Murial's wounded shoulder. Murial was trying to keep her tears back as the pain raced up and down her nerves, her neck on fire. Her mother gave a broken explanation in choppy sentences.

"We were being robbed by four armed men. One of them I recognized from yesterday. Murial stood up to them. Their leader threw a knife at her and it stabbed her in the shoulder, near her neck, when she tried to move out of its way." Charlene and Nora helped to lower Murial down from the stage, sliding her into Jack's arms. Mr. Windgate announced that he could see the doctor coming from around the corner of the blacksmith shop, with Bernard behind him. Dr. Mason held the handle of his medical bag in one hand and motioned for Jack to sit her down on the sidewalk with the other. Carefully, the doctor removed the tightly wrapped cloth bandages, made from Charlene's shift, in order to better assess the situation.

It was a deep gash that penetrated about an inch and

a half into her chest to the left side of her rib cage, near the top of her shoulder and just missed the collar bone. Blood was running onto the floorboards as the pain was increasing with each passing minute. Murial's eyes panned the crowd that was watching her. *I hate being the center of attention,* she told herself. "I am going to have to clean it, making sure that there is nothing in there to cause infection. This is going to be painful at first." Dr. Mason looked from left to right, then back to the left again. "Let us get you into my office for some privacy." Jack carried Murial behind the doctor, leading them over to the one story building that operated as his office in the first two rooms and his house in the back three. Greg held the door open so that Jack could gently place Murial onto the examination table. Nora was the only one allowed to stay in the room, so Jack and the others filed out onto the porch in order to wait and see.

It had only been seven minutes and already the ground in front of the doctor's porch was forming a slight moat from the constant back and forth pacing from Jack's boots. He despised feeling so useless. All he could focus on was the rising anger, escalating into his own need for revenge, and a desire to kill Brewer with every ounce of his being. Remembering the telegram that the clerk had given him, Jack pulled the note from his pocket and silently read over the message. His eyes glazed over when he had finished. Murial screamed from the alcohol being poured onto her open flesh, forcing a knife through his already pierced heart. He would have given anything to trade places with her. It crushed his soul, rubbing his spirit raw, that she had learned about his investigation into her family, leaving her feeling betrayed and cynical against him, and now this? Jack scolded himself for having failed her yet again. *I should have been there to protect her. I should have insisted on going along.*

Seconds felt like minutes and minutes felt like hours. Everyone remained silent. Charlene leaned her head on Greg's shoulder, sitting next to her father. She wished there were words she could say to help comfort Jack, but she knew better than that. It was like looking at a mirror of herself when her mother died. Nothing, no matter how thoughtful or well-intended, would have made her feel any better that night.

"And you said that she shot him after he threw the knife?" Sheriff Bernheight jotted down a few notes on a pad of paper.

"Yes, sir. She most surely did. I did not have a chance to make sure that the man was dead, but he looked that way to me." Mr. Windgate dabbed his forehead with a handkerchief. "We left the other three men wandering around the desert. Those horses, tied on the back of the stagecoach, are theirs. The leader's horse went running off to who knows where."

"Is that how it happened Miss Shetron?" Charlene glanced up at the sound of her name.

"Huh? Oh, yeah, it is."

"Did you happen to catch any one of their names?"

"What?" Charlene was either very distracted by still being in shock, or deliberately acting as though she were absentminded. Jack couldn't be sure which was the case.

"Mr. Windgate tells me that one of the men said

'Remember what blank said' as a warning to their boss. Did you hear the name? He says that you were closer to the man who was talking than he was." Charlene vehemently shook her head.

"No, I did not hear who it was."

"Sheriff." The deputy rode up with four other men at his side. "Swore in the extra deputies like you asked for. We are ready to hit the trail."

"Good. Go half a mile past Eagle Rock and start searching there." With a tip of his hat, the deputy led the others out of town.

"Was this the man they called boss?" Bernheight held up the wanted poster for Mr. Windgate and Charlene to see.

"That's him alright." Mr. Windgate nodded. Charlene looked away, burying her face into Greg's shoulder. A sound coming from right behind the doctor's door caused all eyeballs to be glued onto the worn knob. The handle turned and Nora stepped over the threshold, looking relieved. "The good news is that the doctor was able to stop the bleeding and has stitched the wound up. She is going to spend the night here for observation and then she can go back to the ranch if there is no infection."

"Are you going to be staying with her?" Sheriff Bernheight asked. "I don't think it would be a good idea to leave her alone until my men come back with a report."

"Yes, Sheriff. I will be here with Dr. Mason. Thank you all for your concern, but the doctor says that no one can see her tonight." The group disbanded, after saying their farewells for the evening and best wishes for a speedy recovery for Murial: Greg took Charlene toward the stables to prepare the wagon for the trip back to the ranch, Mr. Windgate shuffled off to the stagecoach to attend to his riffled through luggage, Sheriff Bernheight returned to his office to prep some paperwork and Bernard gave Nora a kiss on the hand before bidding his farewell.

Jack stood awkwardly like a lone tree, staring pleadingly into the space behind Nora. He could see Murial sleeping on the table, her shoulder bandaged. "Jack, no one can see her tonight." Nora gave him a firm look.

"I realize that. It's just…well…I would like to stay here, outside on the bench this evening. To keep watch. We still do not know if Brewer is dead or not." Nora gave him a compassionate smile and placed her hand on his shoulder.

"I think she would like that."

Murial's eyes opened to a room shrouded in darkness. She blinked, trying to find some little dot of light in the midst of her black surroundings. "Did I die?" Her voice sounded weak and unfamiliar. *I'm in a bed, apparently.* Two pillows lay under her neck, giving her the most support at the base of her skull. A headache knocked on the door to the left side of her brain, asking for permission to take over the rest without accepting 'no' for answer. A blanket was draped over her body, despite the room being warm enough to cook a steak, and it's fibers were growing itchy against her skin.

"I certainly hope not. If you did, that would mean that this is either a dream or that we both died from that band of outlaw thieves." Nora's hand stumbled around for the box of matches to relight the candle on the bedside table to her right. After three hours of staring at the unrevealing tell of its light, she had grown favorable to the still darkness. Just like she had done many years before, when Murial had gotten sick at the age of twelve, Nora sat motionless and unwavering in a chair beside the bed as her daughter lay equally as still. In the room devoid of any brightness, time was frozen and Mrs. Robertson was perfectly content with that. The instant she struck the match, a flash of orange flame temporary blinded Murial.

"Now I know I died, because you are cracking jokes." She took a second to readjust her vision. The light appeared blurry, as did her mother's features in its warm glow, but Murial was positive it was her based on Nora's voice. In a crowd of a thousand women, she would be able to pick out that soft, yet authoritative tone her mother always had. Nora blew out the match and laid the used up, burnt piece on the table after successfully relighting the tall candle's wick.

"How are you feeling?"

"Crappy. Like my body was dragged behind a horse for a mile."

"That is normal after what happened today."

"Mother, did I get him? Did I kill Brewer?" Her bandaged shoulder fiercely stung as she tried to change her position.

"You should rest now, Murial. Do not try to move. Dr. Mason stitched your shoulder up from where the knife penetrated." Nora picked up the blanket's edge and pulled it higher up until it covered her daughter's chest.

"I need to know, Mother. Did I kill him?" Murial winced at the headache that was moving toward her right temple while the pain in her shoulder throbbed with an unquenchable ache.

"Yes, Murial, you did. The Sheriff and his deputies confirmed it when the sun was still up. They found his body where the other bandits left it to rot. Just past Eagle

Boulder." Relief crashed upon Murial's soul like a tidal wave. *Finally, it's over.* "I was truly proud of you out there." Nora smiled shyly. "The way you stood up to those men was…I will have to remember to thank Jack for teaching you how to shoot a gun."

"Then you would want to be thanking Uncle Seb for that one."

"I thought Jack…what about all those times I saw both you and him practicing at wooden targets or tin cans?"

"We were having a contest." Murial gave a soft snort. "Whoever shot the worst had to help Katy wash the dishes." Nora's left eyebrow rose.

"Is that why you were drying the plates that night?"

"I only missed out by one, thank you very much." She heard her mother chuckling in the chair. "Glad I could amuse you." Murial was not in a humorous mood for obvious reasons.

"I am so sorry, Murial. I just, well, it is so good to hear you speaking again."

"Me too." Her mind was grinding away, trying to remember the details as to what exactly took place when she was injured. "Did…everyone…make it?" Murial wasn't sure that she wanted to be told the truth. Some parts were a blur, but seeing blood oozing and a hand applying pressure kept coming to the forefront. "I should remember…" She hit her forehead with her left hand as if smacking the memory back would result in doing anything.

"Do not hurt yourself. More details can come back in due time, but it's nothing to be concerning yourself with right now. Everyone did make it out alright, thanks to you and Mr. Windgate."

"Mr. Windgate?"

"The man who shared the stage with you, myself, and Charlene." Nora brushed off her lap. There was no dirt on it to be dealt with, but it gave her fingers something to occupy themselves with as she worked up her courage to say her next statement. "Jack was the one who brought you over to the doctor's office. He was extremely worried about you." She paused to see what Murial's reaction would be. Sensing none, Nora decided to continue. "I know what he said to you on the train. About how his superiors had encouraged him to use his relationship with you to further their investigation. Do you not think that keeping a secret, such as that, tore him up inside?"

"Do we have to discuss this now, Mother? I have just awoken from being stitched up by a doctor after killing Brewer to keep him from kidnapping Charlene." Murial turned her head away, laying her right ear against the top pillow and let out a sigh of exasperation. It was bad enough that her body physically hurt, begging for relief from the throbbing pain that felt as if it was spreading. Why did she have to bring up about her fragmented heart in addition to all of that?

Internally, Murial wanted to hide in a darkened hole where there was no one to see her cry and no one to pour salt on her reopened wounds. *Time heals all wounds.* It was an aloof idea that never seemed to work out well for her. Sure, time eventually dulls the sting's impact after the initial blow, but those scars are permanent and each recut hurt worse than the last one.

"Now is exactly the time we should be talking about this. I understand you're feeling betrayed and confused as to what all to believe, but Murial, did it ever occur to your stubborn head that Jack actually does care about you? That you are the reason he is here?"

"How can you be so blinded? Jack came along in the hopes that he would pick up a lead on their case and nothing more." Nora's nostrils were fuming at her daughter's bullheadedness. It was always difficult to argue with her whenever her mind had already been made up, a trait Murial had inherited from both sides of the family.

"Murial Jayne Robertson! Get your head straight! It is imperative that you stop listening to the fear restricting your ability to view things clearly." Nora stood up, hands on hips as Murial faced her mother with eyes blazing.

"What fear? Jack lied to me and that is the bottom fact."

"No, that's the explanation you are telling yourself." Nora retook her seat and placed her hand on Murial's leg hidden underneath the blanket. "Murial, you are still allowing the past to keep you from moving onward with your life. I know your turbulent experiences with your father caused you to put up walls to shield yourself from further disappointment and suffering. However, while they did serve an original purpose, the time has come for those barriers to come down. After so many years, it can be very difficult to shed those burdens. I have that same issue myself. I am constantly trying to improve after Gerald died, and it is no picnic for me either in that regard, but I am getting better."

"Please bring this talk to a point of some kind."

"Our past can do two things for us: strengthen ourselves or bind us in chains. Jack is not your father. He made a mistake, as we all do as human beings. Do not let your fear of history repeating itself keep you from taking a leap of faith." Murial's rigidness lessened, allowing her mother's words to sink in.

"Where is Jack?"

"He is right outside on the bench as we speak."

"Murial?" A softened male voice came through the door to the recovery room, followed by a few knocks. Murial stirred from the unexpected sound, causing her mother to awaken from her daughter's disturbance. Nora's empty hand rested on top of the bed cover, her body slumped over the bed, and her back screamed in a fit of rage at being in an uncomfortable position for the last four hours. "Nora?" Mrs. Robertson blinked her eyes open rapidly in an attempt to remove the sleep dirt that was crusted on the edge of her eyelids. She stretched her arms above her head until she realized that it was making her spine hate her even more.

"Just a minute." Nora picked herself clumsily up from the chair, walking over to the door to the left of the bed. Turning the knob, she peered around to see who was calling. "Good morning Jack." She gestured for him to come in to the ten foot by twelve foot space. "I apologize for the state of my appearance at this hour."

"That is quite alright, Mrs. Robertson. I was just going to inquire on how Murial was doing?" He asked in a whisper as to not disturb Murial, oblivious to the fact that she was already wide awake.

"I think you can ask her that yourself." Nora smiled, tipping her head in the direction of where Murial laid, who was giving Jack a weakened smile of her own when he turned to face her. "We were just talking about you a few hours ago, were we not, Murial?" Her mother leaned heavily to her right in order to peek around Jack's shoulder, casting her daughter an arched eyebrow and motherly warning in her eyes. Jack pulled his hat off his head, keeping it in front of his stomach and shifting uncomfortably like an alert deer. "I believe that the toilet set could do with some more water. Please excuse me." Mrs. Robertson made her way into the hall, shutting the door behind her to give the two some privacy.

"Won't you sit?" Murial verbally offered the now vacant chair at her bedside. Along with the new dawn, came with it a new batch of pain that was starting to make it's presence known. *Curse that hidden knife of his,* Murial muttered to herself. Jack obliged by sitting his butt down onto the hard wooden surface whilst rubbing his fingers along the wide brim of his hat. She could tell that he was feeling just as awkward as she was at the moment; the unavoidable tension was growing increasingly larger with each tick of the invisible clock. "I wanted to ask you a question."

"Yes, Nora did mention that you wished for me to visit you this morning." Jack watched the small rays of sun being casted upon his thumb from the tiny crack in the pulled drapes of the window. The yellow square traveled around as he repositioned himself on the stiff seat, almost getting his holster stuck in the process. "Are you feeling alright?"

"If by alright, you mean feeling as if a horse ran me over, than that would be correct." She tried to force her lips into another smile, but ended up wincing from the aching pain instead. *It is going to be a long day.* "Why did you not tell me about the investigation into my father after you discovered that I knew nothing on the subject? That is, if you had me cleared as an accomplice at all." Jack almost leapt from his seat to answer her question, but restrained himself from getting overly defensive. Murial had a right to ask and it was not her fault she did not know what was going on. Still, it was not easy confronting the situation head on. In fact, the longer he discussed it, the more desirable it was to just drop the matter entirely and pretend that it never happened. He wanted nothing else but to return to the farm, to the way their lives used to be.

"Because I was afraid to." Murial observed the uncommon way that Jack squirmed about in the chair. She had never seen him act so nervous before, at least for as long as she could remember. It took her a moment to realize just what he was trying to tell her. Her weakened state of energy made it difficult for her head to fully function properly though. Unbelievably, it had not even been twenty-four hours since the time of Brewer's death to the dawn of the following morning. To be sure of her suspicions, Murial decided to be blunt. Considering on the foul mood she was in, pleasantries were not an option.

"What were you afraid of exactly?"

"I was afraid of losing you." Jack starred straight

into her eyes as he said it, causing Murial's heart to skip a beat. "I knew you would react the way you did on the train, when the time came to explain the truth, and I did not want anything to spoil the time we had on the farm. After all of my deception, I just wanted you to know that I do not expect your forgiveness nor your trust ever again. Perhaps it was selfish of me to do, and in that, I apologize."

The puzzle was clearing up for Murial. In some strange way, Jack's actions were making sense. He had been distancing himself from her purposefully. *Not that it was a tasteful tactic.* "I could not keep the secret any longer, and tried to tell you on numerous occasions, but it never seemed like the right moment. Be that as it may, I do not have much time left to solve the case. Marshal Heathrow was the man who deputized me about a year and a half ago. His job spans a four year term, about to run out next year. If he is not chosen to continue in his position, then I will most likely be relieved of my duty as well." Jack's hand fumbled around in his pocket in search for the crumpled up telegram he had received the prior day. He managed to pull it out and unraveled the worn paper from its condensed form, proving to Murial that it was no lie. "I was given this just before the stage pulled into town after Brewer and his men attacked you. It was sent to me by the Marshal, stating that unless there is some progress made in a short amount of time, then he is going to lose his job come next spring. His superiors are applying political pressure."

Murial's tired eyes scanned over the words that blurred into one long squiggly line against the white background. She could feel her energy draining despite having had slept most of the night away. "Do you want to stay on as a deputy?" In the past, Murial had only casually met a couple of marshals while accompanying her father on his travels. She remembered that their tasks varied from person to person, but there was one important characteristic of their job they all shared; a marshal's power resided in a specific territory. If Jack was deputized in Arizona, then his power would be confined to the territory unless there was a special circumstance. *He had offered to resign on the train.*

"That is another issue I have been dithering on." Jack rubbed the back of his neck with his right hand. He picked himself up from the seat and paced over to the window, allowing the slice of the rising sun to land on his face. "I know that I have been more distracted than anything for some time now. It's like my brain has fifteen railroad tracks going in haphazardous directions and the engines are trying desperately not to collide."

"Really? With all that swirling around in your head, I am surprised you could get dressed yesterday." Murial made an attempt at a sarcastic joke to ease the remaining tension. She had found it useful in times when silence was stifling and unseen pressure was plentiful. A gulp caught in her throat as she chuckled, causing her to begin coughing and aggravating her beaten shoulder. Jack was on his way to fetch Nora when she suddenly rushed in from the hallway with a pitcher of water and quickly placed a half-filled cup to her daughter's bottom lip.

"Careful now, careful." Nora spoke in a gentle and soothing voice. "I think that is all for now, Jack." Murial's right hand pushed the cup away after a few sips slipped down her throat.

"No. I'm fine." She croaked out as the liquid was still going down the back of her tongue. "Leave us." Hesitantly, Nora removed herself from the bedside once again, sitting the cup on the stand to her right, and sending Jack a look of caution while she made her way back to the hall. "I had a feeling she would be eavesdropping. Anytime there is a chance for some good gossip." Murial's head shook side to side.

"Like daughter, like mother." Jack teased. For a second, his eyes regained their old snarky self before quickly returning to all seriousness. "I would be lying if I said that I did not enjoy the work, but some other factors have arisen that prevent me from continuing on." In the near empty room, Jack's echoing footsteps filled the space. "However, I need to see this through before I resign. Curt is dead." He gazed up from the floor to see her shocked expression.

"That is why he never notified us about Brewer." Murial's heart saddened. Curt had been kind to her and she knew how much he had meant to Jack. "I am so sorry. I know that he was a good friend and saved your life a time or two." She pulled at the itchy blanket. "Was it Brewer's doing?" All three of them were at the trial, so it was a logical conclusion.

"No. At least Curt's deputy didn't seem to think so. That is what Sheriff Bernheight told me. There may not be any connection at all, to be honest, but I have to find out for sure." Jack walked up to the edge of her bed and knelt down on his knee. "I was going to gather my things up at the ranch and leave today for Conestone." Murial stayed quiet; confused on what to say and even on how to feel about it. Her soul was raw from the hurt he had caused but there was a part of her that still clung to a piece of hope. There was also an unanswered question lurking in her mind to consider. "Brewer is gone now, and it is quite apparent that you did not need any of my help in order to do that, and the doctor has you on the mend from the knife wound."

"I should have checked him for knives. All the rest of his men had them." Murial scolded herself.

"That is alright, Detective. Slip ups do occur."

"Ha-ha. Very funny."

"Anyways, I figured that it would be the best time for me to get going. I made things awkward enough between us already." A soft smirk graced Murial's face.

"I agree with you on that one." Her eyebrows pinched inward in thought. "Did Walter know about all of this? Am I going to have to punish him when I get back home?"

"Some of it, but not all. Listen to me, Murial. Reginald was following a shipment on the train, a shipment that Bernard was carrying out here with him. That is why he was over at the crates when we switched over in Nebraska."

"Was that the crate that went missing?"

"Yes. It was stolen in Los Angeles. I am not sure what all he knows, but I have a feeling that he was just a carrier or perhaps he has no idea what was in it to begin with." Murial studied his face.

"You believe that innocent bit as much as you like cold coffee." Jack pushed himself up from the floor, returning to a standing position, and brushed off his vest with one hand. He stifled a sniffle and blinked back some water in his eyes.

"There is no evidence to suggest otherwise. Oh, and I have a feeling that Walter would deny knowing anything even if he did. He's scared of that death glare you give and your right hook."

"Is that so? I see you cannot ever seem to stay clean for long, can you?" Murial looked over his dusty attire from top to bottom. It was eerily reminiscent of when she saw him in the sheriff's office in Arizona, his clothing caked in the red dirt that was characteristic of the area. "Curt was lucky to have a friend like you, Jack. I know you will track down who killed him."

"Take care Murial." Jack placed his hat on top of his head, tipped the brim at her in a final farewell and turned to leave the room.

"God Bless, Jack." As soon as the door latch clicked shut, a tear streamed down her cheek.

Murial stared out at the far off mountains of the valley, across the empty vastness of the landscape. The calming wind wrapped her up in a comforting embrace before rushing off to sail through the rocks and to push the clouds into new places. A simple sling was tied behind her neck, holding her left arm in place while she slowly walked beside a watering trough. Evening was setting on the third day after the incident, the day Single Tooth speculated there would be a massive storm coming to break the drought. In Murial's opinion, the old man's words were about to come true. Rumbling thunder clouds were advancing across the desert with a booming presence. Lighting flashed amidst the brooding storm, their veined energy pulsating purple highlights of color against the majesty of the forthcoming darkness.

Above her head, the stars dazzled with such wonder. Murial was grateful to see them in all their glory with the Milky Way streaking across the sky.

"The full moon illuminated the landscape before her,
    Hazed, lines were undefined,
      All that remained was light and shadows,
        With three tiny stars to comfort thy night.

  The deep sea of sky, and gray of grass
    Were split only by a forest darkened to hide all foes,
      Small light of guidance pure and strong,
        Will steer me true to one's internal peace."

"Beautiful. What is that from?" Nora walked up behind her daughter. Having spotted Murial through a window in the house, she thought it was best to fetch Murial from wandering about in the dark. Doctor Mason had given her strict instructions to stay rested in bed for a week. That order only survived for two days.

"Something I wrote once." Murial glanced over her shoulder at her mother. She had hoped that the red puffiness of her cheeks were not visible in the nearly extinct light.

"You always have been an astrophile."

"I am not quite sure I would put it that way."

"What would you call your fascination with the stars then?"

"A dreamer." She played with a strand of her long hair. It was cascading freely down her back, dancing in the breeze.

"What are you doing Murial?" Nora dipped her fingers into the warm water of the trough. She watched the ripples domino along the water's surface.

"Watching the storm. Those clouds are harboring a vengeance."

"I overheard what Jack told you."

"I know. You are always eavesdropping in on other

people's conversations."

"And you do not do that too? What were you listening to on the train when I asked you about the missing photograph? Because it was surely not me." Nora placed her hand on Murial's good shoulder.

"Hey!" Her daughter gave her a look of bewilderment as the water soaked into her fabric.

"Sorry." Mrs. Robertson continued without removing her wet hand. "That man truly cares for you and you let him walk away without the slightest attempt to stop him."

"Mother, if you had TRULY been listening, there was no way I was going to even try to stop him. He has to finish his investigation and go after the man who killed Curt."

"All I am saying is…that I saw your discreet sobbing and eye contact avoidances since he left. It hurts me to see you so upset." There was no way Murial could deny that she was carrying a heavy heart. No matter what she told herself, the pain didn't ebb away and depression threatened from the fringes of her mind.

"I am alright, Mother. I will be fine." She removed her mother's damp hand with a smile. "Besides, you never liked the Fulton family anyway."

"No, I do not. To be frank, I wasn't sure about Jack when you both came home from Arizona…which disconcerted me by a margin to see the daughter I sent out with her father come back with a man I have not seen in a few years. I know how his grandfather treated his grandmother and I was afraid that the same thing would happen to you." Nora embraced Murial in a hug. "But I was wrong. He is as different as night and day from his grandfather. And he is not like your father either."

"That is true. Father would have scolded me when I was laying on the sidewalk, bleeding, if he was here."

"He would have. Wrong as it would be, that was just how he was." Both ladies' attentions were grabbed by another flash of lightning. "Nothing in life is simple, especially when it comes to love. Would it not be grand if it sometimes happened like it was written in the fairy tales?"

"Are you sure you are my mother?" Murial joked.

"What?"

"I do not recall you ever being so soulful and caring."

"I am human."

"Yes, but molded into the high society of life. The snobbery ill-mannered and hypocritical judges that were called our 'friends' would disapprove."

"Murial, my father's brother owned a farm where I grew up during the summers of my youth."

"What?!" Murial was flabbergasted.

"Your father would not permit me to admit as much because status was ever so important. However…" Nora shrugged. "Now I am free from all those obligations."

"Took you awhile to leave those chains behind."

"Does a leopard change their spots overnight?"

"A leopard's spots do not change at all."

Nora swatted that detail away with her hand. "Posh. There will be more than my spots changing here soon." She displayed the shiny addition of an engagement ring to her daughter.

"Wow! That is a beautiful stone." Murial faked her delight. "Congratulations."

"Since Brewer is dead, you are safe, and Bernard is cleared of suspicions, I accepted his proposal."

"Oh, well, if that's the only reason…" Murial teased and Nora smirked at her.

"Okay Smart One. I do love him, thank you very much. But I do not believe it to be wise to marry a man if he tried to kill my daughter. Do you?"

"No. That would put a damper on our relationship." Murial's eyes sparkled playfully. She kept her worry hidden, not wanting to spoil her mother's newly found happiness. Brewer had been able to pay for travel across the country, ride on an expensive train, and pay for top tobacco when he was supposed to be on the run from the law. Where did he get the money? Maybe it was from a stash he had buried for a rainy day or perhaps he robbed a rich man to cover his fare. Still, Murial's instincts were telling her that neither one was the case. *He was hired to complete a job. And the bottom fact that he did not succeed, does not mean his employer will stop from getting the job done.*

"We best be going in for dinner." Nora pointed to the system that was headed their way. Its clouds were spiking high in the sky and the damp feeling of rain kissed the air. "That storm is coming in fast and Charlene made us a special treat this evening." Her eyes glistened. "You need to get your strength to heal up before Jack comes back anyhow."

"You know, the funny thing is, that we were lying to each other to keep the same thing." She leaned against her mother. "You think he will?"

"I am certain of it."

"Everything smells so delicious." Nora gazed down at the chicken, potatoes, and cooked tomatoes on the plate in front of her. She picked up the glass of Chardonnay to her right, sipped the dry liquid and toasted Bernard for such fine hospitality. His face beamed proudly at Charlene, sitting to his left at the dining table. Murial shifted in her seat from the uncomfortable task of having to eat with only one hand. "Oh, here. Let me do that." Murial glared at her mother as she cut the chicken into pieces for her. *I hate feeling like a child.*

"I should have done that back in the kitchen. Sorry about that Murial." Charlene rose up from the table and moved over to the other side to make up for the mistake as thunder peppered the outside air. She gently pulled the fork and knife from Nora's hands to finish chopping the poultry dish into fork sized chunks.

"That is alright, Charlene. It is not life or death." Her cheeks reddened in embarrassment as the expression slipped from her tongue. "I mean…it happens. Thank you for cooking this wonderful meal."

Greg stood by the window, watching the storm grow

stronger. "Mr. Shetron, I believe there is a cloud of dust forming in the front of that beast out there. There must be some strong winds behind it. It could get really rough tonight."

"Single Tooth was right, then?" Bernard gave him a cheerful look. "Good thing we did not bet on it. You would be out of some money, my friend. You know, that Sheriff Bernheight informed me that Richard Thompson is denying that he was behind the beating and the stagecoach attack. That man is lower than fleas." The chicken juices got caught on his beard, causing him to dab his facial hairs dry with a white handkerchief. "I must say, Charlene, that this chicken is one of the best you have ever made."

"Thank you, Father. I wanted to cook something special for your big announcement." Charlene's mouth hovered near Murial's ear. "I hope we will become close as new sisters." A broad smile spread on her sweet face. On that cue, Bernard pushed his chair back, rose from the padded cushion and raised his filled wine glass for a toast of his own.

"I am sure that Nora has already told you, Murial, but to make it official, I wish to announce that Nora and I will be getting married just as soon as Murial is feeling better." Greg looked about the room, his attention pulled away from the raging clouds outside, and saw the others smiling with glee.

"Was I the only one no one told?" He sassed.

"Well, consider that you have now been told. Quit whining like an infant and sit down to your dinner. Or do you not care for the meal your own fiancé created for us this evening?" Greg fell for the trap and sat down without another word.

"I just don't like the looks of that storm out there, Mr. Shetron."

"Nonsense, it will be perfectly fine." He observed the issue for himself. "I wonder if that is what that man…Dr. Gravis…no…Dr. Grinchon…no," Bernard pointed into the air with success, "Dr. Gustavus Hinrichs. A teaching man. Ran into him about five years ago, socially you understand, and he was explaining to me a new term for a storm he had been working on. A derecho, if I remember correctly."

"A what?" Murial chewed slowly on a piece of chicken while Bernard explained.

"It has something to do with a long line of severe thunderstorms paired with strong winds that run straight, I believe." Bernard tucked his hand into a vest pocket. "Bet you did not think of me as the most intelligent type of man."

"You are full of surprises." Nora scooted a bracelet down her arm, repositioning it over her wrist nervously. "That storm is certainly coming this way in a hurry." A lightning bolt split across the window, causing everyone to jump, right before thunder roared through the beams and cracked the night like an egg. Brewer's face flashed in Murial's mind. She could see his mustache lording over the devilish smirk he carried on his mouth. Another streak parted the sky, sending Murial into another highlight of the incident. Something was fighting its way to be remembered, straining itself to the forefront of her thoughts. Most of that afternoon remained a mystery to her with bits and pieces slowly being revealed over time in the form of short images. *What is it? What am I missing?*

She shook her head forcefully, trying to rid her vision of the man's distressing memory. "Murial, are you alright?" Nora clutched onto her daughter's arm. "What is the matter?" Brewer's tobacco filled her nostrils. Her mother's voice rang out through the sudden time warp she found herself immersed in. Staring into the ravaging wind, Murial saw a lightning bolt take on the outline of a triangle. *Angle!* It was coming back to her: the triangle in the letter 'c,' the man mentioning the word in reference to a name at the robbery and the cigar remnant in the ashtray back in Chicago. That was the missing link.

Murial returned to the present, looking around at all the concerned faces starring back at her. Four pairs of wide eyes gave her their undivided attention, which would normally have given her a sudden desire to escape, except for this time. "Mr. Shetron, who is Angle?" Fear consumed his face as he instantly shot a look of panic in the direction of the window. Pulling a handkerchief from his jacket pocket, Bernard dabbed at his forehead while trying to keep a calm falsehood up.

"I am quite sure I know no one by such a ridiculous name."

"You need not worry. I did not see him lurking outside the window, if that is the reasoning for your sudden look in that direction." Bernard's bottom lip quivered. His eyes focused in on Murial's confident composure, a complete opposite of his. Charlene lowered her head and silently observed the floor while Greg sat his fork down in confusion as to what was being discussed.

"Really, Murial, I'm afraid that the only 'Angle' I know is the one in mathematics. And, it is Bernard after all. I would not want my future step-daughter calling me by my surname." He spread his mouth out into a toothy grin under his mustache.

"Not until I find out which side you are on, *Mr. Shetron.*"

"Murial, what is this?" Nora pleaded. "What on earth are you talking about?"

"I am talking about the man who hired Brewer." Murial narrowed her sights onto Bernard. Perhaps it was not the wisest move to show her cards out right, with the storm about to beat down the door, but she needed to know right then and now if what she suspected was true. "When Brewer decided to take me instead of Charlene, another man warned him about what Angle had said. Angle was the one you saw at the hotel in Chicago, was he not?"

Bernard gave his daughter a scouring glare. "Angle set that stagecoach heist up and you failed to mention that?!"

"I did not wish to alarm you, Father. You have worked so hard on building this town up that I wished for you to be able to stay here and not for us to have to move, again." Charlene fiddled with her fingers, much like a child would when their hand had been caught stealing a cookie before dinner.

"Would you rather be dead?!" His tone deepened as he snapped at her. Charlene flinched away from his boiling temper.

"But we are safe with all the men outside. He is only one man against our at least twenty."

"No, he is not. That's how he gets you, Charlene. By underestimating his capabilities. If Brewer worked for him, and was on Thompson's payroll, there is no telling how many others he has paid to do his dirty work. Oh, do not get me wrong, mind you. Angle enjoys the killings himself." Bernard pulled his collar from his neck. It was feeling a shade tight at the present moment.

"Wait a second," Greg spoke up for the first time in a while. "The way you reacted to me telling you about that man outside the gates…when I mentioned that he had trouble saying words correctly and all…you made us send that message to Los Angeles because it was Angle who was snooping around here. Wasn't it? At first, I thought it was Brewer who had been hovering around the gate. But his face was not scarred like the man who was here."

Charlene no longer played the guilty daughter as she returned her father's scouring glare in double-fold. "So!" Bernard chewed on his lips. "You knew all along that he was here. That is why you have asked me to stay inside the house these past couple of days. And I quote, 'do not go outside the gate and do not go anywhere far from the house unless you must.' A coyote issue was the made up excuse you gave me." She smacked away Bernard's extended hand. "No. You were all mad at me for keeping a secret and yet, you were keeping one from me as well. The same one, as a bottom fact."

"Angle was your old shipping partner?" Murial broke into the heated conversation.

"Yes, he was." Charlene answered. "He was a silent partner and ran shady deals." Bernard remained quiet. "Are you going to tell them, or am I?" She searched her father's face for a response. "Daddy does not play poker anymore, if you have not noticed. That is because he once acquired a debt to Angle, and at that time, we were cash poor. So, to wipe the record clean, Angle became part owner in the company without anyone knowing and started running smuggling operations under the business's name."

"I saw the crates being unloaded off the train in Chicago. They were stenciled with the insignia of a letter 'C' along with a small triangle in the middle of it." Charlene nodded.

"That was how they could tell which shipments contained the smuggled items versus the regular loads."

"But, what about that story you told us in Chicago?" Nora found her voice after taking it all in. "About you tracking some missing crates stashed away in a cave up near Canada?" Bernard looked straight at his fiancé.

"I did not lie to you in any way, Nora. That captain had stolen some crates of Angle's and we both went there to find them. It is something I was not proud of. A life that I was forced to participate in, elsewise…"

"Angle would have killed him." Charlene finished.

"A point he liked to bring up frequently." Bernard sipped the wine to dampen his dried throat. "I thought I had taken care of him." His hand formed a fist and pounded on the table top. "Can they not keep anyone in jail anymore?"

"What happened?" Murial readjusted her shoulder as a string of pain shot through it.

"Angle was overseeing another one of his smuggling shipments on the dock one night, his usual from Spain. I had notified the police through a messenger, so as to not have anything trace back to me, and installed a backup plan in case something went awry. So, as the cargo began to be unloaded, officers swarmed the dock and a gunfight ensued. Angle killed one of the officers, a judge's son, and it helped secure him a life in prison. Or so, he was supposed to have."

CRASH! Suddenly, a large tree trunk busted through the window and sand filled the room in the swirling wind of the dust storm. Greg grabbed a hold of Charlene while Bernard located Nora and Murial in the gritty chaos. "To the cellar." He coughed out, leading them to the front parlor room and pulling the rug back to expose a trap door. Bernard unlatched the two metal clasps and swung the wooden door open by the small handle. A set of stairs led into a darkened void that gave Murial the chills. Still, it was better than hanging out in the incoming weather.

"Boss?" A larger man with built muscles rushed in from the front door. "I heard the crash." He held up his arm as a feeble shield against the spinning dust.

"Yes, Red. A tree crashed through a window in the dining room and…where's Jared?"

"Here." Another man dressed in blackened attired approached with a handkerchief covering the lower part of his face. "Glad I had this in my pocket."

"See what you two can do about salvaging what you can in the dining room." Just then, a painting sailed by their heads from having been removed from the wall by the wind. "Then join us in the cellar." Both men ventured in the direction of the exposed room while Murial was being helped down the stairs by her mother. She had not told Nora, when they were outside earlier, but she was still very weak from the injury and was fading fast. Once at the bottom of the steps, now being lit by a lantern Charlene located on shelf, Nora eased Murial over to a lineup of crates sitting beside the wall to their right.

"What the…?" Murial felt her dress snag on one of the box's sides and peered down to see the reflection of a metal object in the dim lighting of the lantern.

"Here, hold this." Charlene handed the metal lantern to Nora. "I need to get the other candles and oil lamps lit."

"Mother, here." Murial pointed to the crack in the crate's side wall and lowered herself in order to get a closer look. With her one good hand, Murial pulled at the loosened wooden slat and was able to pry it free enough to identify pieces of extremely fine pitchers and pottery stashed between layers of straw.

"Murial!" Nora whispered and positioned the lantern closer to the crack. To the edge of the newly opened space her daughter had created, there was another reflection of something smooth and rounded. Murial pulled out a handful of straw, gasping in unison with her mother when the two ladies realized that it was the barrel of a gun. Drops of water echoed in Murial's ears, causing her to turn around to see another entrance on the opposite side of the cellar.

"Good job, Charlene." Bernard commented. He left the door for Greg to close, walking carefully down the stairs so as not to trip. "Been a while since I have been down here." Murial quickly re-stuffed the straw into the crate and sat on top of the wooden box like nothing had happened. Charlene struck a match and lit the last lamp by the far side of the cellar. She screamed as a man's face materialized out of the darkness in the flame of the candle.

"I' that any way to treat an old friend?" A husky voice hung in the air. Everyone turned and watched the man leaning against the wall, his guns primed and ready to fire.

The devil in his eye was fueled by rotten hatred, zeroing in on Mr. Shetron. A tan trench coat dangled around his ankles, drenched by the storm that raged overhead and covered up most of his attire. His gun belt was draped over his shoulder in a laissez-faire manner, but his body was rigid as stone. In the flickering light, his saturated beard glistened from the water droplets within the whiskers, obscuring only a portion of his scarred face. Both hands clutched Belgium Texas-Type Revolvers, one aimed directly at Charlene and the other one in the general direction of the group.

"No one is going anywhere. Drop all weapon' gentlemen." He gave his guns a shaking to rush Greg and Bernard along. "Quickly. I have no patience. Ain't that right, Bernard?" Angle took a step closer to Charlene. "Or would you like me to give your daughter a new mouth? In the stomach."

"You used to have the decency to not go after women." Bernard's teeth clenched. The sound of his gun being dropped into the dirt filled the small space after Greg's gun did likewise.

"That was before you decided to play rough with me."

"How did you get in here?" Murial asked. "Through

the house or from the outside?"

"From the outside." Angle looked her over from top to bottom. "Murial Robert'on. Well, well. You're the one who killed Brewer? Apparently he wa' not in prime condition after all." Water continued to drip from the outside door behind the man. Murial squinted her eyes, trying to see if there was an interior lock. If not, that would mean that the door was open and could provide an escape route, as long as they could make it past Angle that was.

"Now…" Angle positioned his gun toward Bernard's head. "Time for payback."

"Two year' I have been dreaming of today! TWO YEAR'!" Angle gritted his teeth. Bernard raised his hands in surrender.

"Shoot me then. But leave my daughter and the others out of this. It is our business, not theirs." Bernard took a step toward Charlene.

"You think I want to kill you?!" Angle laughed full-heartedly at the notion. "Kill you? If I had wanted you dead, I would have done that long ago." His eyes smirked in self pride. "I do admit, I had wanted to pull the trigger. But, I didn't give in to the urge." His scar smiled. "No, that would be too easy for you. Con'idering you were the one who reconfigured my face. Clever thing you did, fixing my gun to jam when the cop' came."

"How did you get out?"

"Oh, that." Angle's stomach contracted as a hearty laugh took over the silence in the cellar once more. "That was a 'troke of geniu'. I overheard a couple of prison guard' talking about how the government wanted any information on a man who 'old gun' to Geronimo. Apparently they don't like that 'ort of thing. E'pe'cially when the gun' were 'tolen from the military."

"But, I did not sell any guns to Geronimo." Bernard inched forward. "You did."

"Well, that would be 'tupid to admit to it. And am I 'tupid?" Angle shifted his stance a couple inches to the right, matching Bernard.

"No, you are not." Bernard watched Charlene out of his peripheral vision.

"Damn right, I ain't. Told them you did it and that I would get you to talk in exchange for my freedom."

"The judge would not have allowed such a deal."

"Oh, but he had no word' on the matter. Federal deal, not local. Oh, and you don't have to worry for him." Angle's lips smacked together and played around as if looking for a tooth that had gone missing. "Anybody have a cigarette or cigar? I u'ed up all of mine last night and I've been aching for another. Liked that cigar Brewer picked up on the train."

The room grew silence once more, everyone searching each other's faces for an answer, or hint, of what to do next. Nora gave Murial a wink with her right eye, hoping to catch her daughter's attention, but the lantern's weak light was not strong enough for her to see her mother's signal. Angle sighed when no one came forth. "Well, that ju't mean' that our talk' over." He trained his right gun at Charlene, holstered his left gun, and reached for the inner pocket of the soaked trench coat. A piece of paper was thrown on top of the nearest crate box. "Write your name."

"What is it?"

"Were you not li'tening? You are going to 'ign it and

give me my freedom." Angle took a singular step. "Now, write." Like a flash, Angle latched onto Charlene's arm and dragged her closer to him. "Write."

"Why? You will not leave me alive after I sign it. I would contend that it was signed under duress and invalidate it."

"I will kill your daughter." Angle placed the barrel of the gun against Charlene's right temple. Her lips trembled as her body shook. She was starting to wish she was back East again, this being the second time in a week she had been caught in such a predicament.

"You are not going to allow anyone to leave this room alive, Angle." Bernard picked up the paper and began to rip the planned confession up. Panic rose in Angle's eyes.

"I wouldn't do that." He pressed the barrel onto Charlene's shoulder, pushing it into her skin through the dress. "Because I will make her hurt before I kill her. If you write your name, I will be merciful." Charlene could feel the tears about to stream down her cheeks. *Oh, how I wish I could have seen my own shop be a success before I died. Selling fabric and making dresses…*an idea dawned on her. Stealthily, Charlene reached into a pocket hidden in the folds of her skirt and gratefully felt the smooth surface of the handles to her scissors. Without hesitation, she gripped onto the metal cutters with all her strength, positioned the blades so that they were parallel with her arm, and thrusted the sharpened points upward into Angle's stomach.

Angle grimaced and shot off the gun wildly into the dark at Charlene as she ran away from him. Nora hiked up her dress and pulled out her own Derringer, unloading both shots into Angle's chest just as Greg planted a knife into the man's heart. Falling backwards, Angle rolled into the dirt before spitting out his final breath. Bernard embraced his daughter, making sure she was alright. Everything remained calm for a spell, the adrenaline still working overtime for each one of them when the outside entrance unexpectedly fell in due to the powerful storm still raging overhead.

Thinking it was someone Angle had hired to help him, Bernard threw Charlene behind him and unsheathed a knife hidden in his boot. Greg dove for the knife that was lodged in Angle's dead corpse while Nora ran for the gun stowed away in the crate as Murial pulled out her Pepperbox. Primed and ready to defend, the crew gave each other a half-smile when it turned out to be Mother Nature as the culprit. To be sure, Greg cautiously crawled up the waterfall filled steps and peered into a sheet of rain. He picked up the water soaked boards of the door and held them up to the opening, practically yelling so that the others could hear him over the noise of the storm. "It seems that the force of the wind broke the hinges. We need something to brace it up to keep most of the rain at bay."

"Will he do?" Murial pointed to the now-dead Angle. Bernard, Nora and Charlene carried the man over to the opening and propped his body up with nearby crates.

"He could do with a good bath." Bernard commented, scrunching up his nose in protest to the foul trail smell the body was giving off.

"Shame he wasn't alive for it." Murial added. She felt awful that her bandaged arm kept her from helping them out. However, she did manage to locate a few blankets stored on a shelf and handed them out as they all sat atop of crates to keep themselves from getting wet from the flooding floor. "When did you get a gun?" Her eyes stayed steadfast on her mother.

"After what happened in the desert, Bernard gave me one for protection." Nora gently laid her arm over her daughter. Murial was full of questions, but she could feel her adrenaline fading fast and decided to ask them at another time. Nestled under the blanket, and the crook of her mother's arm, Murial looked down at the exposed .44 caliber Walker Percussion Revolver that Nora had unearthed from the crate underneath them.

"Why did you reach for that gun?"

"Mine needed reloading and I have no extra bullets with me."

"But it wouldn't be a loaded gun. No one ships a gun ready to fire."

"It can still be thrown at someone or knock a person out by hitting them on the head with the butt or the barrel." Nora gave her daughter a kiss on the forehead. She had never felt closer to Murial before this trip and never so grateful to see her alive.

"Who are you and what did you do with my Mother?" Relief flooded into her soul and lifted the weight that had been compressing on Murial. The next thing she saw was the inside of her eyelids as the rain slowed to mere drips.

"I now pronounce you Man and Wife. You may kiss the bride." The pastor gave his diplomatic smile to the happy couple sealing the marriage vows with a kiss. Roars erupted from the crowd of townspeople who had come out to celebrate the union of Mr. and Mrs. Greg Franklin along with Mr. and Mrs. Bernard Shetron. Murial stood awkwardly in the middle of the two couples at the front of the church, being the Maid of Honor for both brides, and wished for the moment to quickly be over. She had never been to such a public wedding before, since they were mostly privately held family events. But in this town, everyone was family.

"Oh, it is just so exciting!" Murial's ears picked up on a female's Scottish accent from the first row of seats. "I have never been to a double wedding." The woman's eyes glistened in thought in what Murial surmised was to be the lady's own wedding day in her imagination. Waiting until the two newlyweds made their way back down the aisle, Murial felt a twinge of pain in her shoulder. It had healed without any issue over the past month, but it would ache whenever rain was not far off. *Oh, no. Please do not ruin the*

276

reception. Bernard had pulled out all the stops for the cake, food, and flowers to make the day special for everyone in town. It was to be a truly grand celebration that traveled all the way from Los Angeles for the most memorable party this side of the Mississippi River.

Then, she realized it was something else. Seeing Charlene with Greg, and her mother with Bernard, Murial was missing Jack. She wasn't ready for marriage, that she was sure of, and she was fairly certain that Jack wasn't ready for that either. However, he had become her best friend and she missed his jokes he would say. *They are not as good as Walter's though.* A sweet smile shared both sadness and happiness between her cheeks. She allowed the rest of the crowd to file in line on their way outside the church, staring into the memories she had collected from over the past four weeks.

Nora had emphatically insisted that Charlene have her own special day, but she ultimately gave in when her future stepdaughter considered it to be a wedding present to her if they shared the ceremony. "I hate being the center of attention, please…as my wedding present?" Murial made sure to take note on how big the woman's eyes got when she was in the midst of persuading someone to side with her. It was a skill that Murial had only attributed to animals until she saw the enlarged, kitten-like eyes Charlene was able to produce on cue. Both women had grown close during the ample amount of time they had to bond with the house in such disarray. It turned out that Murial and Charlene shared a lot in common and their conversations ranged from childhood memories, to father issues, to reading the latest literature, and who their favorite artists were.

She had even spent time with Bernard to make sure of whom her mother was still determined to marry. It was a conversation she remembered as if it were yesterday.

The sun was high in the sky, shining through the leaves of a Joshua tree. Murial breathed in the chemical smell characteristic of larrea plants after it rains and could see bright orange poppies and devil's nettles dotted around the rocks of where she was seated beside Bernard. "Tell me one thing."

"Anything." Bernard stared at the shadows created from the leaves. Their shape appeared to be a man's face watching over them.

"What made you decide to risk your life and turn Angle over to the law?"

"I moved out here to start fresh, leaving behind that old life." He sighed, his beard moving gently in the breeze. Bernard turned to face Murial directly in order to tell her the answer. "My first wife became very ill, Murial. She was a beautiful angel, my Matilda, and knew nothing about Angle's dealings. It was my fault that he entered our lives to begin with, there was no sense in upsetting her further with his antics. One night, he forced me to come along on his smuggling job to a client in another state. I made up some lousy excuse about being called out for an emergency shipment for the military and left her in the hands of a nurse we employed. By the time I returned, she was gone." His eyes watered. "I wasn't there for my wife when she needed me the most because of what my gambling addiction did to

*me. I missed out on her dying breath, which the nurse told
me was my name, because of that wretched, horrible, man.
Murial, I love your mother and would not do anything to
harm her."*

*She searched his eyes, honest and unyielding. Murial
believed him and prayed that her judgement was right.
"Thank-you, Bernard. I know you will keep your promise.
Although, I don't think you are the wisest man for what you
did."*

"Which part?"

*"Giving my mother a gun." A little laughter was
good for the soul, and helped to clear the air before she
asked him the question that had been burning in her mind
since Jack talked to her in the doctor's recovery room.*

"Murial? Come on. It's time for our photograph to
be taken." Charlene wriggled her way through the hoard of
men, women, and children, to find her new stepsister. The
photographer had come in from San Francisco to take a
picture of the occasion on a celluloid film sheet, a newly
invented way of capturing the image as opposed to a plate.
Murial's smile came off as genuine while the man informed
them all to stand rigid, but all she could think about was the
missing face of her sister that the image would not hold.
Nora had sent an invite to Shannon in the form of a
telegram, only to receive a short and concise response sent
back by none other than Senator Drouther himself.
Apparently his son and his wife were off on a vacation in
Ireland. *How convenient.*

"Everyone, let us all go down main street to continue

with our celebration!" Bernard shouted into the summer air to the delightful ears of the crowd awaiting free food and drink. String was hung over the road, from balcony to balcony, hanging pretty triangular cuts of fabric in a banner up and down the town. The cake was frosted with a sweet icing that completed the chocolate taste of the baked batter inside. Desserts, flavored ice, and ice cream were all dished out for the eager group. Such delicacies were foreign to most of the townspeople, and were widely enjoyed by all ages. Music filled the makeshift dance area with songs played by a violinist, cellist, trumpet player, and a local fiddler.

Everone looked on as Charlene and Greg danced to "Oh Promise Me." Nora walked up beside Murial. "I wish Shannon was here." Her soft voice was almost drowned out by the music playing.

"I know, Mother. And I am sure she would have wanted to as well." Murial stood still as more and more men led their wives and sweethearts onto the dance floor. Bernard laid his hand out for Nora, who accepted graciously and soon, Murial found herself alone again. The whole scene was bittersweet for her, gazing around at everyone having a good time. It was the last night she would be staying in Bracken as she was due to leave first thing in the morning the following day. Walter would be waiting to accompany her in Chicago, where she hoped to catch up with the police regarding Reginald's death and to arrange for the return of the photograph to his brother.

"May I have this dance?" Greg held an outstretched hand in Murial's direction. Charlene nodded that it was alright so Murial politely accepted. They had gone halfway through the next song when Bernard butted in.

"Excuse me, but I believe my stepdaughter wished to talk to me about something." He shot Greg a smirk and whisked Murial away as Nora wove her way over to the refreshment table for a drink of homemade slumgullion that the Shetron's housekeeper made. Bernard's beard had grown about two inches longer since leaving Pennsylvania, slightly tickling Murial's chin. "Now, what was it that you were being so cryptic in reference to earlier? The only thing I am sure on is that you wanted to have it taken care of before you return home."

"Yes. I would like your help in shipping a horse home to the wild plains. His name is Firestorm."

Gazing out of the open window of the stagecoach, Murial watched the railroad station being built by many skilled hands. The design was much simpler than that of Graver's Station back home, but its duties would remain the same: to allow possible travelers to purchase tickets and to relay current train arrivals to everyone concerned. At its present phase in life, Bracken was not in need of such elaborate accommodations that one would expect to find at a station near Philadelphia. However, the desire for a more grandiose building was possible in the near future for the ever-growing town.

Since Murial had arrived, there had been a number of families who had either moved into one of the empty store fronts on Main Street, or claimed a spread of their own among the surrounding land. A few spectators wandered the side alleys most nights with their mules and burros rattling around with all sorts of pots and pans strapped onto their backs after a day's hard search for elusive gold. It appeared that Charlene's dress shop was taking off as orders flooded into her hands from the sudden need to look sharp at the church's first Saturday night dance. Murial found the whole spectacle to be a wondrous achievement. Here, in the middle of practically nowhere, a town had been started, and was thriving through sheer hard work and the determination of the people living there. *It's amazing what a dream can do. And faith for that matter.*

As the horses dragged the stage toward Los Angeles, the town slowly faded from her view and blended into the rocky formations and rolling hills that it called home. Sitting across from her, on the other side of the stage, Nora and Bernard discussed the various theaters they wished to attend on their honeymoon in the big city. Lost in the all of the choices of their own world, Murial was content with remaining in her's for the duration of the ride.

Looking back on all that had transpired throughout the trip, Murial could not have possibly fathomed how badly this journey would have shaken her life. *If I had the chance to do it all over again, knowing what I now know, would I have stepped onto the train?* The situation reminded her of the fable of Pandora's box in a way. In an uncanny parallel, the weight of the truth caused a change in her that could not be undone. *But, then again, God does work in all things good for his children as per Romans 8:28.* Still, knowing that verse did not make her experiences any easier to deal with, wondering as to "why" was only human after all.

Questions flew aimlessly in her mind. They bounced off the contours of thought and logic with no real answer to stop their momentum. With nothing else to occupy herself, Murial found her thumb twitching again to her dismay. It was of no use to sketch while traveling over a rock and pothole filled trail, nor was it any use to write for the same exact reason. Instead of resembling a picture, or a typical journal entry, anything drawn or written would have more in common with a child's random scribblings than with what it had intended to be.

Unbeknownst to Murial, all of her concentration had resulted in her face looking irritated at her mother and new stepfather. "Murial, are you alright?" Nora watched her daughter's disheartened brown eyes, trying to figure out what she was so wrapped up in. Her mind were obviously somewhere else and not on what was being said in the stage.

"Of course I am." Murial produced another fake smile, spreading her cheeks upward in cheerful mannerism. "Whatever gave you the idea that I was not?" After so many years of practice, that one lie was not so hard to perform anymore. But her mother could sense she was being lied to, having the ability to discern between her daughter's genuine emotions and her masks of facade. She longed to push Murial for more details. It concerned her to see her daughter not like her stubborn and enthusiastic self.

"Are you sure?" Nora saw the warning glare she received from Murial and decided to drop the matter entirely. "I hear that you are having Firestorm shipped out to the wild plains so that he may run free." Her daughter nodded.

"It is where he belongs."

"That was a very commendable decision you made, Murial. I know that you are terribly fond of him and that the choice could not have been easy. " Murial shrugged the compliment away with her shoulders, forgetting for a moment that her left side was still sore from healing until a shot of weakened pain reminded her.

"Jack was right that he is dangerous to my hired hands and that our farm was not the right home for him." Silence fell within the tiny box. Murial realized that her comment had dampened the overall upbeat mood without much care. The result was the peace and quiet she had been wanting, desperately wishing to stop the clock, and be able to live in the moment instead of thinking about what was to come next.

After all of this, I am hibernating from society as soon as I reach home. Loud noises pierced Murial's ear drums as different groups of people were raising the volume of their voices to be heard all at once. The station was alive with busy bees swarming the track platform for the train heading East. Nora hugged her daughter with all the strength she could muster, crushing Murial's rib cage in the process and making it difficult for her to get air into her lungs. "Mother, I do need to breathe." She managed to squeak out. Her mother's perfume wafted in the air and drowned her nostrils with its flowerly fragrance.

"Sorry." Nora didn't care that she was tearing up in the middle of the afternoon rush for the weekend travelers as families gathered together in anticipation of having to board in the next few minutes. Panic was painted on a neighboring mother's face, who was dedicated to ensuring that none of her eight children got lost in the chaos. "Now, be sure to let your sister know about the wedding."

"It is hard to forget something as monumental as that, but I will do my best not to." Murial sarcastically smirked. "I will also make sure to send you a new picture of myself when I arrive home.”

“Perhaps you could have one taken with Shannon?” Nora’s face gently pleaded as Murial rolled her eyes.

“Fine. I will have one taken with Shannon.” She knew that would mean having to deal with the Drouthers again and Murial dreaded the very idea the instant her mother suggested it. While she was trying to treasure this moment with her mother, seeing her for the last time before embarking on the return trip home, Murial just wanted to board the train already. Charlene and Gregory had spoken their farewells back in Braken with wishes for safe travels and all of the emotional goodbyes were growing increasingly awkward for her. Nora wiped away the tears from the sides of her cheeks as Bernard gave his stepdaughter a bear hug.

“I am going to miss you, Murial.” He pulled her face from his beard, showing a dazzling grin with proud, fatherly eyes. It was the one thing she never expected to see again since her uncle had passed. A look so rare for her to see cast upon herself and yet, it was the one thing she had craved for so often. Blush stained her cheeks pink as she fought back the water threatening to spill past her eyelashes. She blinked them away and gave him another hug, whispering in his ear.

“Thank-you for everything.” Murial stepped back from Bernard and Nora, waving farewell just as the train’s whistle blasted through the platform of people. She carried her personal bag up the stairs, into the parlor car, and sat down on the west side of the train so she could watch her mother and stepfather shrink into the distance from her seat. The train proceeded along the tracks at a steady pace.

Smoke passed by the window both black and almost transparent. All seemed quiet for a moment and Murial took a deep breath to reassure herself. *Everything is going to be alright.*

Suddenly, a woman plopped down across from Murial noisely. She was wearing a green dress with striped stockings, black shoes, and a few hawk feathers resting under a brown band of a man's black hat. Murial tried not to stare at the woman's eyepatch. "Such a waste."

"Pardon me?" Murial asked. She was not used to hearing such a thick British accent.

"A travesty. That's what it is."

"I am sorry about your eye." Murial ventured a guess as to what the curious lady was referencing to.

"Oh, that? Do not mind at all, really. Just had some surgery, tis all." She gave her a quick, half-grin and produced a hand fan from the pocket of her dress. Fanning herself, the woman looked out the window, ignoring Murial. Around the lady's neck sat two necklace chains laid atop her chest and disappeared under the square neckline of the fabric. One pendant popped upwards after the wheels of the car ran over a stone kicked up onto the tracks from the engine. The pendant was a green gemstone wrapped around by curly metal wires and spring-like metal pieces.

"What an unusual necklace." The woman instantly looked down at the rebellious gem.

"Thank you." She shoved the pendant beneath the lining again without hesitation. "Since we will be together for an extended period of time, I best introduce myself. My name is Vectra Tillerman."

"Murial Robertson. Nice to meet you Miss Tillerman."

"Are you hungry Miss Robertson? My stomach could do with a few little biscuits and a hot cup of tea." Murial declined the offer, so Ms. Tillerman obliged the call for food alone and headed for the dining car. It was going to indeed be a long ride till Walter joined her in Chicago for the last leg of the trip. She would have normally revolted against having a chaperone escort her home, but it would do her some good to have a familiar face to talk to on the way back. *He will be thrilled to hear that Firestorm is going to be leaving the farm.*

Outside the window, Murial watched the land sloping upwards and down, curving and straightening whenever and wherever it pleased. Her mind drifted back to the night they were trapped in the cellar from the storm and the collapsing doors had frightened all of them. *Grabbing for an unloaded gun,* she shook her head in thought. *Glad Mother did not need to use it.* What Murial didn't know, was that that the gun Nora had reached for in the cellar, was in fact, the very same weapon that Bernard had rigged to jam on Angle on the night the police raided the port, and the gun that caused Angle's scars had been intended for her new stepfather, Bernard Shetron.

THE END

Murial Robertson will be back in...
A Counterfeit of Death

Vectra Tillerman's Adventures will begin in...
Written Wings

ABOUT THE AUTHOR:

Sarah Ickes has her Associates Degree in Art and Design. She has always held a passion for writing since her first publication of a poem in fifth grade. Not only does she pursue writing, but she also creates artwork that is available for purchasing, such as the illustrations and book cover of this novel. History is of a special interest to her, as she enjoys learning about the past. Please visit her website for more details or follow her on social media.

www.sarahickesart.com

Thank you for reading my novel and I hope you enjoyed it.